HARRY FLASHMAN
AND THE INVASION OF IRAQ

Dedicated to the memory of those servicemen who deployed to Iraq and did not come home.

Profits made from the sale of this book will be donated to Help For Heroes.

HARRY FLASHMAN AND THE INVASION OF IRAQ

A Novel Based Largely on Real Events

H. C. Tayler

ARTHUR H. STOCKWELL LTD
Torrs Park   Ilfracombe   Devon
Established 1898
www.ahstockwell.co.uk

© *H. C. Tayler, 2011*
First published in Great Britain, 2011
All rights reserved.
No part of this publication may be reproduced
or transmitted in any form or by any means,
electronic or mechanical, including photocopy,
recording, or any information storage and
retrieval system, without permission
in writing from the copyright holder.

British Library Cataloguing-in-Publication Data.
A catalogue record for this book is available
from the British Library.

This book is a work of fiction and, except in the case of historical fact, any resemblance to actual persons, living or dead, is purely coincidental.

ISBN 978-0-7223-4040-0
Printed in Great Britain by
Arthur H. Stockwell Ltd
Torrs Park   Ilfracombe
Devon

Preface

I came to, dazed and covered with earth and mud, spitting blood and with a penetrating ringing in my ears. The trench in which I had been cowering had all but vanished. I had been blown flat on my back, partly buried in debris, and the deafening roar of battle was all around. Another huge explosion ripped into the wall of the trench a few yards away, once more showering me with earth and stones. Machine-gun bullets zipped through the air, sometimes a few yards away, sometimes directly above my position. I could also make out the whistle of mortar bombs overhead, though it was impossible to tell if they were ours or theirs. I was utterly convinced I was about to die and, as might be expected, was terrified out of my wits.

Fear – or rather panic, for that was what it had become – is a great driver to action, and this was no exception. Dying pointlessly in some foreign field is bad enough, but I was damned if I was going to die alone. Hesitation (or cowardice) had kept me in the trench when my Royal Marines colleagues advanced. Probably many of them had paid the price for moving into the open – but I was sure some of them would have escaped the onslaught of shelling, and they were getting further and further away by the minute. I was dazed, bleeding and half deaf – but I wasn't staying in that hellhole a moment longer. Clutching my rifle I kicked away the spoil that was covering my legs, staggered to my feet, clambered over the remains of the parapet, and tore after them like a man possessed.

To my surprise, the line of advancing Marines seemed unbroken and, despite the ordnance raining down on the battlefield, the ground wasn't littered with bodies either. Perhaps this was because of the rapidity of the advance, or perhaps due to the uncanny ability of the Marines to vanish into cover in the split second before the air was filled with incoming fire. I shall never know the answer. But on that bleak day in southern Iraq it seemed the gods of war were smiling on them. I scuttled up in rear in a low crouch, not close enough to the forward troops to be caught in crossfire but close enough to scream for help in the event of anything untoward happening. Bursts of fire rang out from Iraqi depth positions, but the vanguard of 3 Commando Brigade pressed on undeterred. Heavy machine-guns boomed out from our flanks, as the stand-off companies suppressed the Iraqi gunners concealed in the thin stretches of woodland to our front. Large-calibre rounds smashed into the enemy trenches, and for a moment I had sufficient presence of mind to thank my stars that I was on the giving, not the receiving, end of such treatment. Within a few minutes the first Marines were inside the woods, operating first as four-man fire teams and then in pairs as they systematically cleared the network of hidden Iraqi trenches. I hid in a shallow ditch a couple of hundred yards from the edge of the trees, waiting until I was convinced the nearest trenches had been silenced. Eventually, conscious of being the last man left out in the open, I sprinted across the gap and into the copse, hopeful of finding a suitable bolt-hole. Ahead of me the Iraqis were in disarray. Little white flags appeared as some of them surrendered, but for many it was already too late. The Marines swept through the positions with astonishing speed, pouring bursts of rifle fire into anything that moved and posting grenades into the Iraqi trenches to make doubly certain that nothing survived inside. Sporadic bursts of Iraqi AK47 fire came cracking through the trees in my direction, so I wasted no time in diving into an available trench, despite the gruesome sight of its dead occupants which awaited me.

With a sense of horror I realised that there were more Royal

Marines entering the woods to my rear. There was no way they could be sure which trenches had been cleared and, cowering inside, covered in mud and blood, it was a distinct likelihood that I would be mistaken for an Iraqi soldier and shot. I screamed and waved my arms, desperate to be recognised as British. The Marines were taking no chances, ducking from tree to tree, utilising every scrap of cover and scoping the area through their telescopic sights before they moved. Just a few dozen yards away I watched as one of them spotted me through the smoke and cordite fumes. My head began spinning as I realised he was raising his rifle in my direction. In slow motion the barrel rose until it was pointed exactly at my face. He squinted, peering through the telescopic sight, and I closed my eyes as his finger closed around the trigger. I was unable to speak or cry out, but I suppose the abject terror in my face must have made him hesitate for a second. I realised afterwards that I had dropped my rifle and instinctively raised my arms aloft in a gesture of surrender, but with all the adrenaline coursing through my veins I wasn't conscious of having done this. The stand-off lasted for several seconds until the Marine in question finally recognised me, lowered his rifle, shot me a broad grin over the top of his sights, then disappeared into the trees in pursuit of his colleagues. Overcome with relief I collapsed into the trench where I was able to catch my breath whilst resting on the conveniently prostrate corpse of one of its former occupants.

This was Operation James, a nondescript code name for the bloodiest day of fighting since the war began. Fate had dealt me a rough hand indeed, landing me unwillingly at the sharp end of proceedings just as the British advance gained momentum. In my current situation I would be lucky to survive the day unscathed, let alone the rest of the campaign. Home suddenly seemed a very distant land – and despite the horrors unfolding all around me, I found myself experiencing a queer nostalgia for the comforts of Blighty. Perhaps it was simply because I was all too aware of my own fragile mortality. Whatever the cause, I found myself thinking wistfully of London parties, days spent hunting on the South Downs, and boozy nights in the officers' mess. No doubt the boys back at the regimental headquarters were safely tucked up in bed, sleeping off their hangovers caused by the previous night's excesses. I envied the lucky bastards. I really did.

1

It was shortly before Christmas 2002 when the Second Gulf War began for me. And a bloody depressing Christmas it made for too. I had bunked off to Woburn with a couple of chaps from the regiment – Roddy Woodstock and Charlie Valdez-Welch, as I recall – for a round of golf and a bigger round of afternoon drinking. I can't remember the exact date, although I know it was early December and I was supposed to be writing end-of-year appraisal reports for the non-Commissioned officers in the battalion headquarters. For once, my procrastination of staff work was not simply borne out of idleness. A couple of the Staff Sergeants had done me a tidy favour earlier in the year, covering my tracks when a romp in the bushes with the Brigade Commander's undergraduate daughter had been uncovered during the summer ball. That's another story, but suffice it to say that I might not still be wearing my rank on my shoulders if they hadn't thrown up a smokescreen quick sharp. For that, if nothing else, I intended to write them a pretty decent annual report. However, there was really no point reinventing the wheel with these things, and I knew that Julian Pemberton had already completed most of his – first in the queue outside the CO's office as usual, and much good might it do him. The obvious solution was to get the chief clerk to put Pemberton's reports onto disk, and then copy the best written prose straight into my reports. I reckoned I could get through most of the headquarters NCOs in less than half a day by this means, and the time saved would be well spent sharpening up my short game and enjoying a couple of Speyside malts courtesy of Valdez-Welch's father, who was a member at Woburn.

The weather that winter was typically abysmal, dominated by long, wet spells and endless dreary grey skies. The day we spent on the golf course was unfortunately no different – rain squalls were gusting in from the north east and it was icy cold to boot. I was wearing layer upon layer of woollens to keep out the frigid air, topped off with a smart new golfing cap which attracted a good deal of abuse from my playing partners but did a fine job in keeping the rain out of my eyes. The weather may have been grim but happily my golf was on remarkably good form, considering I had hardly swung a stick in anger for almost four months. Roddy, who was immensely proud of his handicap of four, suffered a shocking round and was in a terrible funk by the time we were halfway round the course (I had never bothered getting a formal handicap but usually played off 14). Today though I was thrashing Roddy at his own game and for every shot he dropped, I managed to pull one back, even birdying a couple of par three holes. Charlie and I threw in the odd cheap jibe about his swing needing some coaching, which made him tighten up all the more – it's a glorious feeling, kicking a man when he's down, and I was thoroughly enjoying every minute of it. Roddy's game deteriorated further as we entered the back nine and he even stopped speaking to us after losing a ball in the drizzle off the 13th fairway, while I managed to birdie the hole which only served to make things worse. Anyhow, as Charlie and I strolled towards the 14th tee, with Roddy scowling some way behind, who should we bump into but old Bob Tudor, Honorary Colonel of the regiment, all smiles and bonhomie, and wearing a pair of bright blue tartan plus-fours that would have offended the sensibilities of a Peckham market trader.

"Boys! How unexpected!" he boomed at us, striding across the fairway. "Bit of a shocking day for it, don't you think?"

he shouted at me with outstretched hand. "How delightful to see you all."

We returned the platitudes and he strode off back across the fairway, evidently well pleased with himself for having spotted us through the gloom. 'Bonking Bob', as he was affectionately known, had shot his career royally in the foot when caught conducting an away fixture with his interpreter in Bosnia a decade earlier. I never had the pleasure of meeting the girl but apparently she was a lovely looking filly and the boys thought he had done the battalion proud. Unhappily the dago general running the United Nations show at the time thought otherwise, word got out, Missus Tudor was none too pleased, and Bob returned home with his tail between his legs and his career in tatters. Time is great healer though and the Army has always liked a rogue (I should know); a few years and a lot of settling dust later, and he was welcomed back to the regiment with open arms as the Honorary Colonel. Good on him, I say, although he was an idiot for getting caught.

Anyhow, an hour later and we were back in the Woburn clubhouse, poor Roddy still in something of a sulk after being reduced to 16 over. Charlie and I had beaten him by three and five strokes respectively – my best ever round, as it turned out, and one I still haven't bettered. Woburn, if you haven't been there, is a smashing place, very comfortable and ideal for whiling away a slack afternoon, especially if you have just excelled yourself out on the golf course. Of course it's even more relaxing when someone else is paying. I was the wrong side of a couple of brandy and gingers and just beginning to contemplate lunch, when I was vigorously clapped on the back and asked if I wanted a proper drink. Bonking Bob had returned.

After ordering us several pints of stout ("Shorts have their place, of course, but they do make you look like a bunch of pseudo-intellectual nancy boys...") he plonked himself down on a nearby armchair and launched into a machine-gun diatribe about the regiment (morale high), the state of the mess (shocking), diesel engines in recce vehicles (about bloody time too), and rumours circulating within the MoD about the possibility of a forthcoming Gulf deployment. He was an opinionated old bugger but he was also very well connected within Whitehall, so it paid to listen to what he had to say. A rumour coming from old Tudor was often little short of an intelligence briefing and always a good way of finding out which units were liable to be going where. On this occasion, as so often before, he was bang on the money.

"Of course, you'll have heard the buzz about the Gulf deployment," he started. Ever since the Government had published a dossier giving details of Saddam's alleged chemical weapons the political bun fight had dominated the news, so this was hardly much of a rumour, but more was to follow.[1] "Turns out the bloody Admiralty has done a deal with the Yanks to provide a battalion of Royal Marines. But our Tony has volunteered more troops to the Pentagon, so the battalion is going to become a brigade – it's all over the wires in PJHQ.[2] Word in London is that he wants to send even more – there's even talk of it becoming a divisional move, God forbid." Good, thinks I, send in the Marines, let them spend a few months sweating in the desert while the rest of us get ourselves ready for another season on the polo field. I could think of few places I would like to go less than Kuwait – the obvious exception being Iraq, of course.

"Of course 16 Brigade is working itself into a lather as usual," he continued. The rivalry between the Parachute Regiment troops of 16 Brigade and the Royal Marines of 3 Brigade is legendary and neither enjoys missing out on a deployment at the expense of the other. 2002 was no exception, since the Marines had already seen service in Afghanistan – and me with them, mind you. A pretty pickle that had got me into, I don't mind telling you, but it's a story for another time. While all that was going on, 16 Brigade had fumed at home and the thought of missing out on another deployment would have been enough to have the brigade commander phoning the Samaritans. "CDS is due to hand over at any moment and the new chap will certainly send them if he can."[3] CDS at the time was an Admiral, which was why the Marines (being part of the Navy) had been picked for all the choicest deployments. But his successor was to be an Army chap, so all that would no doubt change. "And if it *is* a divisional move then the last brigade will have to be armoured," continued Bob, "So the heavies are jockeying for position. The smart money's on 7 Brigade, with all that desert history to fall back on." This was both good news and bad. Moving armour to the Gulf would take time and in any case we were part of 4 Brigade, as opposed to 7 Brigade (or the Desert Rats as they were popularly known) so would have a better-than-even chance of staying well away from any shenanigans. But the fact that armour might be going at all was not comforting – staff officers would be dragged from every nook and cranny to make up the numbers in brigade and divisional headquarters. Still, it was too early to get worked up about these things, or so I mistakenly thought as I sipped the froth from my latest pint.

Colonel Bob stayed with us for almost an hour in the end and the old rascal was three sheets to the wind by the time he remembered his luncheon partner and wobbled off in the direction of the dining room. Frustratingly, before departing he embarked on a series of questions about the regiment. I was pretty certain that, through no malice on his part, he would let slip to the CO that he had bumped into us at Woburn and our relaxing day out would be exposed – and punished with a string of extra duties, no doubt.

But, if it happened at all, that would be tomorrow. For the moment we were free to return to giving Roddy Woodstock a hard time over the standard of his golf and of course racking up an even bigger bar bill for Valdez-Welch's old man to pick up.

The following day dawned blustery and bright, and despite a

crashing hangover I felt relatively chipper as I strode from the officers' mess over to the brigade lines. Gaggles of men were forming up outside their accommodation blocks for morning parades and young lieutenants were scurrying around making sure everyone was present before the squadron commanders put in an appearance. The vehicle hangars were already open and lines of Scimitar and Spartan recce vehicles could be seen peeping out. All was well with the world and I had a veritable spring in my step as I made my way towards the headquarters building.

"Morning Sir," called the RSM as I entered the headquarters.

"Good morning to you, RSM," I responded. "Any good rumours to pass on today?" The RSM was one of the best connected blokes in the HQ and was usually good for some chitchat about forthcoming appointments and the like.

"Nothing for you today Sir, but you'll be the first to know when I hear something." For some unknown reason he frequently confided in me, and his information was usually pretty reliable too. In my opinion it always pays to the keep the RSM onside and this one was no different. "Much obliged, as always," I told him, with a conspiratorial wink.

The morning passed easily enough and a half-dozen cups of coffee put pay to my hangover, thankfully. I had a quiet word with the chief clerk who promised me a copy of all Pemberton's reports on disk without even asking why I needed them, and the rest of the morning was spent surfing the Internet looking for a decent second hand GTi to replace the somewhat tired looking model I had been clinging onto since returning from the Balkans years before. All in all it was turning into rather a good day, or would have done if something had not then happened to blacken it beyond all recognition. At that moment there was a knock on the office door and the CO appeared.

"Harry, good to see you on this fine morning," he grinned, not giving me enough time to reply. "Look, something has come up which I think might have your name on it, very much up your street, so I thought I should run it past you, what?" I had an immediate feeling of impending doom. Perhaps it was the hangover still clouding my brain but I failed to come up with a response and instead just sat dumbly awaiting the rest of his pronouncement. "Well look, I haven't got much time but I would like to talk to you about this today if poss. Could you pop into my office after lunch? Thanks." With that he was gone, and the office door clicked shut behind him. I stared at the screen, my mind churning over the various possibilities that could be heading my way. The CO was a straight talking chap and if it was anything trivial he would have come out with it there and then. It wasn't a bollocking – God knows, I'd had enough of them, and I knew what his face looked like when he was about to dish one out. But it wasn't a pat on the back either, which was disconcerting. Probably just some dull staff duty he wants me to take on, I decided, and returned to searching for a suitably entertaining motor car to replace the current toy.

The potential for conflict in Iraq was all over the lunchtime news, with both Bush and Blair pledging to do their utmost to get a UN resolution before committing troops to action. Like an idiot I joined the chaps getting sandwiches and plonked myself in the mess TV room, which did nothing for my nerves prior to meeting the boss. US troops were already building up significantly in the region and, as far as I could see, it was fast getting to the point of no return – in another few weeks the deployment would have generated its own momentum and Bush would have painted himself into a corner whereby he wouldn't be able to bring his boys home without having won some kind of tangible concessions from the Iraqis. And if the concessions didn't come . . . well, there would presumably be some kind of punch-up, and it would doubtless involve the Brits as well as the Americans. I couldn't care less about Joe Iraqi, he could take his oil and burn it for all I cared, and as for human rights abuses, well that was clearly just an expedient excuse for taking action – there was no shortage of dictators around the world after all. But I did care that another Gulf War might involve yours truly, and for this reason alone I found myself silent in front of the BBC footage from Kuwait, rooting for a diplomatic solution to the whole mess. My face must have told a story because halfway through the news bulletin Charlie Valdez-Welch thrust a pint of the cold stuff in my hand and told me I had a face like a wet weekend.

"The CO wants to see me after lunch," I told him. "Don't suppose you know what he wants?"

"Sorry Flashy, I haven't the foggiest," he replied, then added, "Shit, you don't think he's got wind of us bunking off yesterday?"

"No, I don't think he has," I said. "I wouldn't mind too much if it was just a straightforward bollocking. It's something else, and I'm not getting a warm fuzzy feeling about it."

"Well, no point brooding over it. I'm getting another beer. Want one? I mean, if it is bad news you might as well be half-cut when he dishes it out."

He had a point, so I accepted the beer, which in hindsight may have been a mistake. If my wits were more fully about me perhaps I could have come up with something imaginative to counteract the news the CO was about to throw at me.

Straight after lunch I padded along the headquarters corridor which led to the CO's office, passing a series of oil paintings of the regiment's exploits during the 19th Century as I walked. Afghanistan featured several times, as did Persia, which should have been enough to get the alarm bells jangling.

"Ah, Harry, there you are. Do take a seat," said the CO, gesturing towards the leather button-back armchairs that littered the front of his office. The room was enormous, all oak panels and more oil paintings, this time of former commanding officers. His desk was also oak and measured a good eight feet across – ludicrously over the top for a battalion commander, but then it had been in the regiment for well over 100 years. I sat myself down with a growing feeling of unease. "I expect you're wondering what all this is about," he continued. Too bloody right I was. "Well the long and the short of it is that a job has come up with your old friends at 3 Commando Brigade." My heart sank like a stone. I had only returned from service in Afghanistan with the Royal Marines six months earlier – a tour of duty which had hugely enhanced my reputation (albeit not through any of my own actions) but very nearly cost me my life.

"But Colonel . . .," I stuttered, but it was no use, he simply waved an impatient arm to shut me up. "Harry, I know perfectly well what you are going to say. Of course it's jolly noble to think that another chap should be given a crack of the whip, but I have the reputation of the regiment to think of and you have an absolutely first-class track record with the Marines. Just look at the report that they wrote last time around!" He reached into his desk drawer and produced the dreaded document then waved it theatrically at me across the desk. "First-class! Courageous! A clear thinker! Cool under fire! It's all in here Harry. Once I re-read this there was no doubt in my mind that you were the right man – the only man – for the job."

My head was swimming. It seemed only yesterday that I had found myself cowering behind the mud wall of a fort in the Hindu Kush while hoards of Taliban fiends fired AK47s and lobbed grenades in my general direction. In the nick of time I managed to call in an airstrike, although I came within an ace of getting myself shot in the process. I counted it little short of a miracle that I had survived at all and frankly if that was the sort of place the Royal Marines frequented then they could keep it. And yet here I was about to be sent back to the commandos at a time when there was another war looming. It was too awful for words. I think the shock must have affected my speech, for I simply sat staring at the CO in disbelief, not uttering a sound. He probably took this to be a show of steely resolution, the daft old sod.

"Now the Marines," continued the boss, "want someone

who can act as a liaison officer between themselves and whichever armoured unit the MoD chooses to send to the Gulf. Good chaps, the commandos, but they know bugger all about armoured warfare, as I'm sure you remember from your time with them last year." I sat there shivering in disbelief as he droned on. "You'll be attached to Brigade Headquarters, at least at first, but they reckon you'll probably be pushed forward to a commando unit if there is any actual fighting, to advise the CO on the mechanics of tying up with armoured formations for any push into Iraq." He beamed at me from across the desk. "Well Harry, what do you think? Pretty bloody good, eh? We all know how much you enjoyed last year's deployment and working with the Marines. I expect they'll be delighted to have you back – you're becoming something of a permanent fixture within 3 Brigade, eh?" He chortled at his own joke, while my insides turned to jelly. It would mean months spent among officers who, while presumably reasonably competent at their jobs, shared nothing in common with me whatsoever. There was barely an old school tie between them, none of them could ride, polo was a foreign language to them and, while my idea of vigorous exercise was a round of golf, theirs was a 15-mile run followed by press-ups outside the mess. The whole prospect of returning to them was simply too awful for words.

"You'll receive the joining instructions in a couple of days and you'll need to be with them immediately after Christmas leave," said the CO. "I know you'll love every minute of it Harry. Ah, sometimes I wish I was a younger man – this is just the kind of opportunity I would have jumped at."

Lying bastard, I thought, twenty years earlier he was probably skulking around the clubs of London, doing his best to avoid serving in Northern Ireland and bouncing every filly in sight. Which is precisely what I would have been doing this New Year, if this bombshell hadn't just been dropped on me. I bade him farewell and sloped back to the mess, in urgent need of a stiff drink.

NOTES

1 Flashman is referring to the dossier compiled by the Labour Government and the Joint Intelligence Committee (JIC) in September 2002, detailing Saddam Hussein's alleged weapons of mass destruction and including the now infamous claim, subsequently found to be false, that the Iraqi leader could deploy such weapons within 45 minutes. No weapons of mass destruction were found following the invasion and an independent inquiry in the UK, chaired by Lord Butler, found that Tony Blair's cabinet and the JIC had both made grave errors of judgement in publishing the dossier without significant caveats about the reliability of the intelligence contained therein.

2 PJHQ: Permanent Joint Headquarters, the UK's centre of operations, located at Northwood, west London.

3 CDS: Chief of Defence Staff.

2

With the news of my impending posting still fresh in my mind I found myself somewhat distracted during Christmas leave. Even the prospect of brandy, bonhomie and slaughtering pheasants with the chaps from my Sandhurst platoon was not enough to lift me from my sulk and the whole festive season passed me by like a ticking clock, each day bringing me just a little nearer to my departure for Plymouth. The whole situation was too ghastly for words but it did have one saving grace, in that my pained expression was noticed by Roddy Woodstock's rather attractive younger sister, Charlotte, who asked why I was looking so glum. I must admit that I hammed up the answer somewhat such that it had the desired effect and, a couple of stiff drinks later, she insisted on taking me to bed for the afternoon, which was something of a tonic I don't mind telling you. Nevertheless, the two weeks of Christmas leave was over soon enough and on January 3rd I found myself disconsolately packing my bags and preparing myself for life in the desert. This was bad enough in itself and made substantially worse by the Royal Marines' insistence that I bring only one large kitbag in addition to my bergen and webbing. I had always found several bags and my old Wellington school trunk insufficient to hold all my belongings when moving from place to place with the regiment, yet now I was expected to achieve the same result with less than a third of the space. It was absurd and my mood blackened further as I was forced to abandon a perfectly good case of scotch and also, would you credit it, my duvet. (After numerous uncomfortable exercises spent shivering on the Barossa training area I had vowed not to spend any unnecessary nights in a sleeping bag and yet here I was preparing, for the second time in a year, to spend months sleeping in the wretched thing.) In the interim there would be just a couple of nights in the officers' mess down in Plymouth before we set off for the Gulf and I had no intention whatsoever of leaving a room full of clobber for the light-fingered Royal Marines rear party to pilfer while I was gone. Come to that, I had no intention of returning to Plymouth at all and, assuming I made it unscathed through the adventure ahead, I planned to bid farewell to the Marines the minute we returned to English soil. With this in mind it felt a little easier to leave most of my trappings in my room in the regimental mess in the hope that they would be the first possessions to welcome me home, so to speak.

A sharp hoot on a car horn alerted me to the presence of the duty driver outside my window and it was with heavy heart that I heard the latch on my room door click shut behind me as I staggered down the corridor with my bag, bergen and webbing. The staff car – a ridiculously over-pompous term for a car unbecoming of a second-rate sales rep – was right outside the back door of the mess and the driver, lance corporal someone-or-other, was all smiles and good wishes as he loaded my clobber into the boot.

"The duty sergeant tells me you're off back to the Marines, to go to the Gulf, Sir," he beamed at me. "I bet you can't wait. A bit more exciting with the Marines, I suppose, than with the Regiment." Then, realising his perceived disloyalty, he caught himself and quickly added, "Not that there's anything wrong with the QRH of course but, you know, tours of the Balkans can get a bit repetitive for the lads."

I had spoken about almost nothing else for the whole of Christmas Leave so, as you might imagine, I was royally aggrieved that after enduring a fortnight of answering inane questions about the Middle East I should have to face more of the same from an idiot driver. I flew into a rage, told him what I thought of him and, if memory serves me, I think I even threatened to charge him with insubordination if he didn't shut up. Fortunately the obsequious little toad got the message and we drove the route to Warminster railway station in complete silence which, considering the alternative, was absolute bliss. He even unloaded my bags onto a luggage trolley and wheeled it to my platform without uttering a sound, then hovered around, presumably waiting for my train to arrive so that he could load the baggage on-board for me. It was a distraction I could do without, so I shooed him away and spent an enjoyable ten minutes waiting for the train sending Charlotte Woodstock solicitous text messages from my mobile phone.

Once on-board, I found an empty first-class compartment and watched England's rather soggy and not-so-pleasant landscape pass by the window until we reached Exeter St David's, where I had to change trains. Again I had a few minutes to kill and, asides from pestering La Woodstock with yet more lurid messages, I amused myself by counting the number of Royal Marines recruits I could spot on the station.[1] Eventually the Plymouth train rolled in and with a heavy heart and a strong sense of déjà vu I clambered aboard. Less than an hour later and the feeling was stronger than ever, as I shuffled out to the taxi rank in front of Plymouth station, feeling the cold coastal drizzle dampening my cheeks and hearing the cabby's west country burr as he asked where I as going.

"Stonehouse, if you please," I answered.

"I thought you must be goin' there," he responded. "I seen 'em bags of yours and I thought aye aye, that'll be another arrival destined for the desert. There's been plenty of 'em during Christmas Leave, I don't mind tellin' you." Well at least I won't be the only Johnny-come-lately in the mess, I thought to myself, a few more new arrivals to keep me company will be no bad thing.

Stonehouse Barracks was exactly as I remembered it: a

beautiful Victorian stone quadrangle with offices and accommodation mixed higgledy piggledy on all sides, and the entrance to the officers' mess nestling in a far corner. The setting would have had more impact if the centre of the quad had not been used as a regimental car park, but even with the addition of a hundred or so cars it was a very picturesque scene. Plymouth was hardly somewhere I would ever wish to be based but I couldn't help thinking quietly to myself that such a glorious headquarters was somewhat wasted on the Marines, most of whom would have been just as happy in prefabricated squalor dating from the 1970s – as indeed was proven by the living quarters of 42 Commando, just a few short miles down the road.[2] I showed my ID card briefly to the young chap manning the main gate and loped across the courtyard to the mess, where the porter relieved me of my bag (but left me wrestling with the bergen) and showed me to my room (or cabin, as the Marines insist on calling them, in a transparent attempt to remind the rest of the world that they are part of the Senior Service), a pokey little hovel on the ground floor, complete with creaking pipes and peeling paint. Still, it would do for a couple of nights and would no doubt seem the height of luxury compared to whatever deprivations lay ahead. I unpacked the few personal items I had brought with me in a futile attempt to make the room a little more homely. Its saving grace was a proximity to the bar, where I had every intention of spending as much of the ensuing 48 hours as possible. Many of life's little luxuries would probably be lacking in Kuwait and the absence of alcohol was a racing certainty. In addition to a carefully secreted bottle or two in my bags, I planned to smuggle as much out in my bloodstream as humanly possible. Having hung up my kit and partially emptied my bags there seemed little point in loitering around my bedroom, so I made my way through to the lounge to see whether there was anyone else on-board.

As it turned out there were numerous officers of assorted cap badges adorning the bar. A heated debate was taking place and I had difficulty making out what the discussion was about, so I ordered myself a beer and shuffled closer to the group. At first I mistakenly thought the conversation was about whether Britain should be sending troops to the Gulf at all. The UK as a whole was divided by the issue and these debates were taking place in messes and clubs up and down the country. The hawks were determined to sock it to Saddam while the doves reasoned that the UN should be given more time to deal with him and anyway, what was the rush to invade when we couldn't properly quantify the threat that Iraq posed. For Flashy at least, the debate had reached resolution: if I was on the nominal of troops to be sent to the Gulf, then clearly the UK should not be taking part in such folly. I was about to offer my two pennies' worth on the topic, when I spotted the chap at the centre of the group and overheard a snapshot of conversation, accompanied by some emotional gesticulation.

"Well, what can I do?" (Waving of hands and shrugging shoulders.) "We are all in zee military, non? So I must do as I am told. But zat doesn't mean I 'ave to agree wiz it. It's a stupid decision, trés bête. And very frustrating for me, ziz you must understand. I would love to go, of course, I am a professionelle, juste like you."

By this stage I had a clear view of the individual and could see that he was sporting French uniform, which only served to beg the question of what a frog was doing in the officers' mess of 3 Commando Brigade Headquarters. The discussion was quickly halted as said frog spotted me from across the bar and waved the group aside.

"Anyhow, we have a guest," he announced, waving me into the group. "I apologise monsieur, we did not mean to be so rude. You must be new here." He outstretched a hand in greeting, which I shook, in spite of my inveterate dislike of all things French.

I introduced myself to the Frenchman, who I could now see was a captain in the French commandos, and to the rest of the group, which consisted of a Navy doctor, OC Brigade Recce Force, an attached officer from the Royal Artillery, and an assortment of Royal Marines staff officers – the usual group of skivers and drinkers that one finds in a mess on any given weekday afternoon. Funny how quickly a headquarters changes its staff: I could remember none of them from Afghanistan less than a year earlier.

Light was soon shed on their conversation. The French officer was on a two-year attachment to 3 Commando Brigade, and the French government had just issued an instruction that, since their troops were not to be involved in any action against Iraq, he was not to deploy with the Marines. His line, or at least the line he was taking when talking to the British, was that he was part of Brigade Headquarters and should therefore be perfectly entitled to go on operations with them. It takes one to know one, as they say, and I had delivered enough bluff and bravado in my time to have my suspicions of what his real emotions might be. I must admit feeling a fair pang of envy – the lucky swine would presumably waft his way back to Paris and spend a happy six months whoring and drinking Chablis while the rest of us were forced to slog it out in the fetid heat of the Middle East. Amongst his military peers, missing out on the deployment wouldn't matter a farthing, since the French government had already made it plain that no French troops would be committed unless there was a fresh UN resolution which, as they held a veto on the Security Council, seemed highly improbable. Instead the opportunistic bastards would simply sit on the sidelines and wait for the shooting to finish before muscling in on the most lucrative reconstruction contracts, all shrugging shoulders and Gallic charm, no doubt. Fair weather allies, aye, and when the clouds roll in just look at 'em run, I thought to myself.

I invested the remainder of the afternoon in getting quietly sozzled and chatting to the assorted chaps in the room, gleaning as much information as I could about the forthcoming operations and the various characters I would need to interface with. The artillery officer was particularly useful to talk to, since he was also an attached Army rank. He had admittedly completed his

Commando Course so had turned partly native but nevertheless he saw the Corps of the Royal Marines through Sandhurst-trained eyes, which was helpful, at least to me. I knew the layout of a brigade operations room well enough to know that during the deployment, nestling among all the other staff officers and watchkeepers, the artillery (or "Arty") desk would be a pretty central feature. With a bit of luck and a following wind I could arrange for the desk labelled "Armour" to be next door to him, which would at least mean I wouldn't have to speak exclusively with Royal Marines morning, noon and night. A seasoned artilleryman, he had been attached to the Brigade since its return from Kabul a year earlier and was on good terms with almost everyone in the headquarters, and wasted little time introducing me to most of the gaggle involved in that afternoon's conversation.

By early evening the bar had filled up significantly with a variety of souls mainly sporting combat clothing. The Royal Marines have a peculiar obsession with hygiene and widely consider it inappropriate or downright rude to dine without washing and changing first. (Fortunately the Army is a little more pragmatic and has no such hang-ups about eating in work clothes.) Sure enough, as the dinner gong drew nearer, they began to depart, returning en masse a few minutes later sporting jackets and ties and smelling faintly of soap.

I made my way to the bar to line up a last pint before supper and was startled by a swift punch on the arm and a thunderous "Hallo!" I turned around to be confronted by the grinning face of a disgracefully irreverent media liaison officer with whom I had got into several scrapes in Kabul a year earlier. I shook his hand like a man being rescued from a sinking ship. A demon skier, the man had initially been commissioned into the Army back in the 1980s but had transferred his Commission to the Marines almost on a whim after just a few years' service. He had long since been discharged and retrained as a solicitor. But after a short time in civilian life he had joined the Reserves, risen to the rank of major, and become a seasoned war-tourist volunteering (insanely, in my opinion) for deployment after deployment on the basis that it was more interesting work than life in his law practice. He was truly his own man, someone who did as he pleased and took nothing in life too seriously. Keeping him in check was practically impossible – his CO once remarked that he would rather administer bollockings to anyone else in his unit, since it was a racing certainty that they would be ignored, which was not only frustrating but served to visibly undermine his authority too. I noticed that he was walking awkwardly and remarked upon it.

"My back's trashed," admitted my media liaison chum. "I broke it skiing last year. Total nightmare. Had to spend months in a body cast so I'm weak as a kitten at the moment. Can't run either – it hurts too much. Hope no bugger asks me to carry a bergen on this trip, because I don't think I'll be able to lift the thing, let alone walk anywhere with it."

"Then what the Dickens are you doing here?" I blurted out. "Surely you should have been medically downgraded by now?"

He met this outburst with a wry smile. "Of course I should. But I couldn't let the opportunity of a good old-fashioned war pass me by. And the quacks at Chilwell are atrocious, everyone knows that.[3] Admit nothing and they'll never find out for themselves. So I kept schtum, told a few half-truths and ta-da! Here I am, SO2 Media."[4]

"You must be bloody mad," I told him. "A perfectly good excuse to avoid this idiocy and you not only volunteer for it, you hide the fact that you are crippled in order to join in."

We agreed to differ and shuffled through to dinner. In fairness to Stonehouse, one of the absolute joys of being based in Plymouth is the extraordinarily friendly nature of the mess staff. A posse of largely middle-aged women make it their mission in life to fuss over the officers as if they were spoilt children. Nothing is too much like hard work, everything is delivered with a smile and an old-world charm which I have seldom seem matched in the best London establishments, let alone the provinces. Yet another reason why Stonehouse is wasted on the Marines – if it were up to me, I would have the entire place moved to Salisbury Plain and given over to the Hussars. Still, their jollity and eagerness to please, coupled with the company of SO2 Media, made dinner a significantly happier affair than it otherwise might have been. For reasons unknown I was as hungry as a horse and thirsty to boot, so I set about leveraging the goodwill of the mess staff in order to get second helpings of everything, while a couple of the chaps joined me in putting away a couple of bottles of Amarone, which fairly hit the spot.

I was all for whiling the evening away in the mess bar but SO2 Media was having none of it. It was, he pointed out, potentially our last-but-one opportunity to paint the town red and we had nothing to do the following day but the nauseating tedium of traipsing round RM Stonehouse's many administrative offices to draw desert kit, sign forms, and have Lord-knows-how-many inoculations. Not the kind of day which requires much brainpower. He called a cab and we made the short journey to the Barbican, always a good spot for a jar or two and for ogling the local talent which, it being Plymouth, is far from shy. It was a frigid evening but this seemed to have no effect on the attire of the local girlies, who thronged from pub to pub wearing little more than their underwear – a truly enjoyable spectacle. We descended on a wine bar and began working our way through their stock of Italian reds whilst putting the world to rights. After an hour or more I had comfortably settled in and was sporting the kind of rosy glow that comes from coupling excess food and booze with cold winter air, when I felt an unexpected tap on the shoulder and looked up. There, looking down on me with her trademark haughty smile, was Kate Gibson, a filly over whom I had spent many an idle hour fantasising during our days at Sandhurst together. She was vacuous, conceited bitch – but stunningly good looking and fit as a racehorse, which more than compensated for any failings of character, at least in my book.

""Harry bloody Flashman!" she explained. "What the hell are you doing in Plymouth?"

With transparently false modesty, I explained the current situation, leaving little room for doubt that I now stood head and shoulders above my peers in terms of being selected for such an operationally vital mission. She looked less than impressed, while SO2 Media looked suitably quizzical as I introduced him. He disappeared to the bar to get some more wine while La Gibson, before I had chance to ask her, drew up a chair and the two of us descended into the usual "Whatever happened to such-and-such . . .?" conversation that one invariably has with old colleagues. Kate, it transpired, was attached to the Navy for a couple of years on some job creation scheme dreamt up by the Second Sea Lord's office. She was currently stationed in Plymouth and had tentatively agreed to meet an old university friend for a glass of wine that night. At least that was her story and to be fair, I could see no sign of any lingering bloke whom she might be seeing. Equally, there was no sign of the university friend either which, given her unusually friendly overtures, I was rather glad of. SO2 Media reappeared with the wine and three glasses and we set about getting more merrier than we already were. Shortly before we reached the bottom of the bottle, Kate departed to powder her nose and I seized my opportunity to get shot of my Media Ops colleague.

"Look, I wouldn't ask this of you unless you were a real chum. But would you, ahem, push off somewhere else?"

"You jack bastard," he retorted, clearly unhappy.

"You'd ask the same in my position."

"Balls," he replied. "I'd stick to my guns and have a lads' night out."

"Be that as it may, this bird is clearly gooey at the forks – she's putty in my hands! And I've wanted to get stuck into her since Sandhurst. Now be a good sport and disappear, eh?"

With that he got up, called me a tosser, winked, and vanished towards the door. I felt a vague pang of guilt but it soon evaporated when Kate reappeared, all T&A and sporting freshly applied gloss lipstick.

"Where's your friend?" she asked.

"Ah, I'm not sure," I stuttered. "His mobile phone rang and he had to shoot off somewhere."

Kate looked deeply disbelieving but said nothing. Conversation resumed and I plied her with more vino. The evening disappeared in a haze of wine and reminiscing about the bunch of wasters with whom we had passed through officer training. Then, just before the bar called last orders she stood up, looked down her nose at me and held out her hand. I stared at it dumbly, frustrated that she was calling time on the evening.

"Come on Harry," she cajoled. "Let's get back to my place. There's a stash of wine and you might as well spend your last real night of civilisation enjoying yourself."

I chortled at my good luck, downed the remnants of my wine, grabbed La Gibson by the arm, strode out into the freezing night air and hailed a passing cab. A few minutes later we tumbled through the door of her flat, a delightful little place on the Hoe. She practically tore the shirt off my back and I reciprocated by relieving her of her skirt and blouse. My Camberley fantasies were rapidly being fulfilled – she had the body of a gymnast and was clearly proud of it. I pulled down her bra and grabbed a handful of breast while she wrapped her legs around my waist and lowered herself onto me. I was so taken aback by her impatience for a good seeing-to that it took me a moment or two to get into my stride. But before long I was bouncing her for all I was worth, while she cried out like a banshee and dug her fingernails into my shoulders. Her physique was matched only by her stamina and when we eventually called it a night I was a spent force, albeit a very contented one. In the morning I awoke shortly before six, mouth parched from all the wine and the vigorous exercise that had followed it. My previous night's conquest lay tucked under the duvet in blissful ignorance. I shuffled through to the kitchen for a glass of water before getting dressed as quietly as I could manage. Kate still hadn't stirred and I really couldn't be fagged with the usual morning-after pleasantries or any more of her banal twittering, so instead of waking her I stole quietly away, shivering in the chilly pre-dawn sea air.

By the time I had a shower and a shave and presented myself for an early breakfast, the first glimmers of dawn were showing themselves and Stonehouse was brightening up. As usual the waitresses were a joy and, presumably from years of experience, could home in on a hangover from a thousand paces. I was duly plied with lashings of coffee and toast, followed by a full fried breakfast which would have been a challenge for a gang of Irish navvies. By the end of it all I was pressed to work out whether I was fortified or simply more tired and sleepy than I had been at the outset. I didn't have long to ponder the question though as just at that moment my media and artillery brethren appeared, both looking as rough and hungover as me.

"Ah, Flash, you disgraceful excuse for a friend," commented SO2 Media, perhaps justifiably. "And did Sir get lucky last night? Or did the stuck-up cow blow you out?"

I shot him a victorious grin. "I was invited back to her place, if that's what you're asking."

"Don't avoid the question, Flashy. Did you, or did you not, give her the good news?"

I confessed and, at the insistence of the boys, spent the ensuing five minutes giving them a blow-by-blow account of the bedroom gymnastics the previous evening, my story being punctuated by the occasional comings and goings of the mess staff. When I had finished there was a brief silence, eventually interrupted by the artilleryman.

"You fluky bastard," he said coolly. "I've been here for months and nothing that good has happened. You come down here for one night and get the jump of your life immediately before departing for operations. That's not far short of winning the lottery."

Kate certainly wasn't the jump of my life – several conquests vied for that honour and, for all her bedroom prowess, Ms Gibson was not even on the shortlist. However, I had to admit that he had a point – but then his lack of success with the ladies was hardly my problem so my response was not entirely sympathetic. I asked for yet more coffee and shuffled off to catch the morning news bulletin on the TV.

I had a check-list of admin tasks to carry out during the remainder of the day, none too onerous but all frustratingly time-consuming. The first of these was to draw my desert clothing from the stores. I was prepared for a bust-up here, since most of the Brigade had already drawn its kit and there would presumably be a shortfall, especially of larger sized items. My intuition was correct and I departed the stores an hour later only partially equipped. The rest of the gear would be available from the Quarter Master's store in Kuwait, I was assured. I was far from convinced but I had no choice in the matter, so I took what kit there was and dumped it in my room.

Next on the list was a round of paperwork which was dull as ditchwater and took up most of the morning. Military bureaucracy is an incredible thing and seems to grow inexorably, made worse by the small-minded little men who dream up most of the regulations I am faced with these days. But eventually the forms were all filled and the boxes ticked and finally it was time for a visit to the sick bay for my jabs. I knew perfectly well that I was in-date for almost everything but, not having had time to extract my medical documents from the clutches of the Army, I knew equally well that the Navy would take the belt-and-braces route of giving me the inoculations all over again. After a short wait, the doctor called my name (no rank either, the impertinent bastard). Sure enough, I had more needles stuck in me than if I had run naked through a cactus grove. Typhoid, hepatitis, yellow fever, and various other assorted nasties all entered my bloodstream via a syringe. The doctor was an unsympathetic devil too, not slowing for an instant despite my wincing and wriggling. After what felt like an eternity of acupuncture came a line I shall never forget.

"And would you like anthrax, Sir?"

I looked at him in disbelief. Right now I could think of nothing I would like less.

"The anthrax vaccine? Would you like the first shot?" he said, growing impatient.

Happily, my bemused look disguised my complete conviction that, under no circumstances, was I going to accept yet another pathogen in my bloodstream, especially one as lethal as anthrax.

"You must be bloody joking," I responded, scoffing.

The old sawbones looked piously at me. "I assure you I am not," he said, labouring his delivery as if I was some kind of halfwit from the Pioneer Corps. "It's a probability that Saddam Hussein has anthrax in his arsenal and there is a distinct risk that, in the event of hostilities, you may be exposed." With that, he passed me a MoD-published idiot's guide to the issue.

"So your solution to this problem is to expose me to it now?" I retorted. "Well that's a work of genius on somebody's behalf. Thank you for your kind offer, Sir, but if it's all the same to you I shall decline it." I had seen and heard quite enough horror stories of Gulf War Syndrome following Operation Desert Storm back in '91, and I had no intention of joining the poor buggers on the sick list in five years time. Besides, at the back of my mind there was the glimmer of hope that, if the intelligence community did ever manage to prove conclusively that Iraq had stockpiles of biological weapons, then those of us who had refused the jabs might be kept back from the front line. With this in my mind I turned on my heel and strode out of the clinic, leaving the doctor and his anthrax jabs for some other unfortunate soul.

The various vaccines left me feeling rather washed out, so I spent a quiet afternoon and evening tinkering with my kit and feeling ever more sorry for myself. By the time I had finished packing my bergen it weighed a good forty pounds and I had yet to add any field equipment such as a radio or ammunition.

Add the prospect of my webbing and weapon and I would probably be carrying over 80lbs, which is (presumably) fine for Royal Marines but is a stomach-turning prospect for a cavalry officer. That kind of weight is precisely the reason that Land Rovers were invented. I said a quiet prayer that the Brigade Headquarters staff would not travel anywhere on foot further than the distance from the transport aircraft to an awaiting staff car, but in the back of my mind doubts were beginning to grow and I was far from hopeful that this would turn out to be the case. Even a steak dinner and the bonhomie of the mess staff did little to raise my spirits, so I turned in early, hoping to sleep off the nausea which I presumed had been brought on by the typhoid jab. Bloody doctors. I also had a suspicion that an early night might be a good investment, for tomorrow we would be in the hands of the RAF movements staff – and that could make for a very long day indeed.

The following morning dawned crisp, bright and chilly. The watery sunshine brought with it an added air of industry – everywhere were bootnecks doubling back and forth, carrying bags, loading vehicles, drawing weapons, mustering troops and issuing briefings.[5] In short, it was one of those mornings which tells you that a unit is on the move. I joined forces with the other officers and we drew our shiny new SA80-A2 rifles from a rather grumpy armourer who complained bitterly that he was not deploying with the rest of the headquarters but was forced to remain with the rear party.[6] I completely failed to understand his point of view – surely the idiot should have been celebrating, but there's just no telling some people. By 10 a.m. coaches were lining up outside the barracks, accompanied by a line of 4-ton trucks to transport our baggage. After the usual rigmarole of loading, unloading and reloading equipment, we hit the road shortly before midday, armed with a paper bag filled with pasties, sausage rolls, scotch eggs, and other cheap muck procured from the Naafi to keep body and soul together during the coming hours.

By early afternoon we had arrived at the RAF Mounting Centre at South Cerney. Any serviceman who has travelled through this place will doubtless have a tale of woe to tell. I have had the misfortune to pass through it on numerous occasions and whenever I make the mistake of thinking it cannot get any worse, the RAF defies me by lowering its standards once again. For somewhere that most visitors are destined to spend many hours, South Cerney offers facilities that a Scottish Methodist would approve of. A couple of tired vending machines spit out cheap coffee and chocolates, an odd assortment of TVs play worn-out videos, and the waiting areas are equipped only with uncomfortable plastic chairs. Worst of all, there is no segregation of officers and men, so from battalion commanders down, everyone is thrown in together, all at the mercies of a bunch of jumped up little Hitlers sporting Air Force uniform, enjoying their one moment of authority in this life. How I haven't punched one of them yet, Lord only knows. All in all, it's a far cry from the British Airways club lounge at Heathrow. And so we waited. And waited. And waited. Day turned to night and our RAF friends announced that dinner awaited us in the cookhouse (no segregation and certainly no chance of visiting the officers' mess). Through the night, the waiting continued. The following morning, another announcement, this time breakfast. Post-breakfast, more mindless waiting. Then another announcement: lunch. By the time we returned from lunch even the most stoical among us were beginning to make threatening comments to the movements staff. Finally, a mere 24 hours after our arrival, some much-needed progress: a string of buses drew up outside. We were on our way to the airfield at RAF Brize Norton, a half-hour drive away. Unhappily, the waiting game continued at Brize, although this time it was only for a couple of hours.

Eventually, bleary-eyed and unshaven, we traipsed aboard the waiting 747 shortly after dusk. A charter aircraft, its livery told us it was Icelandic but the décor inside sported logos from at least three different airlines. In any event it was manned by an Icelandic crew who handed out more sandwiches and carbonated drinks, and steadfastly refused numerous repeated requests for booze. I dropped into a fitful sleep, awaking some hours later when early morning sunlight streamed through the windows. The aeroplane was banking steeply, so I peered down, surprised to see a sizeable mountain range beneath us in place of the expected Middle Eastern desert. A quick word with one of the hostesses confirmed that we were over Iran, not an especially comforting thought given their propensity for shooting down civilian airliners. The terrain looked spectacular but I was more concerned why we had not already touched down in Kuwait. Even the most rudimentary schoolboy geography told me that we had overshot the target and that Iran lay too far to the east.[7] The 747 completed its long turn and from the position of the sun I deduced that we were now headed west, which was at least the right direction for Kuwait. As the Arabian Gulf came into view beneath our wings we began our descent and a short time later touched down smoothly at Ali Al Saleem airbase.

Spirits rose as we disembarked and I realised that the temperature outside the plane was a balmy 23 degrees or so, not the blistering heat I had expected. Of course it was only January and it would get inexorably hotter during the coming weeks but for the moment it was pleasant enough. My initial burst of morale was soon crushed as we were escorted away from the concrete pan and into the British disembarkation centre, which was a dusty patch of rough ground festooned with row upon row of off-white tents, with queues of soldiers emerging from each one. It was essentially the Kuwaiti version of South Cerney, where logisticians and clerks processed piles of documentation, stamped endless forms, and lost the luggage of countless servicemen. I made my way into a tent marked "Officers Waiting Area", and grabbed a cup of watery tea from an urn perched on a folding chair. Asides from dozens of identical folding chairs, this was the only piece of décor in the tent, so I made my way back outside and sought directions from one of the dozens of loggies floating about. The fellow in question directed me to the back of one of the many queues and so I began the long, slow process of being booked "into theatre". There followed hours of form-filling, ID checks, medical documentation checks, local area briefings, mine awareness briefings, road safety briefings, etc etc. After much hunting amidst a pile of identical looking items I managed to locate my bergen and grip, after which we were segregated into groups depending on our eventual destination. I found myself in amongst the reprobates from 3 Commando Brigade Headquarters once again, our numbers swollen by the addition of numerous ranks destined for 539 Assault Squadron, 59 Commando Engineers, 29 Commando Artillery, and various augmentees belonging to 42 Commando. Weighed down by bergens and baggage we were ushered towards a long line of scruffy-looking coaches and lorries by an escort group of Marines sporting weaponry of all kinds and driving civilian hire cars with darkened windows, which gave the whole convoy a slightly mafia-like appearance. I asked one of the Marines why they were equipped in this manner and immediately regretted asking the question.

"Some of the locals have been shooting up the convoys," he replied. "We think they're Iraqis but nobody knows for sure. The idea is to keep the military profile to a minimum, so there's no Land Rovers." He held up his rifle, grinning. "At least this way we can have a conversation with them if they start anything."

I hefted my bags onto one of the attending trucks and found an empty seat on a coach. Sure enough, all the curtains were drawn so that no-one outside could see that we were in uniform. I had hoped that, if nothing else, Kuwait would provide safe sanctuary during the coming weeks but now even that slender hope had been dashed. I slumped into a seat and dropped into a fitful sleep as the convoy trundled its way slowly along the desert highway.

By the time I awoke it was dark and we were moving along a dirt road – dust was creeping into the coach through the gaps in the windows and my smock was being gradually coated with a film of fine, grey grime. Looking out, I could see vehicle headlights illuminating billowing sand being kicked up by traffic moving on parallel dirt roads. We passed a series of checkpoints and I knew that we had entered a military encampment. It was evidently a sizable camp too, because we drove inside it for quite a distance before coming to a halt. One of the escorting Marines appeared in the doorway of the coach and announced that we had arrived at Camp Gibraltar. Like everyone else on board, this meant nothing to me. I had no idea who was accommodated at Camp Gibraltar or where it was situated within Kuwait. The coach emptied and we stumbled around in the dark until we found the contents of the baggage wagons piled in a heap on the sand. This is a great jape in the military, since everybody's kit looks identical and sifting one bergen from another at night is a tedious and time-consuming job. It gets easier when the pile is diminished though, so I slid to the rear of the gaggle of bodies and cadged a cigarette from one of the multitude of staff officers, while the more eager in our party took on the hard graft of sifting through the pile of baggage and extracting their own luggage from it. After about an hour, all of us had been reunited with our bags and the various commanders in the group had taken charge of their blokes. The previously disjointed swarm of bodies had been transformed into military-looking groups, all stood in three ranks awaiting their next instructions. Somewhere amongst them were dozens of floating officers, myself included, also awaiting a spot of guidance on where to go next. Happily, at that moment, a Regimental Sergeant Major appeared and took charge of proceedings.

"Good evening all, and welcome to sunny Kuwait," he bellowed at the assorted masses. "Since you have no idea where you are staying, I will now tell you. Some of you will be accommodated here, some will be in the next-door camp, and some of you are a few miles up the road, so you'll have to get back onboard the buses." Groans were heard from the audience at the prospect of another night-time move. "Listen in for your formation. 59 Commando ranks, you're staying here." A cheer came up from the engineers. "29 gunners, you are also staying here." Another cheer. "42 Commando, you're next door." He gesticulated with his RSM's stick. "It's about 500 metres, so you'll have to carry your baggage." A groan came from the Marines of 42 Commando. "Lastly, Brigade Headquarters. You're staying in Camp Commando, which is quite a few miles south of here. Back on the buses, fellas."

"Tossers," muttered SO2 Media, who was stood behind me. "They never get tired of the on-the-bus, off-the-bus routine." Grumbling, we dragged our baggage back onto the awaiting wagons and clambered aboard the coaches once again. They bumped back down the dirt roads, again covering us with another film of dust, and eventually we turned back onto the black strip of the tar highway, heading south. In fact we retraced our route much of the way back to the airport, which was infuriating, before turning off the highway, through a Kuwaiti police roadblock, and into another, very different looking military camp. Unlike Camp Gibraltar, which was illuminated only by vehicle headlights, Camp Commando was lit up like a Hollywood film set. Chain-link fences stood 15 feet above us, topped with rolls of razor wire. A wooden watchtower overlooked the entrance to the camp, manned by a US Marine toting a belt-fed machine-gun. More US Marines appeared, checking the IDs of the coach drivers and the passengers. Eventually the barriers were lifted and limestone gravel crunched under our tyres as we entered the camp. Like most American military establishments, it was laid out on an impressive scale. Row after row of tents were interspersed with portakabin-style shower blocks. Hundreds of trucks and Humvees were parked in neat lines, with a similar number of civilian 4x4s also on display. Only one section of the camp remained shrouded in darkness but there was enough light spilling from the surrounding area for me to make out the silhouette of a ridiculously ambitious assault course. We drove past it and the coach drew to a halt outside another gate, this time manned by British soldiers. 3 Commando Brigade Headquarters was a camp within a camp – probably the most secure place in the Middle East, which gave me a much-needed sense of reassurance. I felt much happier at the prospect of being surrounded by British troops rather than their American counterparts, whose gun-toting antics have always made me somewhat ill at ease. Our coach rolled through the gate, proceeded along a gravel road for a few hundred metres, and turned into a large, empty square, bounded on all sides by neat rows of large off-white tents, each measuring easily 30 yards long. We debussed quietly, recovered our luggage from yet another heap of bags and bergens and were ushered towards the accommodation tents by an ill-tempered Warrant Officer who seemed thoroughly annoyed to have been forced out of his bed at that time of night.

"Officers that way," he instructed us, pointing to the nearest tents. "Senior NCOs over there," pointing to our rear, "and all other ranks in the tents along the fence-line. There's no ceremony and there should be plenty of space for all of you, so find yourselves an empty bed and get your heads down."

I fished a torch out of my webbing and set about finding a vacant bunk in the nearest tent. Fortunately there were several to choose from so I picked one that wasn't surrounded by piles of baggage or festooned with damp sports equipment. I shoved my webbing and grip underneath the bed, retrieved my sleeping bag from my bergen, and collapsed into the bottom bunk. It was midnight. Incredibly, the move from Plymouth to Kuwait had taken almost 60 hours. I made a hollow promise to myself never again to rely on RAF movements staff, and promptly passed out.

NOTES

1. If you ever happen to pass through Exeter, keep an eye out for groups of seemingly half-starved youths with alarmingly short haircuts, an air of growing confidence, sporting clothes that any self-respecting football hooligan would be proud of – and you are probably looking at the latest products of the Commando Training Centre, which is located a few miles to the south. To be fair, they do turn out some pretty good soldiers from time to time – if they didn't, these chronicles would never have been written.
2. 42 Commando RM, based in Bickleigh, near Plymouth, is housed in 1970's prefabricated accommodation which is the antithesis of the grandeur of the brigade headquarters at Stonehouse.
3. The Reserves Training and Mobilisation Centre (RTMC) at Chilwell, where (at the time) reservists from all three services passed through as part of their mobilisation procedure before deploying on operations.
4. SO2: Staff Officer, second class (a position usually held by a major).
5. Bootneck: Navy slang for a Royal Marine, which probably stems from the leather collar worn as part of a Marine's uniform in the 18th Century.
6. Following complaints about the poor performance and shocking build quality of the SA80 rifle since its widespread introduction in 1985, the MoD finally admitted in 2000 that the weapon needed improving. The contract went to a German firm, Heckler & Koch, who replaced many of the parts with seemingly identical components machined to finer tolerances from higher grade steel. H&K and the MoD both claimed significantly improved performance from the A2 version of the SA80, but many soldiers who used it claimed it was only marginally better than its predecessor.
7. During the build-up to the Gulf conflict, Saudi Arabia refused permission for coalition aircraft to use its airspace. Many flights were re-routed northwards via Turkey and eventually approached Kuwait via Iran – an unexpected direction for those onboard, as Flashman notes.

3

My first morning in Kuwait, like every other one that was to follow, dawned bright and sunny, if a little cold. Like all new arrivals I had no idea of the layout of the camp and it took me a good 10 minutes of traipsing around in my towel and flipflops before I stumbled across the shower blocks. After shaving off two days' worth of stubble and enjoying a warm shower, albeit in the company of tattooed oiks from 3 Commando Brigade, I felt a little more ready to tackle the rigours of headquarters life. I donned my desert trousers and a sandy-brown t-shirt, which had the effect of making me look identical to the thousands of other Brits in the camp. (The morning air was brisk but I decided to brave the cold rather than wear my green camouflage smock.) Back at the accommodation tent I bumped into SO2 Media and several of the other Brigade staff officers and we followed the growing throng of individuals gravitating towards breakfast. The cookhouse (or galley, as the Marines insist on calling it, with their pedantic adherence to naval terms) was constructed from two of the accommodation tents joined end-to-end. For once the Corps had discarded its liberal attitudes and the top end of the eatery was set aside for officers, which made a pleasant change from being surrounded by the dozens of cockneys, Scousers and janners who seemed to make up the bulk of the Brigade Headquarters. The food, of course, was pure muck – lukewarm porridge, shrivelled sausages of indiscernible origin, scrambled egg which tasted largely of plastic, and a small pot of yoghurt. It was to remain unchanged for several weeks and was vile but there was no other choice, so I washed it down with several pints of coffee and set off to find the Operations Room.

The Ops Room (which was, of course, yet another tent) was situated at the top of the camp and sat adjacent to two identical tents. The first of these had a smattering of paratroopers coming and going through the main entrance, and would shortly be fully functioning as 16 Air Assault Brigade Headquarters. The second, which was for the moment deserted, would soon accommodate the headquarters of 7 Armoured Brigade. I looked forward to their arrival immensely – until arriving in this fleapit I had no idea that the three headquarters would be located next door to one another. I was yards away from a brigade staff which would doubtless house dozens of cavalry officers and which would provide much needed respite from the insane eagerness of the adjacent Marines and Paras.

Just as I was contemplating this stroke of luck the air was filled with wailing from multiple sets of overhead tannoy speakers. The camp erupted into temporary pandemonium, with men running in all directions and several diving past me into the nearest tent. The siren, I quickly realised, was a chemical attack warning. I ducked inside 3 Brigade Headquarters' tent and donned my respirator as I went.[1] Unlike the scene outside, the headquarters was a sea of calm, not the reaction I had expected from a group of men facing imminent death in the form of sarin gas poisoning. Wearing the black rubber gas-masks, everyone looked identical and most of the chaps were taking the opportunity to sit down and relax, with the notable exception of one of the watchkeepers, who was talking volubly into a telephone and trying to find out the cause of the alert. I looked around the room, conscious of the distorted view I was getting through the lenses in my respirator. It was just as I had imagined it – which was mainly because all ops rooms look pretty much identical I suppose. The walls of the tent were festooned with dry-wipe boards and huge maps of the area of operations. Underneath these were a plethora of watchkeeping desks and a host of workstations for all the individual elements that would or could be brought to bear by 3 Commando Brigade once the war got started. There were two Aviation desks one marked "Helo" and the other "F/W" (fixed-wing), an Artillery desk, the liaison officers from 40 and 42 Commando both had desks, Info, Media, etc etc. And there, tucked between the G4 watchkeepers and Artillery, was an empty desk labelled "Armour", prospective home to Captain Harry Flashman QRH for the foreseeable future and as good a place as any to see out a nice quiet campaign.[2] Just as I was contemplating my new place of work the watchkeeper put down his telephone, removed his respirator and announced: "Unmask!" Around the room, human beings emerged from behind the black rubber respirators and I was able to take a look at my new colleagues.

"Another moment of embarrassment for the Joint NBC Regiment," explained the watchkeeper to the room as a whole. "I don't know why they persist with that wretched piece of kit – it catches a cold every time one of our Land Rovers backfires."

The piece of kit in question – name unknown, it seemed, by anyone in the Brigade – looked for all the world like a huge, metallic ice cream cone. It was apparently a device for sniffing the air for any nasties, and was mounted on top of a specially modified 4-tonne truck, the body of which consisted of a sealed unit containing chemical analysis equipment and populated by a team from the Joint Nuclear, Biological and Chemical Warfare Regiment. Unhappily for those of us sharing a camp with them, there were various technical flaws with the kit and our days were punctuated with the frequent wailing of false alarms.

Respirator safely tucked away in its pouch, I introduced myself to the Chief of Staff, who was sitting in a corner, pouring over a 1:50,000 scale map of Bubiyan Island.[3]

"Flashman! I've heard your name bandied around – I gather you served with the Brigade in Afghanistan. Good to have you onboard again." He gestured towards my desk. "Well, you have a home here already, as I'm sure you've seen. You'll be bloody useful to us – bootnecks aren't used to working with armour, so we'll be seeking your advice over the coming weeks and even more so when things get started. We're still not sure how this thing will pan out. If we get the green light over the next couple of weeks, we'll have to make do with what armour is already here, which ain't much. On the other hand, if these political delays drag on much longer, 7 Armoured Brigade will be here in force, so we'll have MBTs coming out of our ears." [4]

It was music to my ears. A cosy desk miles behind the front line, a brigade staff hanging on my every word, and still the glimmer of hope that the situation could be resolved diplomatically. Don't get me wrong, I wasn't about to turn into some kind of peacenik campaigner. In fact I'm all in favour of giving Johnny Foreigner a good hiding every once in a while – just as long as I don't have to put my neck on the line to do it.

I bade the Chief of Staff a temporary farewell and he pointed me in the direction of the clerks' desk where I reported to a burly sergeant manning their workstation. After being issued a pass to enable me to get in and out of the headquarters without endless questions I was met by the stores sergeant and taken to a cluster of steel shipping containers a short distance from the headquarters. The following hour was spent drawing rifle ammunition, although I couldn't see what possible use it could be to me, additional canisters for my respirator, which I certainly hoped wouldn't be of any use, and a host of desert-camouflage bits and pieces including a new, vacuum-wrapped NBC suit, a shemagh (scarf) and a windproof smock. No longer a patchwork quilt of dark green and light brown, I now looked and felt every bit the desert soldier – and a valued member of the brigade staff. It shouldn't be too difficult for me to keep my nose clean for a couple of months, get a decent report from the Chief of Staff, and run back to Wiltshire full of second-hand anecdotes to share with the boys in the mess. Life was looking up – or so it seemed at the time.

As I strode back to the accommodation tent, arms laden with sandy-brown camouflage clothing, I witnessed a bout of all-too-frequent Royal Marine madness, in the form of at least 40 members of the headquarters staff – mainly officers, but accompanied by a fair assortment of NCOs – doubling past in PT kit. Early in the year it may have been but the midday sun was still plenty hot and there was, at least as far as I was concerned, absolutely no need to go punishing oneself further than was necessary. Perspiration was already trickling down my back just from walking around the camp and the thought of voluntarily donning training shoes and dashing about the place was quite abhorrent. As I watched, the attendant PTI barked an order and in one movement every man among them dropped onto the gravel surface of the square and began pushing out press-ups at an alarming rate of knots. A second order was bellowed out a short time later and in one fluid movement the group flipped onto its back and began doing sit-ups quickly enough to make me feel physically sick. I naively assumed that this was a test of some kind, so I slithered away, conscious that if I lingered any longer I might suffer the ignominy of being invited to join in. Over the ensuing days I discovered that it was simply part of the daily routine, open to anyone daft enough to join in. I gave it a stiff ignoring during my time in the brigade and I'm none the worse for it. In fact I suspect my knee joints are considerably better off as a result.

There are some bits and pieces that every staff officer should have and one of them is a decent map of the area of operations. There will always be an enormous map pinned up somewhere in the ops room, but one is never enough – it pays to have your own version ostentatiously pinned up behind your own desk. Once an operation heats up the headquarters becomes a veritable hive of activity and the staff are expected to have the answers to a thousand questions at their fingertips. The trick is to anticipate as many questions as possible and a good map is key to getting the answers right – plus it makes you appear far more crucial to the proceedings than your peers. The last element of the winning formula is to ensure that you are off watch when the real fighting begins, so that some other bugger can deal with the pressure of the Brigade Commander bearing down upon them. Shortly after lunch I made my way to the Intelligence Cell to requisition a map and, after forcing my way past the corporal manning the door, I was met by a somewhat flustered looking young chap, 20 years of age at the outside, clutching a heap of transparent map traces.

"Can I help you?" he enquired.

I drew myself up to my full height, looked down my nose at him, and announced that I needed a map of the brigade's area of operations.

"Yeah, and so does everybody else," he replied curtly. "We haven't got any spare."

"Then perhaps you'd like to explain that to the Brigade Commander," I suggested, "I'm giving him an update on armoured dispositions later today. You could join us if you wish, and you can tell him yourself why there isn't a map for a mission-critical briefing."

It was complete bluster of course, but it had the desired effect. He visibly crumpled in front of me, mumbled an apology of sorts and led the way back into the Intelligence Cell with me hot on his heels. The place was a treasure-trove of maps and overlays of all kinds, depicting areas of land stretching from Saudi Arabia through Kuwait and Iraq and northwards into Iran. It took him a few moments to locate the relevant sheet, a 1:50,000 scale map that covered the Al Faw Peninsular and which stretched west as far as Umm Qasr and north beyond Basra. He rolled it up and thrust it into my hands, clearly eager to be shot of me and get on with his work.

"I'd like a trace to sit on top of it too," I added.

Fortunately there was no shortage of sheets of transparent

plastic, so my assistant rolled one up for me and ushered me towards the door.

""There now, that wasn't so bad after all, now was it?" I commented sarcastically. "You should work on your customer service though. Try smiling a bit more often." I turned on my heel and left, leaving him wrestling with his map traces and muttering to himself.

I had plenty of time to kill, which I used to familiarise myself with the layout of my new home. One never knew when things might take a turn for the worse so I made a mental note of the locations of all the nearby Scud shelters, which were dotted around both the British and American sides of the camp. A well-worn footpath followed the perimeter wire of the US base so I set off on a circuit of it, which took me the best part of an hour, such was the scale of the place. Upon arrival we had been informed that the place was called Camp Commando, an absurd moniker that I assumed the misled US Marines had given it in honour of their British colleagues. However, it transpired that the nucleus of the camp – the towering assault course – belonged to the Kuwaiti commandos, and it was from this facility that the place had gained its name, long before the Americans or the British had arrived. As I approached the assault course, I saw that it was being used. Around a dozen terrified-looking individuals were huddled together atop a 60-foot tower which marked the dispatch point of the aptly-named death slide. I joined the dozens of open-mouthed yanks who had also stopped what they were doing in order to observe the spectacle. As we watched, a body exited the tower and shot down the rope slide, finishing around 50 yards from the base of the tower. Unlike any British equivalent I had ever seen, the Kuwaiti death slide did not descend all the way to the ground, so this heroic individual was left dangling in space. Another, smaller, rope dropped from his body and he quickly abseiled the last 20 feet down onto the gravel surface below him. I presume he was an instructor, since he immediately turned towards the tower and began shouting exhortations to his colleagues to follow his lead. To a man they seemed reluctant to come down the rope. Eventually one was dispatched, presumably against his will, since he screamed in terror the whole way down. Another man followed and he too bellowed with fear as he came down. To this day I have no idea what the supposed military value of this training facility might be, other, perhaps, than to provide entertainment to the watching Brits and Americans. The first display had been somewhat comical but the ones that followed were all too much for me. I began to chortle, quietly at first but then louder and louder as the yanks either side of me also began to see the humour in it. The Kuwaitis stared at us, apparently horrified that we should be laughing at their bravery, but this just made it all the worse. In the end, ruddy-cheeked from laughing so hard, I forced myself to continue walking around the camp, the shrieks of terror still ringing out behind me as I left. I made a point of sharing the story with the headquarters staff and over the ensuing days a visit to watch the Kuwaiti commandos in action quickly became a common method of raising one's morale.

Back outside the accommodation, a new feature adorned the square, in the form of an old-fashioned olive-green canvas tent. Throngs of personnel were clustered in front of it and there was an unexpected air of bonhomie about the place. A neat, hand-written sign announcing "Des & Kit's Café" dangled from the apex of the tent poles, occasionally obscured by a waft of steam emerging from within. Inside were two of the oldest chefs ever to don Her Majesty's uniform, providing an endless stream of tea and coffee to the attendant masses. God alone knew how many campaigns this pair had served in, but they certainly knew how to add value to a headquarters. Here, at last, was a legitimised venue for exchanging gossip and avoiding work – no wonder it was proving so popular with the boys. After all the puffed-up self importance of the crowd in the Ops Room it was gratifying to see the effect on morale of such a simple facility. And it came as no surprise whatsoever that my media and artillery chums were already in the thick of the crowd, supping tea from polystyrene cups. I jostled my way through the throng to join them.

"This is a bit of a result," commented the artilleryman, nodding in the direction of the tea tent. "It's as close to civilisation as we're going to get for a few weeks," he added, "so we might as well make the most of it, eh? Much better than hanging around the Ops Room trying to look busy." I had little difficulty agreeing with that sentiment, and pushed on past to get myself a cup of tea, only to find my way barred by one of the chefs brandishing a ladle.

"Sorry Sir, no pongos," he announced gravely. "3 Commando Brigade ranks only." To illustrate the point, he waved his ladle at the sign above his head where I could see small print reading "No PT kit, No Pongos".[5]

"An army officer I may be," I replied, equally gravely. "But I am part of the Brigade, attached to the headquarters to advise on all things armoured."

He stepped smartly to one side and waved me into the tent. "In that case, Sir, be my guest. Help yourself to whatever you want."

I rejoined the boys outside, clutching a cup of tea, and we spent a slack hour putting the world to rights as the sun went down. The tea tent was closed at sundown and we dawdled over to the dining tent to while away more time over a rather paltry supper.

During the ensuing days it became rapidly apparent to all of us that Camp Commando was home to an awful lot of people with not a great deal to do. The planning staff were one of the small groups working at a frenetic pace, although I couldn't fathom our why they bothered because the assets available to them, not to mention the intelligence picture, changed almost daily. Also working flat-out were the Intelligence Cell and the NBC boys, although in the latter case I rather suspected that this was to avoid future embarrassment rather than in the interests of furthering the war effort. Whatever their activities, the false alarms continued to sound on a frequent basis, sometimes several times in a single day, which was tedious to say the least. The political process was still dragging on, with British Foreign Secretary Jack Straw having public debates with his French counterpart Dominique de Villepain, in which neither side made any headway and the prospect of a much-discussed further UN resolution never got any nearer. Blair and Bush continued their posturing, Kofi Anan added his comments on a daily basis, Hans Blix and his team of weapons inspectors were used as a political pinball by both sides – and all the while, we were left to sweat it out in Kuwait. I stayed a mile away from the feverish planning taking place in the Ops Room and counted my blessings that as an attached rank, no-one really seemed to notice or mind my absence. Instead I made a point of ingratiating myself with the Media Ops boys, who had their own miniature operations tent, access to the Internet via some highly-technical satellite dish and, best of all, a fleet of hired civilian 4x4s. I worked a fairly simple routine, in that I was by now receiving a steady supply of single malt whisky, posted in old lemonade bottles from Valdez-Welch and the boys back home, and unknowingly delivered to Kuwait by the good old BFPO. The supply of grog was well appreciated by the Media Ops team so it came as no surprise that, after a couple of weeks, I was invited to join them on a visit to Kuwait City. I visited the armoury to exchange my rifle for a pistol, stuffed a scruffy set of civilian clothes into a small grip, and four of us exited the camp in air-conditioned luxury, no questions asked. Cut from the same cloth as the SO2 and unashamed military tourists, most of the team were veterans of several recent campaigns – indeed, I knew a couple of them from Afghanistan days. A well-drilled unit, they changed into civilian clothes whilst on the move, stopping only momentarily to allow a new man to take the wheel so that the driver could also get changed. By the time we rolled into Kuwait City we looked for all the world like four nondescript tourists – which to all intents and purposes, we were.

My Media Ops comrades had a vague schedule of events

worked out but I insisted that before we went anywhere, we should treat ourselves to a slap-up lunch. The camp food was poor quality, repetitive and dull and the opportunity to fill my belly with decent fodder was too good to pass up. We ducked into the Hilton hotel, ordered the biggest steaks in the house, then settled down to enjoy not just the food but also the novelty of clean cutlery, starched napkins, marble floors, the surrounding greenery, and the omnipresent air-conditioning. Unhappily, Kuwait's hospitality doesn't stretch to a decent bottle of wine, so we had to settle for coke, with a crafty shot of Scotch thrown in for good measure by yours truly. I'm sure the serving staff must have suspected us for we were all half-cut by the time we left. The awful thought of being arrested and publicly flogged as a drunken infidel briefly flashed through my mind, followed by the thought that even without the flogging, being arrested would in itself result in a court martial and return to UK in disgrace. Fortunately the waiter had the good sense to turn a Nelsonic eye to our increasingly liquid state and held his tongue. We tipped him handsomely in return.

Bellies full, we set off on a shopping spree of epic proportions. Like most Arab capitals, the residents of Kuwait City are fairly dripping with money and there is no shortage of outlets for them to spend it. We ventured into an enormous air-conditioned shopping mall. The boys scattered into the nearest shops, emerging sometime later with a collection of goodies including new clothes, CDs, personal stereos, and an assortment of cigars and cigarettes which, asides from their obvious value as smokes, would be useful for bartering back at the camp. On the assumption that we were going to war and I might want to preserve some of the memories for posterity, I splashed out on an unfeasibly tiny digital camera, easily small enough to slip into my hip pocket in the event of anything worth recording taking place in the Brigade headquarters. Then it was back to the car and, I wrongly assumed, back to camp. My hosts, however, had other ideas, and we set off south on the highway out of Kuwait City, completely the wrong direction for a return to the Headquarters, changing back into military attire en route.

Our destination, which was only a short drive down the road, was Camp Doha, an enormous, permanent US base, constructed shortly after the first Gulf War, and home to literally thousands of troops. Situated under the smoking chimneys of Kuwait's biggest power station, it sprawls across miles of desert with lines of steel buildings, concrete missile bunkers, temporary accommodation blocks and countless vehicles of all kinds stretching as far as the eye can see. At first glance the security appears to be tight but, like most American establishments, you can bamboozle the guards with any old ID card and they wave you straight inside. This was clearly not the first visit for the Media Ops team for we didn't stop once to ask directions, zooming through the maze of roads inside the camp at speeds far in excess of the widely-advertised 10 mph speed limit. On either side of us, parked in precise straight lines, were literally hundreds of trucks, 4x4s, armoured personnel carriers and main battle tanks of all kinds. The firepower residing inside Camp Doha was probably greater than that of the entire British Army – and the helipad was equally imposing, housing several squadrons of Blackhawk and Apache helicopters. The most impressive part was that none of this equipment had been specially shipped to Kuwait for the imminent conflict – it was all permanently stationed there.

The first stop on our Camp Doha jaunt was somewhat unexpected. Instead of visiting the numerous eating venues or the shopping mall, we drew to a halt outside a row of scruffy looking temporary buildings, hidden in the shade of an enormous steel hangar. The Media Ops boys jumped out, pulled a series of large bags from the boot of the 4x4 and disappeared into the nearest hut. It transpired the buildings were home to Doha's laundry facilities and rather than persevering with the hand washing routine that prevailed at

Camp Commando, the Media team had got into the routine of getting their clothes clean courtesy of Uncle Sam. Next stop was the huge shopping mall, where hundreds of overweight, under-employed American soldiers spent most of their free time buying junk food with which to supplement their dietary intake, an amazing feat since their cookhouses already provided meal portions large enough to feed a whole family. It seemed somehow churlish not to partake so, despite feeling overfull from the steak lunch, I bought myself a grotesquely extravagant ice cream and entered the enormous department store that lay immediately beyond the food hall. Were it not for the obvious fact that all the clientele inside were in uniform, we could have been at any downtown US shopping mall. Everything from Harley Davidsons to Hershey bars was on sale inside, augmented by the usual collection of jingoistic paraphernalia that always accompanies the US forces – from T-shirts to tattoo parlours, this place had it all. I suspected that Camp Doha was largely populated by logisticians and headquarters elements who would see out their war without even entering Iraq, but that wasn't stopping the shopping mall from doing a roaring trade in Gulf War 2 souvenirs – and the fighting wasn't even likely to begin for several more weeks. Mercifully we stayed in the mall only a short time before retiring to a nearby Starbucks and soaking up some of the late afternoon sunshine whilst supping cappuccinos. I had to hand it to the Media Ops team, their well-worked day trips certainly made a refreshing change from the drudgery of Camp Commando. As the sun set over the desert sands we piled back into the 4x4 and bade farewell to Uncle Sam and his recreational shopping facilities. I made a mental note to remember to bring my laundry with me next time.

That night brought an unusual hum, or rather, rumble, of activity to Camp Commando, as the lead elements of 7 Armoured Brigade rolled into town.[6] The first vehicles arrived in the middle of the night, as seems to be the norm with any British military move. During the early hours I became vaguely conscious of the ground vibrating and tracks squeaking but failed to fully wake up or realise the significance of the noise. By daybreak the relative tranquillity of the camp had been shattered by the roaring of large numbers of diesel engines as vehicle after vehicle entered the square in front of the accommodation tents. The loose gravel surface was kicked up into clouds of dust which quickly covered anything and everything not kept under cover. Row upon row of armoured vehicles took up position within the square, eventually forming a rough oblong around which were rolled coils of barbed wire, sealing in the vehicles and leaving a single entrance some 50 yards from the dining tent. I watched as two signallers erected a large wooden sign featuring the familiar silhouette of a jerboa and reading "HQ 7 Armoured Brigade – The Desert Rats". As a cavalryman I found the sight of all these newly-arrived tracked vehicles a joy to behold, even if they were largely made up of rather aged armoured personnel carriers dating from the 1970s. Accompanying the headquarters vehicles would be more cavalry officers and I had little doubt that the social life around the camp would improve dramatically as a result. I spent much of the morning watching the remaining vehicles arriving and looking forward to evenings spent drinking shots of scotch in the company of officers from the Hussars, Lancers, Dragoons and the like. As soon as they had all arrived I made a foray inside the wire and immediately bumped into a couple of chaps from the 9/12th Lancers with whom I had served in Bosnia. I dragged them off to lunch and before long our table had become a proper little cavalry club, with attendees not only from my home regiment but also from Sandhurst days. Life really was looking up.

The following morning my spirits were still running high from the combined effects of a day spent in relative civilisation and the arrival of my armoured brethren. I felt myself to be well ensconced in an undemanding and relatively sustainable job which, for the time being, involved minimal time in the Ops

Room and maximum time enjoying myself on one spurious mission or another. On balance of course I would rather have been back in merry England but, on the whole, I felt a sense of quiet confidence that I could see out the war in the headquarters without too much drama. I should have known better than to drop my guard but I was utterly unprepared for the next turn of events. Post-breakfast, feeling somewhat bleary-eyed and still clutching a mug of coffee, I made my way over to the Ops Room, primarily to see whether I had any more mail packages from the UK rather than to do any planning work. My pigeonhole was empty so I mooched into the Ops Room to see whether there had been any significant developments during the previous working day. I opened my mouth to say a cheery hallo to SO2 Media, who was (for reasons that elude me) manning the central G3 watchkeeping desk, when I noticed a fresh-faced young RTR captain sitting at my desk.[7] [8] He spotted me and stood up, looking somewhat abashed. At the same moment, the Chief of Staff appeared at my shoulder.

"Ah, Harry, there you are . . ." I wondered momentarily if I had been missed the previous day, then dismissed the thought. "Meet George Thomsett, your replacement." Young George stuck out his hand which I duly shook. My mind was racing and for one hopelessly positive moment I even thought that this could be my ticket home. But the optimism within me was quickly crushed. "I've been looking at the orbat of our two commando units,"[9] continued the Chief of Staff. "It seems to me that 42 Commando will be working almost constantly with elements of 7 Armoured Brigade. There's no-one with particular armoured knowledge within the commando group, and I'm bloody keen that we get them the required expertise quick sharp. You're the obvious candidate for the post, so we're sending you there pronto." My head was spinning and I felt faint. Far from going home, my cosy headquarters job was evaporating before my very eyes and I was to be pushed forward into a fighting unit which would shortly be engaged in the first thrust into Iraq. This was the worst possible turn of events. I was caught completely off guard and momentarily lost for words. I began to mouth a response, but the Chief of Staff beat me to it. "You may be wondering why young George doesn't go in your place." Mouth dry, I could only nod in agreement, hoping in vain for some kind of reprieve. "Well, George has spent the last year in 7 Brigade's headquarters. He knows the ropes, and we need a first-class brigade-level liaison officer. On the other hand, everyone knows your track record, Flash, and there's no doubting our first choice to go to a commando unit. I can see that you're raring to go – you've probably got your bags packed already, I should imagine!" He roared with laughter and clapped me on the back so hard that I spilled coffee onto the floorboards. I stared bleakly at George Thomsett. Under other circumstances I might have stuck my fist in his face for having the insolence to pilfer my job. But it was hardly his fault that these idiots thought I actually wanted to go to a commando group, back to the kind of lunatics with whom I had barely scraped out of Afghanistan a year earlier. No sooner had I made myself comfortable in the brigade headquarters than fate – assisted by my undeserved reputation for derring-do – had intervened. The Chief of Staff had made his mind up and there was nothing further to be said so, attempting not to show my inner despair, I simply turned on my heel and walked out.

NOTES

1 With the Iraqi border less than 50 miles away, Flashman was easily inside the range of Saddam's Scud missiles and the prospect of a gas attack was very real. Most military units encamped in Kuwait experienced at least one false alarm per day during the build up to the invasion. Every man was required to keep his respirator with him 24 hours a day.

2   The UK (and US) armed forces use a series of alphanumeric codes to denote different job functions. G4 refers to logistics.
3   Bubiyan Island is situated in the northern Gulf, just off the Kuwaiti coast. Subject to frequent flooding, it is an expanse of sand and mud which never rises more than a few feet above sea level. Being close to southern Iraq, it was used to site the British artillery positions during the initial invasion.
4   Main Battle Tanks.
5   Pongo: less-than-affectionate naval slang, used to describe anyone in the army.
6   Flashman fails to note the arrival of 1 UK Division Headquarters, which took over the reins of the deployment from 3 Commando Brigade shortly before the arrival of 7 Armoured Brigade. Commanded by a 2-star general, the division's fighting assets consisted of three formations: 3 Commando Brigade, 7 Armoured Brigade, and 16 Air Assault Brigade.
7   G3: operations.
8   RTR: Royal Tank Regiment.
9   Order of Battle, i.e. the manning structure.

4

When SO2 Media heard my sorry tale, he was hardly the sympathetic listening ear I had hoped for. He was perched on his bunk, deep in some trashy paperback, headphones in his ears, in a little world of his own when I walked back into the accommodation tent. Seeing my downcast expression he unplugged himself and enquired what was wrong.

"I'm being moved on," I told him. "Some tosser from 7 Armoured has got my job, I'm being sent to 42 Commando."

His response was typically bootneck, typically idiotic. "You lucky bugger! Good God, a couple of weeks swanning around here, then off to a commando before the fighting begins. I don't know what you've done to deserve this, Flashy, but there's plenty of blokes who'll be gutted to know they're staying here while you move on."

The silly thing was that he was absolutely right, there were dozens, probably hundreds, of chaps in the headquarters who would give their eye teeth to be joining a commando group. And despite having all these people to choose from, I was the one who had been picked, probably the only man in the brigade who would have paid good money to avoid the front line. Still, the decision was made now and there was no point letting a fellow staff officer get a glimpse of my yellow liver. I put on an air of resigned determination for his benefit and that of the other chaps in the accommodation tent whom I was certain were eavesdropping.

"It's not joining a commando unit that worries me old chap, it's the thought of leaving you buggers without the benefit of my leadership and experience. War can be a terrible thing you know, and you boys back here will doubtless have a hell of a time of it . . ."

His paperback book came flying in my direction.

"Bloody hell, you really have a cheek sometimes," he chortled. Then, with mock gravitas, added, "We all know it will be a struggle without you, but we'll do our best to soldier on in the face of adversity. I should think the bigger question is whether 42 have got enough blokes to stop you getting into trouble. If the CO has got any sense, he'll have you making tea in the ops room and not let you out of his sight for the duration."

I set about packing up my limited worldly belongings. It didn't take more than a few minutes and I found myself with best part of an hour to spare before my driver was due to turn up. I whiled away most of it outside Des & Kit's café, saying a fond farewell to numerous members of the brigade staff whilst ensuring that I maintained the famous Flashman stiff upper lip. I might be quaking inside but there was great PR mileage in joining a commando group, so I took the opportunity to milk it for all it was worth. Eventually the laughter and bonhomie was interrupted by a loud hooting from a nearby Land Rover horn, and I spotted my driver looking impatiently at me through the heat haze and dust. I strode over to him.

"Are you looking for someone?" I enquired.

"Yes Sir – you," he replied. "Land Rover to Camp Gibraltar?"

"Right, well I suggest you get out and give me a hand with my bags. If you're not too busy, that is," I added.

He looked for a moment as if he was about to say something, thought better of it, and reluctantly climbed out from behind the steering wheel. I strode off towards the officers' accommodation, the driver trailing in my wake. Inside the tent I passed him my grip and webbing, leaving him wrestling with both as I carried my bergen and rifle out to the vehicle.

"Bloody hell, Sir, I'm a driver not a bag-carrier," he grumbled as he caught me up.

"Really? Well I'm a cavalry officer and you'll be a bloody toilet attendant if you don't shut up and start providing some assistance," I retorted. "I'm only asking you to carry a couple of bags, not parachute naked into an enemy minefield. I thought you were supposed to be a commando?" Peeved, the fellow just shot me a sidelong glance and went into a sulk.

Camp Gibraltar, the place where my arrival coach had stopped briefly a few short weeks earlier, was around an hour's drive north of Camp Commando. The desert on either side of the highway was picture-book yellow, featureless and flat, punctuated only by the occasional camel train barely visible through the heat haze. My thoughts drifted as the Land Rover sped along the highway. It was still only February and already the air was starting to warm up viciously during the middle of the day. Carrying heavy loads, wearing body armour and NBC clothing and breathing through a respirator is difficult enough in any conditions, but the stifling heat of the Middle East meant that our troops would become physically degraded within a very short time. It didn't take the brains of an archbishop to know that the war would have to begin before the real heat of the summer arrived – I reckoned the end of March was the latest possible kick-off date, perhaps even earlier depending on how quickly the hot weather snuck up on us.

After a time, through the dust, I made out a criss-cross of dirt roads cutting through the desert sand, and the earthwork ramparts of a temporary military encampment in the middle of nowhere. The Land Rover slowed and then veered off to the right hand side of the road, bouncing onto a dirt track running perpendicular to the highway. The driver quickly slid shut his window and closed the air vents as dust kicked up around the vehicle. I did likewise but nevertheless the leaky nature of the Land Rover meant we were covered in a fine film of dust even before we reached the first checkpoint, just a quarter of a mile from the tar road. A bedraggled looking soldier wearing goggles and an ill-fitting helmet asked us for some ID, which we duly displayed before driving on along the dirt road. At first there seemed to be no sign of the camp but then I saw that our dirt track was running parallel to the earthwork ramparts once again. We passed a large sign announcing the presence of the Commando Logistics Regiment, then shortly afterwards another announcing the home of 59 Commando Engineer Squadron. Finally, we swung into a gateway where a young looking Marine asked us for our ID again. Inside was row upon row of tents, many of which were flying union flags with a few Welsh dragons and St Andrew's Crosses thrown in for good measure. The headquarters was positioned at the far end of all the accommodation tents, evident primarily from the numerous vehicles parked in close proximity. This, then, was the home of 42 Commando – and a more desolate armpit of a place one couldn't have wished for. Beyond the earth walls of the camp there was nothing but empty desert for dozens of miles. Inside the camp there was nothing but the tents, a fistful of shipping containers, and a couple of portakabin-style buildings which functioned as the ablution blocks for over 700 men. My spirits, already low, took a further battering as I realised the paucity of the living conditions compared with the Brigade Headquarters, which itself was hardly the lap of luxury. It was exactly the kind of isolated, frugal existence that the Marines would love, especially as it ensured that officers and men would share living quarters. (For reasons I have yet to fathom, this holds immense appeal to the egalitarian ranks of the Marine Corps.) Still, this wasn't the moment for moping – there would be plenty of time for that in the weeks to come. I needed to introduce myself to the CO and his staff, and find myself a bed-space somewhere.

My sulking driver dropped my bags outside the headquarters tent and sped off, presumably in a hurry to get away before I had the opportunity to task him with any more work. A stiff breeze was scudding across the camp, blowing little puffs of sand along the floor and ensuring that vehicle tracks and footprints disappeared almost as rapidly as they were made.

On the far side of the camp a squad of Marines in PT kit ran along the perimeter wall, sand and dust billowing up in the breeze from the combined action of 20-odd pairs of training shoes. Overhead, the sun was beating down and I could make out the dull thump of distant rotor blades from a passing transport helicopter. Asides from that noise though, the camp seemed remarkably quiet. I lifted the flap of the tent and stepped inside.

The commando headquarters tent was divided into three discreet sections. There was a large briefing area, into which I stepped, which also housed the duty signallers and the chief clerk. Beyond it lay a smaller briefing area, which housed a large map table and various workstations adorned with dust-covered laptop computers. This area was a hive of activity, with around a dozen officers and warrant officers all poring over a huge black-and-white aerial photograph of, I presumed, some not-too-distant part of Iraq. At the back of this briefing area hung a large curtain, beyond which was housed 42 Commando's intelligence section. Nobody challenged my entrance to the ops room and all inside seemed engrossed in their various activities, so I placed my rifle in the rather homespun wooden rack provided and then stood for a few seconds and earwigged at the ongoing conversation.

". . . if the Iraqis launch an armoured counter-attack, they've really only got two possible routes to follow – here, and here. We can get a blocking force deployed on those routes pretty bloody quickly once we hit the ground. That's got to be our first priority. Then we can start sending probing patrols north and west to find out where the enemy depth positions are . . ." I peered into the group, but could not make out any of the detail of the air photograph they were examining. However, I knew from the Brigade Headquarters briefings that 42 Commando was flying directly onto the Al Faw peninsular, right on Iraq's south-eastern tip. Equally, I knew the strategic significance of grabbing the Al Faw oil installations intact. It was a distinct possibility that the Iraqis would blow the high-pressure oil pipelines, thereby flooding the northern Gulf with crude. The environmental damage would be huge, and so would the PR damage back home, so the pressure was on to ensure that whoever landed on the Al Faw did it quickly and cleanly, and allowed the Iraqis the least possible opportunity to create any deliberate collateral damage. 40 Commando – the sister unit to the one I found myself in – would lead the assault, while 42 Commando landed on their north-western flank to deal with Iraqi depth positions and block any possible counter attack. The wide open spaces inland from the tip of the peninsular were potentially good country for armoured warfare, so 42 Commando was to have an attached squadron of Welsh Cavalry to provide an armoured recce screen to their north and west.[1]

The conversation in front of me continued with further gesticulating at the aerial photographs: "What anti-tank assets are we deploying here? We can't claim to have deployed a blocking force if we've only got blokes with light weapon systems, and we can't get our vehicle-mounted Milans in until the LCACs are functioning."[2],[3]

This was immediately countered by someone else in the group. "Well, we can deploy man packed Milan if we have to. Or maybe we could bring in underslung vehicles by helicopter?"

This was answered by a tall, sandy-haired figure standing at the top of the planning table, whom I quickly realised was the Commanding Officer. "We could do that if we absolutely had to – although we'll need to find out whether the American helicopters can undersling our vehicles – but I'd rather explore other alternatives first. It seems to me we can have a pretty effective block in place just by using the organic assets of our close-combat companies, plus UMST."[4]

There was a murmuring of assent to this last remark, although clearly there was still some concern about the unknown enemy dispositions on the Al Faw. The problem was exacerbated by the date palm plantations and other greenery on the northern side of the peninsula, where fresh water from the Shat-al-Arab waterway was used to irrigate the land. I vividly remembered from my Kosovo days how easy it had been for the Serbs to hide their tanks in the wooded areas of southern Yugoslavia. All the air photographs in the world were no good if your enemy chose to position his armoured formations in woodland – and frankly they would have to be pretty stupid to do anything else. Yet here we were, about to embark on an opposed landing in country which was home to hundred of acres of date palm plantations. I shuddered quietly at the idea and consoled myself with the thought that while 42 Commando's fighting companies would be slugging it out on the Al Faw, the Commando headquarters would presumably not fly in from Kuwait until the area was deemed relatively safe.

The planning group broke up and, their eyes no longer fixed on the photographs and maps, they noticed there was a stranger waiting for them. I stepped forward and introduced myself.

"Ah, Harry, nice to meet you," exclaimed the CO, holding out his hand. "Were we expecting you?" Then, looking over his shoulder at the adjutant, "Were we expecting him?"

"Yes, Colonel," responded the adjutant. "I got a phone call this morning from Brigade to say they were sending him up."

"Well why wasn't I bloody told about it?" grumbled the CO. "I'm always the last person to know about our new arrivals. It's faintly embarrassing not knowing who all these people are." But it was all said in good humour and it seemed that he was genuinely pleased to have me on board. I guessed – correctly, as it turned out – that 42 Commando was being deluged with new arrivals in a similar way to the brigade headquarters, and I was therefore just the latest in a long line of unexpected visitors. The adjutant later made a count of them and the total was in the dozens with cap badges including the Royal Navy, RAF, Joint NBC Regiment, Royal Engineers and now, of course, the Hussars. Before I could depart the CO invited me to lunch in his tent, which turned out to be much less formal than it sounded. The tent was a scaled-down version of the standard accommodation marquees which now littered Kuwait, and the furniture was limited to four canvas camp beds. Lunch was even more meagre than the offering at Camp Commando, consisting only of mug of lukewarm tea and a disgusting American ration pack – but I was famished, so I ate the thing anyway.[5]

"Tell me a bit about yourself," asked the CO. "Your knowledge of armoured manoeuvre will be in demand in the headquarters, so I'd like to know what experience you've got."

I wasn't expecting a job interview but managed to stutter out a rough summary of my military CV: Bosnia, Northern Ireland, Congo, Kosovo, Sierra Leone, Afghanistan, plus a few exercises and the ubiquitous pass at Junior Staff College. The CO seemed entirely unimpressed, which rather took the wind of out of my sails.

"All very good, but what else have you done?" he asked. Then, to clarify, "Frankly, any medal-collecting war tourist could have managed a raft of peacekeeping operations. They're two-a-penny these days. What I'm interested in is your tactical knowledge of armoured deployments. What makes you a particular expert on armoured warfare?"

This was much harder to answer as so much of my time had, as he alluded to, been spent away from my regiment. I waffled out a rather weak answer and pointed out that I had spent some time in both Germany and Bosnia with a Challenger squadron back in the mid nineties. I was expecting another stiff questioning about my exact role but the answer seemed to placate him and the conversation moved on to the current political situation and the impending hostilities.

"So how long do you think we'll be stuck here?" he asked, his impatience transparent through the question. "You've come from Brigade, what's the word on the street about when we'll cross the start line?"

This was potentially stony ground. I was rapidly realising that the ambition of most Royal Marines was simply to get stuck into a good fight sooner rather than later and this mindset wasn't limited to the boys, it was reflected throughout the hierarchy as well. I was savvy enough to know that my inner craving for a peaceful solution to the situation – not to mention a rapid (and safe) return home to Blighty – would be as welcome as a jobby in a swimming pool. No, this was a time for a spot of the traditional Flashman bravado.

"Well Sir, there's a huge air of expectation and impatience at Camp Commando," I answered. "Division is keeping tight-lipped about the start date, but then most of those wankers are more interested in writing their own CRs than getting on with the war."[6] The CO chuckled conspiratorially and I sensed I may have struck a chord. "The Americans are more forthcoming though. They'll tell you pretty much everything over a cup of tea and a sticky bun – to the point where Div has gone apeshit about Marines talking direct with them – and they reckon we'll be in Iraq in the next couple of weeks."

"Well that's heartening to hear," he replied. "It's bloody hard graft keeping 700 blokes motivated day after day. The Unit is doing well at the moment, but these interminable delays will inevitably take their toll on morale in the end. We've been ready to go for weeks. As far as I'm concerned, the sooner we get the green light, the better."

Before I departed Camp Commando, I had taken time to find out a little about 42 Commando's CO. A mountain leader by trade, he was something of a task-master who led from the front and had a reputation for expecting – and getting – the highest standard of work from all around him. Expecting high standards from his men didn't faze me too much (although given the opportunity I generally prefer to shirk a day's work wherever possible) but I was much more worried by his background as a mountain leader. Royal Marines mountain leaders are a rare breed of lunatic whose trade involves scaling slippery, rain-swept cliffs at night, snurgling around in the dark like so many cat burglars and throttling unsuspecting sentries. They are an altogether unsavoury mob whose attitude to risk is significantly more cavalier than the rest of humanity. In itself that's not necessarily a disaster: if a fellow is determined to kill himself in some ill-conceived enterprise, that's his business and all power to him, I say. But when that same fellow is given command of

700-odd souls and told to take them into battle, the alarm bells start jangling. I hoped that 42 Commando's staff would keep him reined in but in my heart I suspected that when push came to shove, we would be shoved firmly into harm's way.

My interview – for that was what it felt like – with the CO over, I made my way blinking out of his tent, momentarily dazzled by the strong desert sun. I now felt as if I had formally joined the battle group but still had no accommodation and only a faint idea of the geography of the camp. It was time to find a home and get my bearings. I set off in search of the QM whom I assumed would be the man in charge of accommodation. When I eventually tracked him down, his answer was less than satisfactory.[7]

"Bloody hell, another new joiner." I looked suitably dismayed, but he quickly shook me by the hand, welcomed me to this "armpit of a place", and assured me he'd find some kind of accommodation before the day was done. I wasn't entirely reassured but set off for a walk around the camp while he went in search of spare tentage.

Camp Gibraltar was essentially nothing more than a huge rectangle of earth walls, separated into three equal sections by dividing earth walls. It took me almost an hour to walk all the way around, my feet slipping in the loose sand that had already been churned up by hundreds of Marines running countless laps of the perimeter. In the section of the camp nearest the road lay the Commando Logistics Regiment and 3 Brigade's Command Support Group. The place was full of shipping containers, fuel tankers, tents and vehicles, and festooned with radio masts, satellite dishes and other assorted communications paraphernalia. Fork-lift trucks and flat bed lorries moved ant-like around the camp, shifting endless supplies of food, water and ammunition from one place to another. Sensibly, most of the troops I could see were sitting under canvas shade awnings with their feet up, relaxing in the midday heat. Logisticians seem to have an innate ability to know when it's time to get busy, and that time was clearly not now.

The middle portion of the camp housed the gunners of 29 Commando Artillery Regiment, the Commando Engineers of 59 Squadron, and the Brigade Reconnaissance Force. A long line of howitzers ran parallel to the central dirt track, their barrels all neatly elevated to precisely the same angle. This was the artillery support for 3 Commando Brigade and they would be tasked with pounding southern Iraq with shells before the Marines flew in. The more HE they dropped, the better the chance that Joe Iraqi would be ancient history before I arrived, and that could only be a good thing as far as I was concerned.[8] It was, therefore, quite a heart-warming sight to see so many guns lined up and ready for action. Beyond them lay numerous accommodation tents, and on the far side of the camp I could discern small groups of men tinkering with the machine-gun mounts on a number of stripped-down Land Rovers. The vehicles alone would have marked them out as the Brigade Recce Force but there were several other obvious giveaways too. Several of their number were sporting beards, something which would never be tolerated outside a special forces environment. And all of them were wearing old-fashioned, hooded, russet-brown windproof smocks which looked remarkably like Luke Skywalker's Jedi cloak. I had no idea what the attraction of such a garment should be, but it certainly served to tell the world they were something different. As I got closer I could also see that they had spray painted their rifles in various shades of desert yellow, something which run-of-the-mill soldiers would certainly not be allowed to do. It was the job of these foolhardy idiots to push miles forward of the commando units, deep into enemy territory, to assess Iraqi troop dispositions and to find suitable targets for airstrikes. And for this highly dangerous mission, they would have no armour whatsoever and be equipped only with open-top Land Rovers. The very thought made me shudder and I silently wished them luck as I made my way eastwards past the Royal Engineers' tents that were sprinkled throughout that portion of the camp.

Beyond the dividing dirt wall, 42 Commando's set-up looked

remarkably like the mounting centre for a battalion engaged in the Zulu wars, rather than a 21st Century fighting force. The tents were arranged in serried rows, unit and Union flags fluttering from the apexes. Everything within the camp had been arranged in straight lines and neat squares. Even the portaloos stood proudly together in one long line. It smacked of a tight-knit, well-drilled unit and appealed immensely to the career military man in me. Unhappily, it also smacked of the kind of unit which would be first across the start line which, since I was now a part of it, was a deeply troubling thought. I pushed it out of my mind as I strode through the sand and instead focused on watching another group of Marines doubling past in PT kit, sweat-drenched t-shirts stuck to their backs while words of encouragement were shouted by the troop commander trotting alongside. You had to hand it to these fellows, they may be foolhardy but they were bloody keen too. My attention was diverted as I heard my name being shouted from across the camp. I picked out the QM who was stood outside a line of shipping containers, waving his arms at me and hollering. When I got to him, I was more than a little dismayed to see that he was stood atop a ragged bundle of dark green canvas which, he explained, was to be my accommodation.

"I've looked into it Harry and all the accommodation tents are toppers," he explained. "This is your only option mate." I stared down at the canvas bag in disbelief. "The good news is, you won't be lonely. We're expecting a two-man combat camera crew to join the unit this afternoon and they'll be sharing it with you. You might as well wait until they arrive to put it up, as it's not really a one-man job." I made no attempt to hide my disappointment – but at least I would have a roof over my head which was, I supposed, the main thing. The QM suggested I join him for a cup of tea which was undoubtedly the best idea I had heard all day, particularly since I was parched after my circuit of Camp Gibraltar.

Much like Des & Kit's place at the Brigade Headquarters, 42 Commando boasted a communal tea and coffee facility in the middle of the camp. Adjacent to the dining tent, this little haven of calm was frequented by everyone in the battle group and was consequently the centre of gravity for information exchange and gossip of every kind. Admittedly there were no good natured chefs doling out hot drinks but the self-service variety tasted almost as good and the very fact the facility existed gave an air of legitimacy to those wishing to while away hours doing very little. I was sure I would be spending much time there over the coming days. As the QM made tea, I eavesdropped on a conversation being held by a bunch of NCOs, which centred around the Commando's newly-issued weaponry.

". . .and bam! I got the shot off, then just waited and whack, a couple of seconds later, down he went. Proper job, hit him right in the middle of the chest – killed outright, he was." I was sure I recognised this fellow and later I realised why – he had served in Afghanistan at the same time as me a year earlier, which is where his story came from. The conversation continued apace.

"That's gotta be bollocks about the range – I'm bloody certain you couldn't get a kill at over a mile," countered his colleague.

"Pukka gen," came the reply. "I know cos I used the laser rangefinder to find out. It's cos the air's thin at altitude, the rounds can travel further."[9]

"I get that bit, but 1800 metres is still over the top. And anyway you have trouble hitting targets at 300 metres on a range so what chance have you got of topping anyone at over a mile?"

This was met with a good-humoured tirade of abuse and the conversation moved on to the state of the camp food. The QM returned with two polystyrene cups brimming full of tea.

"So what brings you to 42?" he asked.

I told him the tale of how I had come from a cavalry regiment to be attached to the Brigade Headquarters, and how that had eventually metamorphosed into a job with a commando unit. He seemed far from surprised.

"There are more people being shifted from one job to another at the moment than you can shake a stick at. Half the augmentees here were mobilised to do a different job. Under normal circumstances I'd say the whole G1 plot was a mess, but I suppose these aren't normal circumstances."[10] I agreed with him here – divisional deployments didn't happen every day and most of the planning staff had never been through this process before, or at least never on this scale. "The good bit is the quality of blokes we're getting – most of them seem to be mega switched-on, which is a good thing, because we're going to need some good blokes when this thing kicks off."

I took the opportunity to get a brief on the camp layout and who the key movers and shakers were. Quartermasters, in my opinion, are usually a highly reliable source of information. Anyone who needs equipment usually has to interface with them – which means they quickly get to know almost everyone in the battalion. Plus they typically have over 25 years of service behind them, which means they have seen a thing or two and can often make good judgement calls about the quality of the people around them. They typically come in two forms: the approachable, nothing-is-too-difficult type, and the stand-offish, don't-bother-asking-because-I-won't-be-any-help type. Judging by the reception I had been given, and the number of blokes saying a friendly hullo in passing, 42's QM fell squarely in the former category. Unfortunately I didn't get as long as I would have liked to get a full download on how he saw the current situation, since he drank his tea in record time and disappeared back into the headquarters tent at a rate of knots.

An hour or so after the QM left me, I spotted a dust-covered Mitsubishi 4x4 entering the camp, which heralded the arrival of the combat camera team. I strode over to greet them and was surprised to discover that the two-man team consisted of a Royal Marine corporal and a Royal Navy lieutenant. Neither of them had served with 42 before so they were as new to the set-up as I was. I explained the accommodation problem and pointed to the scruffy canvas bag still lying in the sand where the QM had dropped it. Neither of them seemed remotely perturbed by the situation and with barely a word they started unravelling the canvas bundle. I pitched in and in a matter of minutes we had a slightly wobbly aluminium frame assembled, over which the heavy canvas outer needed to be dragged. This done, we hammered dozens of steel pegs deep into the loose sand, in the hope of giving the thing some stability in the event of the wind picking up. I dragged my bergen and kitbag inside and they emptied the contents of their 4x4 into our new home. Next stop was a much-needed cup of tea over which I was able to impart most of my new-found knowledge of what life was like in the Commando. When I mentioned the food, my Navy roommate just laughed and gestured towards the Mitsubishi parked outside. "I wouldn't worry too much about that," he said. "Camp Doha isn't so far away and the wheels are ours for the foreseeable." It was music to my ears. I had only been in this dusty hellhole a matter of hours, and already we had an escape vehicle. My spirits soared. By early evening we had arranged the inside of the tent to resemble something like a home. Camp beds were erected, we had purloined a couple of folding chairs, and the combat camera chaps had produced their piece-de-résistance, a roll of carpet which did a neat job of stopping sand getting kicked into all our kit. Or at least, it slowed down the process.

As the sun dipped towards the western horizon, we joined the throng of officers heading for the CO's evening briefing. The headquarters tent was jammed with bodies, with only enough seating for the first dozen or so. The remainder perched uncomfortably atop storage boxes and trestle tables, or stood in the corners of the tent on either side of the doorway. It was pretty phenomenal to realise just how many officers there now were in the unit, and gave a good idea of how much the Commando had grown from its peacetime complement. The CO kicked off proceedings by introducing the day's new arrivals to the assembly, myself included, before asking his various branch officers to give a series of successive briefs on the issues of the day. The evening briefings would follow the same format almost every day for the ensuing months; the points were always delivered in the same order: manning, intelligence, all the operational issues (including any news on the armoured front, which was my part of the show), kit and equipment, signals, and on and on until every aspect of life in the battle group had been covered. On relatively quiet days in the build-up to war, the briefings would last around an hour; on busy days they were well over two. Personally I saw no gain in dragging out the proceedings so I tended to offer a "no comments" line when it came to armoured warfare. Besides which I had typically done no work and had little idea what the Division's armoured assets were up to. But almost everyone else in the battle group was seemingly embroiled in an endless quest for perfection, so the briefings got longer and longer as the war got closer. If the effectiveness of the troops is reflected in the attention to detail of their officers then God help the Iraqi army, I thought to myself, the poor buggers will be slaughtered in droves. I should have known better than to allow myself such optimistic thoughts.

The daily routine in Camp Gibraltar followed such a repetitive format that the days swiftly blurred into one another. Mornings dawned bright and chilly and the day's activity began with a swift trot to the shower block. I chose to rise early simply to ensure that I could enjoy a long, hot shower before the limited supply of hot water ran out. Since there was essentially only enough hot water for around half the men in the camp, the shower blocks were festooned with notices beseeching us to take minimally short showers and thereby conserve the limited supply. Well bugger that, thinks I, a hot shower is one of the few luxuries attainable in this joint, so I jolly well made the most of it, royally soaking myself each morning and getting rid of the sand and grit that had inevitably glued itself to me during the night. Ablutions were followed by a visit to the dining tent and breakfast, which was undoubtedly the lowest-quality meal of the day, consisting largely of grey scrambled eggs and disgustingly shrivelled sausages of unknown origin, widely suspected of being made from camel meat. Much of what was on offer I would ignore, but at least there was coffee in abundance. Breakfast over, the rest of the morning would be taken up by a trip to Brigade Headquarters, transport permitting, or, if I was feeling in more of a social mood, I would wander through the camp to the QDG lines and enjoy putting the world to rights with the squadron officers. By the time I joined them for a cup of tea, usually taken away from prying eyes under a series of camouflage nets strung out from the recce vehicles, the camp would be awash with Marines undertaking training of all kinds. Squads of men could be seen scurrying around the camp brandishing weaponry of all kinds, assembling radio masts, practising grenade throwing, planting dummy Claymore mines,[11] running through drills on their anti-tank rockets, setting up machine-gun nests, etc etc. The place was a veritable hive of activity and, after a couple of months of this routine, I had little doubt that every man in the Commando was more than proficient with every item of equipment. My cavalry colleagues took a slightly more sanguine view of proceedings and, as long as their vehicles were in good condition and they were confident in their skills, the pace of life was usually a little less frenetic than that of their Royal Marines colleagues. By lunchtime the desert sun would be baking the sand once again and as the temperature soared the pace of activity declined accordingly. Lunch, in the form of MREs, would be taken sitting on camp chairs outside the accommodation tents, usually wearing little more than a pair of shorts and a t-shirt. A hardcore element of the Marines would ditch their t-shirts and eat lunch prone on their camp beds in a seemingly endless quest to get an ever deeper tan. Afternoons consisted largely of physical exertion of one kind or another, something which I successfully managed to avoid throughout the deployment. Squads of them would double around the camp in full battle kit, being overtaken only by their fellow Marines who chose to run in shorts and T-shirts. A shipping container full of weights and rowing machines had been brought over from the UK, and this provided a rudimentary gym, which was permanently overcrowded. Following hours of exercise, late afternoons were designated as admin-time, in which the chaps could do whatever needed doing to keep them and their equipment in full working order. To a large extent this consisted of a growing obsession with spray painting everything desert yellow. With the exception of their rifles, which they weren't allowed to deface, the Marines' equipment changed colour in its entirety. Webbing, bergens, vehicles, radios, jerrycans and carry-cases of all kinds all received liberal spray-gun treatment. Over a period of weeks, the entirety of 42 Commando's equipment metamorphosed from dark green to yellow/brown. But the time could equally be spent exchanging broken or damaged items of kit, cleaning weapons, and doing the thousand and one little jobs that keep a man and his equipment in good working order. Admin completed, the evening briefings would begin, followed by dinner which, in my case at least, often meant a jaunt to Camp Doha with the combat camera team, since the food at Camp Gibraltar was consistently revolting and best avoided. Then back into our shabby green tent for bed and a fitful night's sleep, before the whole daily cycle would begin again the following morning. Despite the indefatigable cheerfulness of the Marines I found it a dismal, repetitive existence and any little break from the routine was cherished.

After a couple of weeks of workaday life in the camp, the Operations Office announced at an evening briefing that the unit would shortly begin rehearsals for the helicopter assault that would eventually land us in southern Iraq. This was a significant step forward in the run-up to war and there was an immediate buzz of excitement among the officers present at the briefing. The repetitive routine of camp life had started to take its inevitable effect on morale and it would, according to the company commanders, be much easier to motivate the men in the knowledge that action was drawing nearer. I was in two minds about this development. On one hand, any break from the daily grind would doubtless be a good thing. But on the other, rehearsals for an assault meant that the real thing was getting a lot closer, and that was disconcerting news in the extreme, made worse by the discovery that we were to be flown into Iraq by the US Marines. Their fleet of helicopters was decrepit – many of them had been commissioned in the early 1970s and had seen service in Vietnam – and I suspected the quality of their pilots would match the aircraft. The British helicopter effort had, it seemed, been devoted to 40 Commando, so we were stuck with the Yanks. Rehearsals were due to start in a couple of days and would begin with company-sized daylight lifts, and progress to multiple-company lifts at night. The next announcement from the Ops Officer was the load plan, which was essentially a list of who would fly in each wave of helicopters and where they would land. The first wave was unsurprising, consisting largely of lunatics from Brigade Recce Force, forward air controllers, artillery spotters, and other Special Forces types. Then came a much bigger wave of assault troops, led by the men of J Company augmented by snipers and the Unit Manoeuvre Support Group.[1][2] No surprise there either – until the other augmentees were added to the list. I practically fell of my chair in shock when I heard my name included, and managed to splutter out a protest before the list continued further.

"Good God, lead assault wave, are you sure?" I croaked.

"Don't be so bloody modest, Harry," came the response from the CO. "You'll be in the thick of it, and for very good reason. QDG will be coming ashore by landing craft at the same time as the helicopters land, and we need some educated eyes on the ground to tell them which way to go. If you stop and think about it, it's absolutely necessary." Murmurs of consent filled the room and I felt bile rising in my throat as fear gripped my innards. I nodded weakly in agreement and slumped back into my chair, stomach churning, unable to pay attention to the remainder of the load plan, which in any case was irrelevant to me.

The start of the rehearsals was marked by the beating of rotors overhead, and the arrival of numerous American transport helicopters, all painted battleship grey and bearing the stencil "Marines" along the side. Their landing was marked by clouds of dust and sand being kicked up into the air, obscuring the landing site and the other approaching helicopters, many of which were forced to circle until the dust had settled and they could see their approach more clearly. Once they had landed outside the camp, we were formed up into sticks of 8, 16 or 32 men depending on what type of helicopter we were flying in, and marched out beyond the perimeter to a series of forming-up points marked by light sticks and sandbags. The American air crews disembarked and some of them strolled over to meet their passengers. I was curious to meet these fellows, particularly now that my wellbeing depended on their piloting skills, so I made sure I was in the path of an approaching pair.

"Pleased to meet you Sir," grinned the pilot in a southern drawl, arm outstretched. I shook his hand as if my life depended on it, which I suppose it did to some extent. "Captain Chester O'Grady, U-nited States Marine Corps, at your service."

"Captain Harry Flashman, Queen's Royal Hussars," I responded. "Delighted to meet you."

"Hussars?" he asked quizzically. "I thought we was flying in the Royal Marines."

"And indeed you are," I reassured him quickly. "I am simply attached to them at the moment."

"So you're not a Marine?" he asked. Clearly I had just plummeted in his estimation.

"I'm a cavalry officer," I retorted, more than a little miffed at his reaction.

"Whatever. As long as you're prepared to climb onboard, we're prepared to git you to I-raq."

I detected a note of self-doubt in his voice which prompted some questioning. "You sound as if I shouldn't climb aboard?"

"Nah, you'll be fine with us. S'just we don't have a lot of

rotor hours right now, so some a' these crews, well, we're a little rusty just at the moment."

The alarm bells were jangling loudly now. Was this man really telling me he wasn't confident flying a helicopter? "When you say 'rusty', what exactly do you mean?" I asked him.

"Well we're a reservist company, and most of us only got out here a few weeks back. It takes a little time to get used to flying these old birds agin, I can tell ya."

"You mean, you don't fly these helicopters all the time?"

"Hell no!" He was warming to his theme now. "I fly 737s for United outta Houston, Texas. Of course, I'm qualified to fly choppers too, but I only do that a few times a year to keep up ma qualification, y'unnerstand?"

I understood all right. This man and his colleagues were sham amateurs, airline pilots who had made the mistake of joining the US Marine Corps Reserves and had now been rounded up to fly helicopters into a battle zone. Their commercial flying skills were no doubt laudable, as long as there was an autopilot to do the difficult bits like taking off and landing. But they had probably never flown in a big formation before and had very little experience of flying in the desert or, for that matter, at night. I realised now why the rehearsals were starting in the day before we made the transition to darkness; it had nothing to do with familiarising the embarked troops and everything to do with getting the pilots some much-needed practise. I could barely conceal my disgust for this loathsome creature whose transparent lack of flying ability was jeopardising my very existence, so I strode quickly away to rejoin the rest of my stick before I said or did anything rash.

We eventually boarded our respective helicopters half an hour later, little snakes of men trudging through the sand towards the aging behemoths that sat on the landing site, rotors drooping idly. Most of the helicopters were the inappropriately named super stallions, a big lump of a thing manufactured by Sikorsky, vaguely similar to the "jolly green giant" of Vietnam fame. Other than size there was nothing super about them, unless the description referred to the age of the airframes or the dirty streaks of corrosion along their flanks. Fortunately our captain was someone other than Chester O'Grady, although I had little doubt that he too would be a reservist rather than a full-time helicopter pilot. We were herded inside in two rows and sat astride our daypacks, rifles gripped between our knees. It was cramped and crowded and I wondered whether it would even be possible to get everyone inside once we were carrying our full battle equipment. We sat in a sweaty silence for a few minutes before the turbines began whining and through the open rear door I could see the huge rotor blades begin to turn in a lazy circle. I stuffed a pair of foam hearing protectors into my ears as the din steadily rose and the aircraft began to shake from side to side – a sensation unlike any other helicopter I have flown in, and quite unnerving. Eventually the rotors reached the required speed and sand was kicked up in enormous volumes as we rose into the desert sky. Peering through a dust-covered window I could see another super stallion flying about 200 yards off to our port side and I assumed there was one to our starboard as well. The pilot flew us around in a large oblong, eventually returning to the landing site some 20 minutes later. We sat in silence until the turbines stopped and the rotors ceased turning, then quietly shuffled out blinking into the bright sunshine, relieved that everything had passed off without a hitch. Follow-on rehearsals were scheduled for the following day, and this time we would embark and disembark with the rotors still turning; there was much more scope for errors and, judging by the subdued nature of the troops, everybody knew it.

The second set of rehearsals began with the same sticks of men being walked out into the desert, but this time they formed into huddles, lying on top of their equipment and weapons to stop anything being blown away by the downdraught from the rotors as the huge helicopters came down right next to us. At least, that was the plan. We formed up in a huddle, this time sporting skiing goggles to keep the sand out of our eyes, as well as the ubiquitous ear protectors. The vast, grey bulk of a super stallion appeared in the sky above us, but failed to stay in a hover and began to creep towards us as it descended. I looked up at the animated face of the loadmaster, who was hanging out of the side door, shouting into a microphone to help guide the pilot in his descent. His shouts of instruction were in vain though, as the roaring beast dropped ever closer to us. At the eleventh hour I realised with abject horror that the pilot would miss his landing spot altogether and was destined to land directly on top of the group of men huddled underneath him. The danger was spotted by the Marines as well and our tight-knit group dissolved in a second, every man for himself as we scrambled to get away from the descending bulk of the helicopter. I vaulted over the pile of kit and sprinted into the desert as fast as my legs would carry me, brushing aside a couple of Marines who, in my opinion, were not moving nearly quickly enough. Propelled by the downdraught I ran quicker than ever, glancing back over my shoulder to witness the pilot achieve an absolute bull's-eye, landing squarely on top of the equipment we had abandoned just a few seconds earlier. Daypacks and other items of equipment flew past us as the wind blasted them into the desert. I came to rest, chest heaving, around 50 yards away, sobbing with relief that I was still in one piece, face down in the dirt to shield myself from the stinging sand grains that were still being blasted out by the spinning rotor blades. Face buried in the sand I lay still, cursing the incompetence of the American pilots, the British planners who had agreed to use US helicopters, and the nightmarish series of events that had landed me in the position of having to fly with them. Eventually I became aware that the din from the super stallion had died away so I picked myself up, shook the sand from my smock, and walked back towards the gaggle of Marines that had regrouped next to the helicopter.

"Bloody close shave, eh Sir?" commented one of the sergeants in the group.

"Too damned close by half," I answered angrily.

"Incompetent bastards," muttered a Marine alongside the sergeant. "Why the bloody 'ell can't we have British pilots?"

"Cos 40 Commando have got 'em all," came the reply. "We've got to make do with the yanks, so let's just get on with it shall we? Stop moaning and get on board."

Sullenly, sporting worried looks, the group of men filed on board the chopper and the rotors began to turn again. The rest of the rehearsal went off without a hitch – but at the back of everybody's mind was the prospect of night rehearsals, which would start the next evening.

The following day, while everyone remained preoccupied by the flight rehearsals, 42 Commando grew in size yet again. This time the arrivals were civilians, in the form of a brace of journalists and a two-man TV crew from ITN in London. Bill Neely and his cameraman Dave Harman would shortly broadcast live footage of the war to audiences around the world, from inside a front line unit. Their arrival was another clear indicator that the start of the conflict wasn't far away. They were accommodated in another newly-erected scruffy green tent adjacent to my own, where they spent most of the day fiddling with satellite broadcast equipment or barking instructions to the editors in London via Bill's mobile phone. I had to take my hat off to the media foursome, they were either brave or stupid, having arrived with only a modicum of equipment and virtually no training in how to use it. Benevolent Marines took pity on them and they received some rudimentary training in how to don their respirators and chemical warfare suits. The thought of entering a hostile country armed to the teeth was worrying enough; what kind of fool would voluntarily do it armed only with a microphone, I wondered. The local ITN production crew was staying in Kuwait City, so I made a point of befriending the TV crew in the hope that this would give me a further excuse (if any were needed) to get out of the camp once in a while. Bill's soft, Northern-Irish drawl made his anecdotes all the easier to listen to and he had visited many of the same trouble spots as me over the years. He was a likeable enough chap and certainly pleasant company for whiling away the occasional hour over a cup of tea, although his dogged insistence on joining the Marines running around the camp each afternoon made me question his sanity somewhat. While Bill was out running his bustling cameraman would set up their satellite antennas and the broadcasting equipment in preparation for their daily bulletin on the news back in the UK. As the sun fell to the horizon, inquisitive Marines would gather behind the camera to listen to what was being said to the outside world about their preparations for war. Bill's broadcasts were highly complementary about the Marines, which quickly endeared him to the men of 42 Commando. Given that he was unarmed and the Marines would soon provide his sole protection from the advancing Arab hoards, I was hardly surprised that he waxed lyrical about their competence – I would have done exactly the same.

The arrival of the journalists provided a welcome distraction, but the time for the night rehearsals was on us before we knew it. This time we would be carrying our full battle equipment which, in the case of many of the Marines, meant rucksacks weighing well over 120lbs. All the weapon systems were also lugged out to the landing site, including machine-guns of various sizes and calibres, long range sniper rifles, mortars and anti-tank rockets. My own bergen was a little lighter than most, since I had declined to carry any troop equipment or ammunition (in my opinion this should be the job of the enlisted men rather than the officers) and had stripped my kit of any unnecessary clutter. In fact, my rucksack was three-quarters filled by my sleeping bag and was almost embarrassingly light to carry. I could see little point exhausting myself during the rehearsals when the real operation would be upon us soon enough. It was a cold, clear night with just a light breeze blowing over the camp as I joined the survivors of the near miss the day before, many of whom were chuntering about the prospect of entrusting their lives yet again to our incompetent pilot. Laden with enough equipment and weaponry to make Al Capone think twice, we trudged out of the camp towards the landing site. After the various debacles of the day before, some sensible soul in the planning staff had decided that there was no need for us to embark while the rotors were turning. Instead we were lined out in a holding area and left to sit on our bergens while the huge fleet of helicopters came clattering in and landed. Once all the engines had fallen silent, lines of men yomped out into the desert to clamber onboard their respective aircraft, many still loudly voicing their opinions of our American colleagues. As I had suspected, whichever genius had done the sums on the load capacity of the US helicopters had failed to take into account the enormity of the equipment the men were carrying. The first two attempts to emplane failed, as the hold became completely filled before everyone was onboard, with several of our number still standing at the foot of the tail ramp. The helicopter was emptied and we started again. On the third attempt, with men and equipment squeezed into every nook and cranny, everyone managed to get inside. The tail ramp was eventually raised and with a familiar whine the engines began to turn; my stomach turned with them. I had a sudden feeling of impending danger, a feeling which over the years I have come to trust and rely on. On other occasions I might have been tempted to cut and run, but here I found myself trapped between two enormous Marines and several feet from the exit, so I had little option but to stay put and pray.

As the pilot ran the turbines up to full power the huge Sikorsky began to shake violently from side to side, just as it had done during the first rehearsals. I leaned forward, craning my neck to see through one of the tiny porthole windows. Outside, a maelstrom of sand was being kicked up into the rotors. As it struck the whirling blades it created an eerie circle of white sparks dancing above the helicopter, and for a moment I forgot the predicament we were in and thought to myself what an attractive sight it was. Then we were airborne, rising gently into the night sky. Through the window I could make out the silhouettes of other helicopters flying alongside us and, as we banked over to the right, I could see the lights of Camp Gibraltar several hundred feet below on the flat desert plain.

For the next twenty minutes everything went swimmingly. Flying in formation at around three hundred feet, we described a large square, first south, then west, then north, eventually eastwards back towards the camp. I kept an eye out for the other helicopters in the group and caught occasional sight of them, seldom more than a couple of hundred yards away. Then I felt the speed drop away, the rotor noise lessened slightly and we began to descend. Through the porthole I could see the lights of the camp not half a mile away. We were not hovering, as is normal with a helicopter landing, but moving gently forward and descending at the same time. I braced myself for the bump of landing, but it never came. Instead, the turbines began to screech ever louder and I realised that our descent had ceased – instead, we were climbing. I had no idea why this should be, but I could guess. Looking through night vision goggles, the flat surface of desert should have been clear as day to the pilot. But as the helicopter approached the ground, sand flying up would obscure the landing sight, meaning that the pilot would need to descend using his instruments. Not competent enough to maintain a hover, the pilot was unable to gauge the speed of his descent and had aborted the landing. Sure enough, as soon as we had climbed a few feet, the helicopter swung round in a circle and we began our approach again. Some of the more experienced Marines were exchanging worried glances, while their younger comrades grinned nervously and exchanged the hand-signal for "wanker" in the direction of the cockpit. The second approach was an action-replay of the first; just as I braced myself for the impact of landing, we overshot the aiming mark, ascended, and went round in another circle. Third time lucky old son, I thought to myself, let's see you get this crate on the deck and then we can all bugger off for a cup of tea and bed. It wasn't to be. The third attempt was no different to the first two. And so it continued, for a fourth, fifth and sixth time. Sooner or later the pilot was going to have to brave it, trust his instruments, and get his steed on the ground. I braced myself as we went in for the seventh time, and it was a bloody good job I did, for we hit the deck so hard it fairly knocked the wind of me. A land bang sounded from the undercarriage, the helicopter bounced off the hard sand floor and we were airborne yet again, this time with the engines wailing louder than ever as our inept cabbie struggled to get his machine out of harm's way. By this time the Marines were sporting faces like thunder and it would barely have surprised me if they had rushed the cockpit. We continued to climb and I realised fairly quickly that we had ceased travelling round in circles and the helicopter was now moving on a linear path, south east if my sense of direction was anything to go by. Just then the loadmaster stepped forward and gestured to the nearest Marine to remove his ear defenders. A message was passed back through the cabin. I listened with disbelief as I was told that we had hit the ground so hard that part of the undercarriage had sheared off. Unable to land safely in the desert, we were to make an emergency landing at Ali-al-Saleem airbase, almost 100 miles away. I was momentarily filled with rage, until I realised that we would at least be able to land safe and sound on tarmac and I therefore had a better than even chance of seeing the night through without serious injury. It was almost an hour until we eventually touched down on terra firma, with fire trucks left and right of us and the helicopter listing over to one side, minus one of its landing wheels. It was rapidly becoming apparent to everyone on board that it would take a minor miracle for us to even reach Iraq intact, let alone fight a battle once we got there. Thirty-odd Marines clambered out of the helicopter and onto the tarmac of Ali-al-Saleem, swearing blue murder if they ever got their hands on the aircrew who, conscious of self-preservation, had beat a hasty retreat and were nowhere to be seen. A coach and baggage truck were waiting for us so we wrestled our equipment onboard and clambered inside the coach before being driven back to Camp Gibraltar in complete silence. I have seldom seen a troop of Marines so morose as that one – they had been given plenty of reason to contemplate their own mortality recently and we had got no further than the rehearsals; the prospect of doing it for real was looming large in everyone's mind.

The following day nothing was said openly about the debacle of the previous night's rehearsals, and during the afternoon I paid the ops room a visit in order to check my pigeonhole for letters from home (I maintained a smutty correspondence with Charlotte Woodstock throughout the campaign, writing frequently of my intentions towards her upon my return, which were anything but honourable. Credit where it's due, the little minx matched me stroke for stroke and some her letters were blue beyond belief.) Whilst there I caught wind of a heated debate taking place over the map table and quickly realised there was a conversation taking place between the officers of the Commando Planning Group in which the possibility of using British helicopters was being discussed. From behind the partition curtain I silently urged them to make the decision but the consensus was that there weren't enough British helicopters to facilitate the lift and anyway it was too political at this point to make such a move, so we had to stick with the yanks come what may. Bloody fools, it was all I could do to keep myself from crying out in frustration, but the decision was made so I skulked back into my tent. None of us knew it, but it was a decision which very nearly cost 42 Commando its place in the invasion.

Later in the day I noticed the CO disappearing out of his tent for his afternoon run with a wry smile on his face and a distinct spring in his step. The Ops Officer and BGE were also in high spirits and I began to suspect that something sinister was afoot.[12] My fears were confirmed during the evening briefing, when the Ops Officer announced that the unit had been put on 48 hours notice-to-move, and that Brigade were fully expecting the assault to begin before the week was out. My innards turned to jelly as the damned fools in the headquarters cheered out loud. I joined them with gusto of course, there was no merit in letting them see me for the coward I really was, but I wondered briefly if the day wasn't fast approaching when Flashy should don his civilian clothes and slip quietly over the perimeter wall. With a fistful of dollar bills, a credit card, passport and a little good fortune I could probably be back in Blighty inside a week. But then of course there would be the ignominy of facing a court martial for desertion and all the humiliation that went with it, not to mention being black-balled out of the mess and barred from the Cavalry Club. No, I would have to take my chances with the commandos and hope that I would be able to stay out of harm's way once we were in Iraq. The briefing left me entirely without appetite so I sloped back to my accommodation in a blue funk in order to avoid all the gung-ho joviality that would doubtless fill the dining tent that evening.

For once my timing was spot-on, for shortly afterwards Bill Neely appeared, asking for a ride to Kuwait City. I rounded up the combat camera team and the four of us piled into their Mitsubishi and exited the camp at speed. Bill had spent much of the previous days shooting background footage of the boys training and wanted to deliver the resulting video cassette to the ITN production team in the Kuwait City Hilton. It was a first-rate opportunity to spend a few moments in the civility of an air-conditioned building and get some decent tucker at the same time. After the traumas of the past couple of days I could think of no better tonic for the general insanity that was sweeping Camp Gibraltar.

The ITN production team, clearly frustrated at being miles away from the "action", greeted us like returning heroes and laid on a fair old spread of sandwiches, fruit, chocolate deserts and the like. The only thing missing was a decent drink, but that didn't stop me from tucking into the chow as if my life depended on it. Bill interrupted our feeding frenzy to introduce some of his colleagues, including a couple of fellow reporters who had not managed to obtain military clearance and were therefore stuck in Kuwait City. One of them was clearly anxious to make a move north towards the Iraqi border before the fighting began.

"Harry, would you mind if we tailed your car north along the highway?" he asked. "We've tried to get up the road several times but the police roadblocks always turn us back." I couldn't fathom whether the man was brave to the point of stupidity, or simply insane. Here he was surrounded by every creature comfort known to man, with the perfect excuse to avoid the oncoming melee, yet all he wanted to do was get himself, unarmed and unescorted, into the thick of the fighting. However, it made precious little difference to my life if some news reporter wanted to put himself in the line of fire, and anyway they were paying for the tucker, so I readily agreed.

Some time later, replete with dozens of canapés and deserts lining my gut, we set off into the night back towards Camp Gibraltar, with the ITN reporter and his cameraman glued to our stern in their silver 4x4. With no military pass in the window, their status as civilians was made transparent by the letters "TV" stuck on the bonnet and doors of their car in black masking tape. Sure enough, as we passed the first Kuwaiti police checkpoint on the highway north, flashing blue lights appeared in our mirrors and the ITN crew was stopped. We pulled up hard and reversed back towards them. I bailed out and remonstrated with the local plod, explaining that we were on our way back to 42 Commando and the camera crew was travelling with us. The policeman clearly didn't believe a word of it, for he motioned everyone to get out of the cars and began babbling in Arabic into his radio. Fortunately for us, his controller seemed to think it was a perfectly acceptable set of circumstances, for when the reply came over the radio a few moments later, he stepped back, saluted smartly, and waved us on our way with a smile. The ITN man broke into a broad grin and shot me a wink as he jumped back into his 4x4, and we roared off up the highway. At the turn-off to Camp Gibraltar they sped on into the night; the last I saw of them was a grateful wave emanating from the passenger side window. A couple of weeks later I heard the pair had been killed in crossfire between Iraqi troops and a US armoured column during one of the first actions of the war. Brave buggers – it's not the sort of job I would ever volunteer for, and it makes one appreciate the risks the media take to get the great British public ringside seats of such a punch-up.

The following morning, still feeling smug from my dramatically improved rations in Kuwait, I arose late, choosing to avoid breakfast and focusing instead on enjoying a leisurely cup of tea in the QDG lines. The camp was surprisingly quiet considering we were on 48 hours notice to move – but then all the preparations for war had been completed and there was very little to do other than wait for the "go" signal. Squads of Marines ran past, some carrying kit and weapons and others in shorts and T-shirts. Brigade Recce Force troops fiddled with their vehicles and machine-guns. Soldiers sat in the shade of camouflage nets, stripping and cleaning their weapons. The only clue to the advanced likelihood of action was an increased buzzing overhead from the motors of the US and British unmanned drones – pilotless planes used to take aerial photographs of enemy territory. It was still fairly early in the morning when we heard the crump of a huge explosion several miles away, and a rushing noise in the sky overhead. It may strike you as odd, reading these notes years after the war, but I thought little of it at the time and neither did my peers; we were well used to flashes and bangs on the horizon and the roar of jets overhead, and Camp Commando retained its air of quiet preparation, at least for a short while. It was only when I made my way back to the ops room that I discovered the explosion had been a Scud missile landing, and more missile strikes had been reported from Kuwait City. Saddam had launched a pre-emptive strike at the coalition and I knew it would precipitate our invasion. Sure enough, the signal arrived from Brigade just minutes later: the assault would begin that night.

As word spread, the camp erupted in a frenzy of last-minute activity. Throughout the day, all non-essential equipment was placed in storage. Our personal kit was placed into civilian hold-alls and dumped inside the empty shipping containers which just a few short weeks ago had brought weapons and ammunition to Kuwait. I waved a fond farewell to the last of my creature comforts as the steel door slammed shut, and prayed I would be reunited with my worldly goods sooner rather than later. Weapons were mustered, ammunition issued, accommodation tents dismantled, equipment checked and re-checked, rifles cleaned and tested one last time. As the sun dipped towards the horizon, lines of Marines trudged through the sand to a corner of the camp to form up in a vast, hollow square. In the centre, perched on a trestle table, the commanding officer addressed the assembled mass. Other men, I am sure, found his speech inspiring. For myself, it cemented my view of Royal Marines officers as criminally insane and served only to loosen my bowels. For several minutes he talked about relying on one another, trust, unquestioning loyalty to one's comrades, maintaining momentum, and absolute commitment to the task in hand. The only task I was concerned about was getting out of this mess with my skin intact, but self-preservation seemed far from the minds of 42 Commando that night. He left us with an old Gurkha expression, which I retain to this day as a psychological scar: "Lose money, lose nothing. Lose pride, lose much. Lose courage, lose everything." The Marines loved every word of it, they even cheered the irrepressible old bastard at the end, the bloody fools! I stood frozen to the spot, knees knocking, hoping for divine intervention to prevent the impending madness. It never came, of course, and shortly after sundown, laden with weapons and equipment, we trudged through the eastern gate of the camp and out to the landing site to await the American transport helicopters. The war was about to begin.

NOTES

1. The unit to which Flashman refers is the Queens Dragoon Guards (QDG), the self-styled "Welsh Cavalry" on account of their strong regional recruiting base. Many of the squadron's vehicles can be seen flying the Welsh flag.
2. Milan: a medium-range anti-tank missile.
3. LCAC: Landing Craft, Air Cushioned – i.e. a hovercraft.
4. UMST: Unit Manoeuvre Support Troop. A small, mobile unit within a commando group which can rapidly bring additional anti-tank and machine-gun capability to reinforce a position.
5. US ration packs are more usually referred to as MREs, an abbreviation of "Meals Ready to Eat". Universally unpopular, they are frequently referred to as "Meals Rejected by Everyone".
6. CR: Confidential Report.
7. QM: Quarter Master.
8. HE: High Explosive.
9. "Gen" is Royal Marines slang for "genuine", i.e. "not exaggerated"; "Pukka gen" is an even more emphatic version.
10. G1: manning/personnel.
11. The Claymore mine is a simple device consisting of an oblong piece of plastic explosive measuring roughly six inches by twelve, in which several hundred ball bearings are embedded on one side. Designed to provide perimeter security or for use in ambushes, it is detonated either on command or by trip wire; anyone standing the wrong side of the mine is riddled with high-velocity ball bearings.
12. BGE: Battle-Group Engineering Officer.

5

As the last glimmer of daylight disappeared over the western horizon, laden down by a huge rucksack and with my webbing pouches stuffed to bursting, I shuffled out into the Kuwaiti desert once again, along with the rest of 42 Commando. Despite the crushing pain in my shoulders I took a quiet moment to look about me, for an entire battle group on the march is not an everyday sight. As far as the eye could see, hundreds of Marines were lining out in the desert, sporting sufficient arms and ammunition to raise Cain. Most of them had passed out of training years earlier, while many of the NCOs had been with the Corps for over a decade. For all of them, this was the zenith of years of service, a once-in-a-lifetime opportunity to put endless training and countless exercises into practise and wage war on a legitimised enemy.[1] One look at their faces told me all I needed to know – morale had never been higher. Had they been given the choice between a holiday in Barbados or boarding the helicopters into Iraq, I had little doubt that every man in the Unit would have cheerfully jumped onboard his helicopter. I felt a crushing sense of claustrophobia and wondered, not for the first time, how on earth I had got myself into this fix.

Many of the Marines were carrying in excess of 120lbs on their backs and some were carrying considerably more (notably the heavy machine-gun crews whose equipment weighed in excess of 150lbs), so once we reached the helicopter landing site no-one needed any coercing to ditch their packs and sit down. My experience of military undertakings, whether exercises or operations, is that they invariably involve long periods of hanging around waiting for activity and this one was no exception – our flight was not due to commence until shortly before midnight so I had several hours to kill. It was a perfectly calm, clear night, with just an occasional cloud above us to obscure the Milky Way and the lightest of breezes blowing over the desert. The landing site was almost eerily quiet; most of the men were fiddling with their equipment, eating rations, or taking the opportunity for a nap, but almost nobody was talking. Somewhere off to a flank a short wave radio was tuned to the BBC World Service which was giving a blow by blow account of the "shock and awe" bombing campaign which was raining down on Baghdad. I listened for a moment to accounts of Tomahawk missiles pounding military installations and hoped the Al Faw Peninsular was also getting a softening up before our arrival. (It was, too – I discovered later that the gunners of 29 Commando pumped over 17,000 artillery shells into the area before we arrived, God bless 'em.) Thoughtful soul that he was, the QM had dumped piles of ration packs and water bottles around the landing site, which was a bloody marvellous piece of foresight on his behalf since none of us knew when we would get our next meal, so I shovelled a boil-in-the-bag dinner into my face before crawling into my sleeping bag and dropping into a fitful doze. I awoke a couple of hours later to the beating of rotor blades and the landing site erupting into a frenzy of activity. It seemed the arrival of the American cabs had spurred everyone to get up and get going, but one look at my watch told me that we wouldn't move for at least another hour so I hunkered down in my sleeping bag and attempted to sleep for a little while longer.

 I gave up the unequal battle some time after 10 p.m. Asides from the disturbance of the comings and goings around me, my nerves wouldn't allow me to sleep and I became increasingly on edge as the moment of our departure drew nearer. Eventually it was time to board the choppers and I squeezed into the rear of the behemoth with the rest of my stick, listening as the advance wave of helicopters departed into the night sky, carrying the men of Brigade Recce Force and various Forward Air Controllers and the like. Shortly afterwards our own engines began to whine and the rotors started to turn above us. After the rigours of the rehearsals there was an air of tension among the men – as a rule I'm not a religious fellow, but I said a few prayers before take off, I don't mind telling you. A couple of minutes later the rotors were spinning at full speed and the aircraft began its customary shaking. I readied myself for lift-off then listened in delighted disbelief as the engine note dropped sharply, the shaking stopped, and the rotors began to slow down. A couple of minutes later the helicopter stood silent again, with its cargo of Marines chattering nervously among themselves, all wondering what the problem could be. In a moment of wild optimism I wondered whether the whole operation had been cancelled. What a stroke of luck that would have been – but of course it was nothing more than wild fantasy on my part. Eventually word came from the aircrew that one of the helicopters in the advance wave had gone down. They weren't sure whether the crash had happened in Kuwait or in Iraq and were waiting on more information from the squadron commander. The obvious inference was that the thing had been shot down, so I guessed that the lift was on hold until the anti-aircraft threat could be properly assessed. A few minutes later, still with no news, the aircrew ushered us off the helicopter and we filed silently across the sand back to the holding area once again.

I collected another boil-in-the-bag meal and ate it lying in the darkness, listening once again to the World Service. My aspirations of the invasion being called off were immediately dashed as it became apparent that US forces had already breached the Iraqi border in several places, and UK forces were reported landing in the south east of the country. This was a veiled reference to 40 Commando and it made difficult listening for the Marines of 42, whose job it was to protect their flank and prevent an Iraqi counter-attack. For one Captain H Flashman, it was enough to know that while the bullets were already flying, I was nowhere near them. As far as yours truly was concerned, the longer we stayed safe and snug in Kuwait the better. For the moment at least, there seemed little prospect of us going anywhere.

Eventually a more complete picture emerged of the helicopter crash. Far from being shot down over Iraq, the crash had been caused by either pilot error or mechanical failure (I had my opinion of which it might be, as I'm sure you can guess) and had happened on Bubiyan Island, a flat, featureless mass just off the Kuwaiti coast which rises barely six feet above sea level, and which was currently playing host to the artillery pieces of 29 Commando, many of whom had seen the fireball as the helicopter hit the deck. Tragically, eight of our number had been onboard, including the charismatic officer commanding Brigade Recce Force. Mad as a hatter, like most of his breed, his devil-may-care attitude made him hugely popular in the mess and with the men of BRF. News of the crash brought a sombre air to 42 Commando that night, but it did nothing to reduce the growing impatience of the Marines who were desperate to get out of Kuwait and get stuck into the fighting in Iraq.

The urgency to get the battle group into action was also reflected at the top, with the CO getting more and more animated in his dealings with the American helicopter crews. Now that the details of the crash were confirmed there was no need to delay entry into Iraq a moment longer – or so he felt. However, the US aircrews, already lacking in confidence in their own abilities, had gone into a sort of collective shock. Four of their number had perished in the crash and they were frozen by fear (I know how it feels, I've felt it myself often enough) and refused to undertake the journey into Iraq. For 42 Commando the crash had been a tragedy but it was no reason to delay the commencement of operations. Through the small hours the CO tried every line in the book to cajole and persuade the

Americans to fly, but to no avail. Eventually, around 4 a.m., exasperated and angry, he took the unprecedented step of sacking the lot of them and demanding they remove their helicopters from his landing site. The British divisional air reserve was urgently requested and within minutes of the US helicopters departing a makeshift mob of RAF helicopters was on its way north to our position.[2]

As the first glimmers of dawn brightened the morning sky, a formation of much smaller helicopters appeared on the horizon. The RAF had managed to cobble together seven Pumas (each capable of carrying nine men) and a single Chinook, which could manage upwards of thirty. In a sudden moment of lucidity I realised the huge reduction in carrying capacity meant that numerous men originally earmarked for the first lift would be forced to remain behind in Kuwait. To ensure I was among them all I needed to do was to make sure I was forgotten when the new load-plan was devised. There was no time to waste so, abandoning my bergen, I quietly stole away from the Marines in my stick and made my way towards the group of men furthest from both the Commando Headquarters and the arriving helicopters, creeping up and down the lines in search of an unobserved spot in which to sit myself down and let the morning take its course unhindered. At that precise moment I bumped into the adjutant coming the opposite way at speed.

"Harry!" he exclaimed, brimming with enthusiasm, "The very man!" My heart sank like a stone, for he had that look in his eyes of a man fired up by the prospect of war and I instinctively knew that whatever was to follow would mean trouble. "We've almost sorted the new load-plan and we've got the whole of J Company sorted out, plus most of the attached ranks too. Just one hitch though: we couldn't fit you in with the main body of men so you're in the lead Puma with the snipers – I hope that's okay?" He didn't wait for my reply but added, "Problem is, old boy, they're being inserted to the north of everybody else because their mission is to push northwards on foot through the date palms. The rest of J Company will be going south and east from where the helicopters land. Obviously we couldn't rely on an inexperienced man to make his way overland and link up with the rest of the company, so we've picked you for the job."

I nearly spat in his eye. Far from avoiding the ride, I was being thrust deep into enemy territory and, unbelievably, I was expected to make my way overland on foot, alone, to link up with the main body of J Company.

"Good man!" enthused the adjutant, "I knew you'd love the idea. Enjoy!" And with that, he strode off towards J Company headquarters.

Disconsolate and increasingly nervous about what lay ahead, I made my way across the sand back to my bergen and sat down in a blue funk. I didn't have long to worry about the situation though, as the shout went up almost immediately to "saddle up" and climb aboard the helicopters. The lead Puma was, of course, furthest away from us, and I was sweating profusely by the time I reached it – although whether from exertion or fear, I couldn't tell. The snipers were already there, sitting on their packs and enjoying the warmth from the first rays of sunshine, and a rough bunch they looked too. Already smothered in camouflage cream and sporting the scruffiest clothes I have ever clapped eyes on, they wore the look of men prepared to risk everything in order to accomplish their mission – it's a look I've seen a few times over the years, and it invariably leads to trouble. I introduced myself with a bluff smile and they looked me up and down, presumably wondering why a cavalry officer of all people should be joining them on their flight. I explained briefly and, to a man, they looked even less impressed.

"That'll be interestin' for you," quipped one of them in a northern accent. "At least we'll be going in pairs – you'll have to watch your own back I s'pose. Still, it shouldn't be more than a half mile back to J Company. You'll just have to hope there's no jundies between you an' them!"[3]

At that moment the RAF aircrew arrived, consisting of a

pilot, co-pilot and door-gunner. A jovial bunch, they exuded confidence and were clearly delighted at their elevation from air reserve to front-line flying. I shook them warmly by the hand, delighted that whatever other risks we may be facing, pilot incompetence was not likely to be among them.

"It's nice to see a British aircrew – and a new helicopter," I commented, gesticulating towards the immaculate machine, the smart appearance of which was in stark contrast to the corrosion-streaked hulls of the US machines. The pilot's reply came as a complete surprise.

"Oh, this thing isn't new at all – it's just had a recent paint job. In fact it's ancient," he laughed. "It's not even British. It used to belong to Argentina – until it was captured it in the Falklands. One of the spoils of war. Still, give it a British registration number and paint a couple of RAF roundels on it, and no-one's any the wiser, eh!"

Bemused at the thought of flying into Iraq in an Argentine helicopter, I followed the snipers and clambered aboard, squeezing into a tiny canvas seat alongside the door gunner, who was busily loading a huge belt of ammunition into his machine-gun. For a few moments the only sound was the pilot and co-pilot running through their various pre-flight checks. Then the turbines began to whine and I felt the wind rising as the rotors began to howl above us. I pulled my goggles down over my eyes and gripped my rifle, mouth dry with nerves, and feeling more than a little nauseous. Then we were away, speeding northwards at over 100 knots with the desert flashing by just 20 feet beneath us. Through the open side door I could see the other RAF helicopters close alongside and to our rear, maintaining perfect position in the formation. I glanced about inside the cabin, wondering whether the Marines onboard were experiencing the stomach-churning sense of apprehension that I was feeling. If they were, their faces gave nothing away. Below us, sand gave way to mud flats and then water – we were leaving Kuwait. Sunlight danced on the estuary below, then we were once again flying over mudflats and I knew we had entered Iraq. Below us, the muddy ground was littered with thousands of small craters, which made it look faintly like the surface of the moon. (I discovered later that these were shell craters dating from the Iran-Iraq war some twenty years earlier.)[4] A few moments later the helicopter banked sharply left, the speed fell away, and we came briefly to a hover before landing in the mud. In seconds the snipers were out, pulling on their bergens and moving swiftly away from the helicopter. The pilot gave us a cheery wave, then the engine note rose once more and he was gone. I looked about me, hoping for an obvious route towards the other helicopters which I could make out in the distance. The terrain was almost entirely flat, made up of sand and mudflats crisscrossed by drainage ditches and dykes. A handful of derelict buildings dotted the skyline and to the south east I could make out the pipelines and storage tanks of the oil installations, where 40 Commando was located. A hand slapped me on the back and I wheeled around to see the grinning face of the last of the Marines from the helicopter – the rest of the snipers had already set off towards the palm trees.

"Good luck, Sir," was all he said, and then he too was gone. I felt horribly alone and exposed. In the distance I could hear the heavy rotor blades of the Chinook taking off – the Pumas had already departed. As the beating of the rotors subsided I realised I could hear the sound of distant gunfire coming from the direction of Al Faw town and the oil pumping station where the assault troops of 40 Commando were busy tackling the Iraqi defensive positions, some of which were proving a little more truculent than anticipated. I had barely taken a couple of steps forward when I heard the sound of a motorcar engine roaring along the road just behind me. A small blue and white car crammed full of jundies was fleeing Al Faw town in an attempt to get away from the onslaught of 40 Commando. Unhappily for me, its passage had not gone unobserved and suddenly bullets were flying all around me from the direction of 42 Commando. I let out a yelp of fright and threw myself face first into the mud, cursing as my smock and webbing became liberally coated in the stuff. Several rounds smashed into the car but presumably none hit the driver for it showed no sign of stopping and tore on in the direction of Basra. I scraped myself out of the mud and trudged on, hoping to find some hard standing on which to clean myself up. There was none, and my bedraggled appearance caused no little mirth when I eventually caught up with J Company. By that time, the company had shaken out into a series of troop formations and was fanning out across the landscape with the express intention of meeting out violence to any Iraqi troops they found there. I tagged onto the rear and fervently hoped that the troops to my front would dispose of any trouble before I became embroiled.

Before long, the bulk of J Company, including the headquarters elements, had made their way to a large road junction which marked the western most boundary of the oil installations and also the boundary of 40 Commando's patch. The Marines of 40 Commando seemed genuinely pleased to see us, which was unsurprising given the tense night they had endured clearing out Iraqi soldiers from the surrounding area. There were a fair few enemy corpses lying around which bore testament to the overnight fighting, but the area was quiet by the time I got there and it seemed a reasonably sensible spot to settle down and recover my breath, so I accepted the offer of a cup of tea from one of the boys and sat on my pack, content to soak up the sun and let the war take its course for an hour or two. I had barely taken a sip from the mug when the quiet was shattered by a series of mortar bombs exploding next to the position. I dived behind an earth rampart, spilling hot tea all over myself in the process, and listened as several more mortar bombs screamed into the area. Fortunately for me, their effectiveness was dramatically reduced by the muddy ground, which absorbed much of the blast. Still, with no idea where they were coming from and, more importantly, no idea how many more might follow, I decided it was high time I moved somewhere safer. The heavy bergen cut into my shoulders as I started to trot north, but a bit of short term pain seemed infinitely preferable to being blown to pieces, and I scampered along the track with the aim of being as far as possible from the road junction before the next mortar stomp arrived.

Among J Company's objectives were a series of crossroads on the various roads and tracks leading to and from Al Faw town and the oil installations. Common sense dictated that any Iraqi armour would be forced to follow the roads, since tanks would quickly get bogged down in the muddy terrain elsewhere. I soon caught up with the rearmost group of Marines, made up of 3 Troop and elements of UMST, which was heading to the smallest of these crossroads, just to the north of the main Al Faw-Basra road, close to the Shat-al-Arab riverbank. As far as I was concerned, the smaller the junction, the less the odds on Iraqi troops using it, plus it was the furthest away from the fighting around the oil installations, so it seemed a sensible destination for yours truly. The downside was that it involved more walking, but working on the premise that sore feet were preferable to being shot, I buried myself in the middle of the formation and trudged north along a dirt track, sweating profusely, for best part of a mile. The landscape remained flat and empty, mudflats and drainage ditches stretching to the west as far as the eye could see, with the exception of a series of large farm buildings situated next to the Al Faw-Basra road, towards which we were advancing. (I discovered later that they were not farms but water desalination plants, built to turn the brackish water of the estuary into drinking water for the locals.) As sweat trickled between my shoulder blades and hot-spots formed on the soles of my feet, I began to yearn for an opportunity to drop my pack. I didn't need to wait long.

Bam!-bam!-bam!-bam!-bam! A burst of AK47 fire came from an upstairs window of the nearest building, perhaps 250 metres away. Men dived for cover on either side of the track, dropping their bergens as they went, and all hell erupted. Sharp cracks of high-velocity rounds sounded all around as the Marines began to pour rifle fire into the buildings. Mud and earth spattered up around me as the Iraqis blasted away in our direction.

Fortunately for me they were lousy shots and could generally be relied upon to hit anything but their targets – but that didn't make the experience any less nerve wracking. I lay quivering in a ditch underneath my bergen, hoping their aim didn't improve. A few seconds later the rifle fire was drowned out by much heavier thumping from our machine-guns. The increased firepower knocked lumps out of the building, the windows disappeared within seconds, shards of glass spraying left and right, and pieces of wood and brickwork flew in all directions. An eternity seemed to pass (which in reality I suspect was probably no more than a few minutes) until I realised the Iraqis had stopped firing at us. That didn't stop the Marines though, the gung-ho bastards were still punching holes in the building with everything they'd got. I peered over the top of the ditch to discover that the men either side of me had disappeared – only their bergens remained. The lead sections of 3 Troop were already sprinting towards the buildings in small bounds, diving for cover every few yards in the ditches and dykes that crisscrossed the muddy ground, while their mates continued to riddle the place with holes. Good bloody luck to 'em, I thought to myself, content to lie in my ditch until the area was declared safe. Just then, somewhat surreally, I caught sight of a navy blue taxicab making its way along the main road towards us. To my amazement, blissfully unaware of the bullets flying around him, the driver turned off the road and drove around the back of the buildings. Unfazed, 3 Troop's advance continued unabated – they had closed to within 150 metres and showed no sign of slowing. A few seconds passed during which I could see the Marines inexorably closing on their objective, while rifle and machine-gun fire continued to blast away in support. In less than a minute they would be posting grenades through the shattered windows and kicking down the doors. But the glory of a frontal assault was denied them, for just at that moment, the taxicab reappeared from behind the buildings and lurched back onto the road towards Al Faw town, laden with Iraqi fighters. Faced with the prospect of an assault by dozens of highly aggressive Brits and lacking an escape plan, the jundies had simply phoned for a cab to get them out of Dodge. (All credit to them for using their initiative but very low marks for execution; how they ever thought an aging Nissen was going to outrun 7.62mm bullets beats me.) Alongside the driver, three men were jammed in the front, five on the rear seat, and a further two in the boot. Engine straining, the overloaded car tried to accelerate away from the scene and I waited in horror for the inevitable bloodbath that would surely occur once the Marines opened fire on it. It never came. To their eternal credit a handful of the closest Marines sprinted across the mudflats and onto the road, flagging down the car at gunpoint. It screeched to a halt and the occupants – including the protesting cabbie – were dragged unceremoniously out onto the road. It took me a moment or two to work out why their appearance was faintly ridiculous, until I realised that most of them were only half dressed. In desperation they had ditched the majority of their military clothing, presumably in the hope of passing themselves off as civilians. The black boots were a bit of a giveaway though, as were the numerous rifles and grenades in the boot of the taxi. In any event, the Marines wasted little time in searching them and dragged them off to the side of the road, where they were made to sit cross-legged until transport was found to take them to the prisoner of war processing centre, which was conveniently housed in the oil installations. To a man, they looked royally pissed off with the proceedings – I suspect they didn't realise how lucky they were to be alive and unharmed.

The excitement momentarily over, 3 Troop trudged back through the mud to collect their bergens, sporting adrenaline-fuelled grins. I grinned back at them and made noises of approval whilst explaining that I would, of course, have joined them in the assault but I would only have got in the way, added to the confusion, wished I had worked with them before, etc etc. Not that they cared two farthings about my ramblings; the only thing that mattered to the men of J Company was that they had won their first fire-fight hands down and had acquired a taxicab into the bargain, which was already being used to ferry the troop commander back to company headquarters for a briefing.

Bergen on my back once more, we set off on our intended route towards the river, dropping off an eight-man section to cover the crossroads where the track crossed the Al Faw-Basra road. North of the main road, the landscape immediately changed. Here, irrigation ditches brought water from the river and the grey, lifeless mudflats gave way to green grass and palm trees. It sounds absurd now, but it never occurred to me that these were the same palm trees I had seen on the air photographs, or that there might be Iraqi troops positioned in the only place where there was cover from view. Instead, I simply plodded on, hopeful of finding a spot where I could spend the night in relative peace and safety. I should have known better.

The country became gradually greener as we ventured northeast, until eventually, peering through the trees, I could make out the sluggish flow of the Shat-al-Arab waterway. Across the river, some three hundred yards away, lay Iran. There was no sign of any activity on the Iranian side, but there were some ominous-looking watchtowers poking up from between the palm trees, so I guessed they were keeping a sharp eye on proceedings. Then we stumbled across the crossroads which was our objective and the patrol came to a halt. I was delighted to note that, as suspected from the air photographs, the tracks that made up the crossroads were small and insignificant compared with the main road we had crossed earlier; there was little chance of encountering a tank formation coming this way. To our right, perhaps half a mile away, lay Al Faw town, from where it was still possible to discern the occasional crack of rifle fire as 40 Commando methodically swept through the government buildings. I pulled off my bergen and sat down on it, relieved to have an opportunity to dry my sweat-drenched shirt.

"Okay, let's have a look north and south to establish whether we're alone here," instructed the troop commander as he bounded energetically up and down the line. "3 Section, you can go north – no need to go further than the next irrigation canal, because 2 Troop is operating up there. 1 Section, crack on south. But don't go anywhere near the town because you'll run into 40 Commando." I sat motionless, allowing the late afternoon sun to warm my aching back muscles, fully expecting to be left behind and looking forward to a slack hour or two as a result. Then came the rejoinder: "1 Section, you can include Captain Flashman, because he needs to get his eyes on as many of the local roads and tracks as possible."

I stared at him with baleful eyes, which he probably mistook as rugged determination, and slowly rose to my feet. "Actually old boy, I'm quite happy to stay here with troop headquarters – no need to give your blokes more work than they need. I'll only get under their feet."

He gave a good-natured laugh at this. "Sir, you're obviously more than capable of looking after yourself, and I'm not worried about their workload. And anyway the company commander has insisted we get you out and about as much as possible."

I gave a moment's thought to pulling rank on him and simply refusing to move, then dismissed the idea and dejectedly shuffled off to join 1 Section, who were already shaking out along the track ahead of me. Fortunately they were leaving their bergens where they lay, which made the task of yet more patrolling a great deal more palatable.

The southbound track was evidently used by vehicles, albeit infrequently, since it principally consisted of two deep muddy ruts. It looked to me as if it had lain dormant for a while; there were certainly no fresh tyre marks that I could discern. We walked for some little distance through pleasant countryside, green meadows interspersed with little copses of bushes and marsh grass, all dotted with swaying palm trees. The Marines halted every few yards, diligently scanning the countryside through the optical sights on their rifles or through binoculars, while I enjoyed the feeling of my shoulder muscles loosening without the weight of the rucksack pressing down on them. In front of us I could hear distant loudhailer messages emanating from the town as 40 Commando exhorted the last of the Iraqi fighters to give up without further bloodshed. (Many of them did as they were bid, but some stubborn fools inevitably refused. By the time the Marines stormed the Ba'ath party building in Al Faw town, a camera crew had been flown in by helicopter and the assault, including an incident in which a Marine was injured by an exploding gas canister, was broadcast live on UK television.) But close at hand, the only noise was the rustle of the evening breeze through the palm fronds and the occasional chirrup of birdsong. The low afternoon sun had dried my shirt nicely and I was just contemplating a cup of tea and a boil-in-the-bag supper when a shout went up from the head of the patrol, shots were fired, and I dived into a ditch, thereby soaking my trousers and filling my boots with water.

Over to the east, on the bank of the river, a white three-storey building was just visible through the palm groves. Invisible, at least to me, was the group of jundies who had just exited it and who were making their way south at some speed, parallel to our track. A crack of rifle fire sounded from their direction, followed by the staccato of semi-automatic fire from the front of our patrol. Shouting ensued and the Marines began to leapfrog forward, pairs of men taking it in turn to provide covering fire as their colleagues sprinted a few yards to the next piece of cover. The enemy rapidly disappeared into the greenery, frustrating the efforts of the Marines who were keen to get to grips with them. The Iraqis, it seemed, had spotted our patrol coming and, knowing what was good for them, were fleeing faster than we could advance. Some further shots were fired but the engagement was over in a few minutes.

The patrol regrouped and, despite my exhortations to return to the troop headquarters, the section commander would not be satisfied by anything less than a thorough search of the house and the surrounding area. The Marines fanned out and warily approached the building, lest there be some soldiers remaining inside. I was feverishly worried about the prospect of mines and booby traps and crept through the undergrowth nervously looking for any signs of skulduggery. No such worries seemed to dog my colleagues who pushed on impatiently, primarily motivated by the opportunity to knock seven bells out of any recalcitrant Iraqis they might find lurking in the house. Disappointingly for them we didn't find any, though there was a fair old treasure trove of souvenirs inside. Most of the fleeing Iraqis had shed their uniforms, items of which were scattered around inside. Webbing belts and clips of AK47 ammunition were also in evidence, as were tin helmets and old black leather boots. But the biggest prize was a highly polished 80mm mortar tube complete with base-plate and sights, and an assortment of bombs to match. It seemed a reasonable assumption that these had been the jundies who had mortared us earlier in the day, back near the helicopter landing site. For a few seconds I was livid that we had allowed them to escape; we should have shot the devils when we had the chance. But it was too late now for retribution – instead I consoled myself with the thought that their southbound escape route meant they would in all probability run into 40 Commando and get their come-uppance anyway.

It was early evening by the time the patrol wound its way back along the track to be reunited with the rest of the troop. UMST had also appeared and, with the exception of a few sentries lying forward and aft of the position, the men were chatting and enjoying the opportunity for a brief rest. I had a quick chat with the troop commander about the prospects for the night ahead. He was an eager young thing and I had every desire to rein in his ambitions for world domination and get settled in the palm groves, where the foliage might mask the light from our stoves and I could therefore enjoy a hot meal and a cup of tea. Happily, he agreed without too much argument and we moved en masse away from the vehicle tracks and into the undergrowth, where I spent a desultory few minutes digging a shell scrape with a couple of the Marines. I toyed with the idea of getting them to dig it for me, but decided to show willing on the premise that if anything kicked off during the night I would probably be grateful for their support – better safe than sorry in these situations, I always think. Happily the sandy soil was remarkably easy to dig and within minutes we had a workable foxhole over a foot deep. By the time I had dragged my webbing and rifle into the shell scrape, a stove was lit and rations were being heated. (For all the numerous occasions I have served with the Marines, I never cease to be amazed at how quickly they can rustle up a hot drink and a meal. It's a remarkable attribute – and it makes no difference whether one is in the arctic or the jungle, the service is always the same.) Unhappily, the benefits of the hot rations were undone somewhat by the attentions of the Al Faw's mosquitoes, which dined out in some style that evening, leaving me wondering whether there was any malaria in Iraq (not that I had any anti-malarial tablets with me in any case). Full and exhausted from the day's activities, having ducked sentry duty (which in any case is not the role of an officer, no matter how my egalitarian Royal Marines counterparts may feel about it), I unrolled my sleeping bag and crawled inside, looking forward to some much-needed sleep.

    I don't know how long I dozed for but it couldn't have been more than a couple of hours before I awoke to the sound of heavy machine-gun fire. Thankfully it wasn't coming in our direction, but it was close enough to be disconcerting. I crawled out of my sleeping bag and demanded to know of the troop commander what was happening.

    "Not sure yet," was his muted response. "I've sent some blokes forward to have a look. Can't work out where the firing is coming from, or who they are shooting at."

    A few moments later a brace of Marines appeared breathless from the undergrowth, having just scrambled the distance from the river.

    "Sir, I think you'd better come and see this for yourself," was their only utterance.

Out of curiosity I followed them back towards the riverbank, to witness a scene of unexpected barbarism. In the middle of the Shat-al-Arab waterway, struggling against the current, was a small wooden boat, 20 feet in length at the most, crammed with civilians. It was a few hundred metres downstream from us and difficult to see clearly but there must have been a score of people onboard, including women and children. Presumably frightened by the fighting in Al Faw town, these poor souls had decided to flee across the river to Iran. The Iranians, however, were having none of it. The machine-gun fire was coming from an Iranian watchtower several hundred yards back from the shore (it occurred to me afterwards that they may have assumed the boat was a military vessel; nervous soldiers who had witnessed 24 hours of fighting over the border could easily jump to such a conclusion). The first shots may have been delivered as a warning, in an attempt to get the boat to change its course. But since it had continued on towards Iran, the heavy calibre gun was now trained on the vessel; each burst of fire was smashing into the boat and into the civilians onboard. Screams and cries for help rang out across the water, barely audible above the echoes of the machine-gun fire. Engine cut, the boat circled erratically in the eddies of the river. It was riddled with holes and slowly began to sink, listing to one side as the uninjured occupants, many of whom seemed unable to swim, threw themselves into the water. Several of their number remained in the boat, either dead or too badly injured to attempt to swim ashore. The machine-gunners didn't let up though, and bullets continued to rip into the water, killing several of the swimmers before they had got more than a yard or two from the boat. I don't know if any of them made it back to Al Faw that night – the current took them downstream and out of sight before the firing ceased. I'm not easily shocked but I returned to my sleeping bag in silence, feeling faintly nauseous from the sight I'd seen. It wasn't the last we would hear from the Iranians.

Soon afterwards, a crackle came over my radio from

company headquarters, informing us that there would shortly be a series of air strikes in our vicinity. Several targets had been identified, primarily by the snipers operating to our north. Sure enough, a minute or two later, the air reverberated to the sound of beating rotor blades and a brace of Cobra gunships appeared over the horizon, flying fast and low as they passed over our position, bristling with rockets and cannons. I lost sight of them in the gloom as they continued north, but the huge explosions caused by their missiles destroying Iraqi tanks was music to my ears.

As if to demonstrate the wealth of firepower available to them, more American aircraft appeared a few minutes later, this time in the form of A10 "warthog" tank-busters, their huge engines making a uniquely low-pitched drone as they passed overhead. The booming from their cannons rang out over the palm groves as they made multiple passes over their targets, before turning and heading for home. As they came back over our position (it's always a nervous moment when a US aircraft appears overhead – one can never be entirely sure when they will open fire, or in what direction), the lead aircraft barrel-rolled into the night sky, popping anti-missile flares from its belly as it went. The burning phosphorous illuminated the whole area, casting a pale white light over the palm trees and creating an odd sensation of motion as the shadows moved in harmony with the falling flares. It was harmless showboating on the part of the pilot but made for a fairly spectacular fireworks display that lent an odd feeling of security to our situation, for which I was very grateful.

With the aircraft departed, the area fell into an eerie silence. Our position was in utter darkness, just the way I liked it, and the Marines were silently manning the sentry positions. I returned to my sleeping bag, hoping the night brought no more surprises, and fell into a deep sleep.

At some point in the small hours I awoke to the sound of more machine-gun fire, again emanating from the Iranian side of the river. Unlike the incident with the boat, this time the bullets were zipping overhead, smashing into the trees and bushes and thumping into the earthworks around the shell scrapes. Fortunately the firing was only intermittent and the gun was more often trained on targets to the north and west of us. For my part, I cowered in the bottom of my shell scrape, praying that the one-foot depth of the position would provide sufficient cover. (If you've ever been unfortunate enough to be shot at by a large-calibre weapon, you'll know just how frightening it can be. If you've not had the experience, believe me, you're better off without it.) Over the radio I could hear animated chatter between 2 Troop, to our north, and the company commander. The gist of the conversation was that 2 Troop, who were receiving the brunt of the attack, were understandably eager to give the Iranians a taste of their own medicine. The company commander, however, was taking the slightly more cautious view that Operation Telic was only supposed to involve the invasion of Iraq and he thought it somewhat beyond his authority to open up another front with Iran. 2 Troop held their fire and eventually the Iranians ceased shooting – at least for a short while. Occasional bursts rang out across the river throughout the few remaining hours of darkness, ensuring that nobody got much sleep.

By first light the Iranians had stopped firing altogether, although I remained jolly wary about venturing anyplace I could be seen from across the water. Eager to get away from the riverbank, I tagged onto a detail of men making their way back towards company headquarters to pick up a much-needed water re-supply. It was a chilly morning, the sun had yet to rise, and the landscape was shrouded in a thick, damp morning mist. I reasoned that a quick stroll would serve to get the blood flowing again and, since I was almost out of water, I wanted to ensure I was first in the queue when the new supplies arrived. Other than our patrol, no-one was on the move and the mist served to deaden any noise, leaving the area completely silent save for the crunch of our boots on the dried mud. As we approached the Al Faw-Basra road, I heard the noise of an engine approaching from the north. From the haze, travelling at speed, appeared a faintly ghoulish sight: the Company Sergeant Major, sporting helmet and goggles, travelling at speed astride his quad-bike, towing a trailer on top of which lay the rigid corpse of an Iraqi soldier who had died the previous day in a firefight with 2 Troop. To my mind, the only good Iraqi soldier was a dead one, and I should have had no compunction whatsoever in leaving them where they fell; it would save our efforts and might serve as a useful warning to others. The Sergeant Major thought otherwise though and, deciding it was unhealthy to leave bodies all over the battlefield, had undertaken the grizzly task of collecting and burying them. With a grin and a wave he zoomed off along the road in search of more work. The quad bike and trailer combination became a regular sight over the next couple of days, bouncing around the battlefield as the Sergeant Major went about his morbid business.[5]

We had barely ventured more than a hundred yards further when another droning motorcycle engine sounded, again from the north. Unlike the powerful quad-bike engine, this was the sound of an asthmatic two-stroke struggling to cope with a heavy load. Out of the mist, perched precariously atop a shiny red motorbike and grinning from ear to ear, appeared the lead sniper pair with whom I had flown into Iraq just a day earlier, long range rifle dangling by the side of the pillion passenger. On the course of their travels they had come across the bike, which had apparently been abandoned by fleeing civilians. There were no keys but after a bit of creativity with the wiring it had started at the first attempt. They juddered to a halt alongside the patrol.

"Morning fellas," grinned the rider. "Anyone know where Unit Headquarters is located?"

"Not a clue," I told him, "though I imagine it's somewhere back towards 40 Commando's location. Nice bike you've got there."

"It beats walking," he replied. "The boys have shot all the

jundies they can find up there, so we're hoping to get re-assigned somewhere new. We called in a hoofing air strike last night – did you see it?"

He didn't wait for a reply but gunned the engine and was off, spluttering away into the mist. It was clearly going to be a very surreal day.

It transpired that the water re-supply had already been dropped off at the next road junction, which saved our legs somewhat. There was far too much to carry, so the taxi-cab commandeered during the previous day's fighting was utilised to distribute it around the troops. I cadged a ride in it myself, thinking a visit to company headquarters might be timely, as I wanted to know a little more about the wider battle and anyway I owed them a brief on the state of the roads and the likelihood of any armoured movement along them. Riding in the taxi was certainly more comfortable than walking, although it smelled like a Spanish brothel and due to a wiring fault it was impossible to switch off the car radio, which played an unceasing medley of tuneless Arabic wailing. It was quite a relief to get out at the other end, especially as I was greeted by the company signaller wielding a freshly-made a cup of tea.

The company commander was, as expected, full of the joys of spring. All his objectives had been taken swiftly, his men had won a string of fire-fights, and the snipers, who currently fell under his command, had slaughtered everything in sight to our north, not to mention calling in a highly effective series of air-strikes. Not bad for a couple of days' work, so I suppose he had every right to feel pleased with himself.

"Harry!" he exclaimed. "Good to see you – I gather you have been having fun with 3 Troop. Doesn't look as if there's any danger of an Iraqi counter-attack just at the moment, so I guess we'll just stay put for a little while. The LCACs have been putting QDG ashore all morning so I guess you might be sent to join up with them, but I haven't heard anything over the radio."

For my part, now that I knew the area was safe, I was

entirely happy to remain with J Company, especially as QDG's mission was literally to go looking for trouble. The prospect of advancing northwards in a lightly-armoured recce vehicle, seeking out Iraqi main battle tanks and the like, was not a comforting one.

"Anyhow, now that the sun's up, I'm off to take a look at the boys," grinned the company commander, donning his helmet and goggles. He gunned the engine of his quad-bike and shot off up the road, leaving me to enjoy another cup of tea courtesy of his signaller.

The taxi returned a short while later and, not being one to look a gift-horse in the mouth, I cadged a lift back along the road towards the palm groves and my shell-scrape, hoping I might catch up on some of the sleep I had missed the previous night. In the event, my ride halted at the junction with the Al Faw-Basra road, where 3 Troop's morning was beginning to liven up. Extensive patrolling and house-to-house searches by 40 Commando had created a small exodus of Iraqi troops fleeing to the north. Overnight, 3 Troop had managed to acquire a set of loudspeakers and, from their checkpoint on the road, Arabic messages exhorting the Iraqis to surrender were blaring southwards towards Al Faw town. Much to my surprise, these appeals had already proved successful, and several Iraqi prisoners were sitting cross-legged under the watchful eyes of the Marines, on a flat patch of wasteland close to the shell-scrapes that 2 Section had dug the previous evening. More were making their way disconsolately towards us from the town, holding aloft a series of white flags and pennants. Since no transport was available to move these souls, they faced a long, hot day in the sun – or a long walk to the PoW handling centre. 3 Troop were in no hurry to move the Iraqis; their number was swelling by the hour, so it made sense to wait until they had all been rounded up. The various rifles and pistols they had surrendered were heaped in a pile just off the road, which I was idly looking over when I noticed the ominous little spikes of a Russian land-mine poking up through the earth. Frozen to the spot, I glanced around me and was horrified to notice several others, not all as well-concealed as the first – in fact, some were simply lying on the surface of the mud-flats. I pointed them out to one of the corporal present, who simply laughed at me.

"Yeah, we spotted them last night," he told me. "A bit worrying at first, but they're bloody ancient – probably from the Iran-Iraq war. We just tried not to step on 'em or hit 'em with a shovel. Anyhow, none of 'em have gone off, which is all that matters, eh?"

Ancient they may have been, but I didn't fancy chancing my luck, so I gingerly retraced my footsteps back onto the road and made a mental note to watch where I was putting my feet in future.

More Iraqi fighters gave themselves up as the day wore on, until eventually there was a tidy little group of them all awaiting processing. Now that the shooting had stopped, civilian traffic also began to appear on the road, ancient cars and vans coughing their way towards Basra with cargoes of anxious passengers keen to find news of their relatives. The boys routinely searched these vehicles at the checkpoint, but none were carrying soldiers or weapons, so they let them go about their business.[6] I used my smattering of Arabic to chat with some of the locals and find out their thoughts about the invasion. Happily, most of them seemed to give it the thumbs-up which, after almost three decades of persecution was, I supposed, unsurprising. I'm not given to sentimentality – sometimes an old-fashioned dictatorship seems to be the simplest way of dealing with these foreign types – but some of the stories I heard were enough to make my toes curl. One chap pulled up in a small van, with his wheelchair-bound friend loaded in the back. The pair of them were all smiles and the driver used his limited English to announce, "Good Bush! Good Blair!" at the top of his voice, presumably in the hope that we would thereby allow him through the checkpoint. I asked what was wrong with his passenger.

"What is wrong?!" he shouted, gesticulating wildly. "Saddam! Saddam is wrong! One year ago, this man could walk fine. He was a fit man, who worked as a mechanic in the town." More gesticulation, this time in the direction of Al Faw. "Then one day, this man makes the mistake of criticising the Ba'ath Party in front of a customer. The next day, Saddam's people come to the garage. They say this man has insulted Saddam and he must be punished. You know what they did? They cut his legs. Here," he pointed behind his knees, "and here," pointing behind his ankles. "All tendons cut. So he can never walk again. So, my friend, it is very good to see you!" At this, he thrust out his hand for me to shake. It was filthy and he looked singularly unhygienic, so I declined, but I did wave him through the checkpoint without further delay.

Shortly afterwards, with a roar of dust and diesel smoke, a remarkably new-looking six-tonne Iraqi army truck pulled up alongside the checkpoint, sporting a British vehicle marker panel on the bonnet. At the wheel, grinning like a Cheshire cat, sat the lieutenant in command of 3 Troop.

"Thought you might want a hand transporting the prisoners!" he bellowed at one of the corporals above the engine noise. "We just found this hidden up at one of the farmhouses. Get the jundies loaded in the back and let's get them to the prisoner handling centre."

"No offence, Sir, but are you sure you know how to drive that thing?" asked the corporal.

"Well I've made it this far without crashing, haven't I," retorted the officer. "It's just like driving a car, only bigger. Now stop dripping and get the Iraqis loaded in the rear."

Chortling with laughter at the unexpected trophy, the Marines swiftly rounded up their prisoners and loaded them onboard. A couple of the boys clambered up with them, rifles at the ready, but it only took one look at the dejected Iraqis to know that escaping was the last thing on their minds. Most of them looked as if they had barely eaten in a week – I guessed they didn't much mind where they ended up, as long as there was the prospect of some food and a cup of tea. The lorry roared off up the road towards the oil installations with its tailgate still hanging open, leaving the remaining Marines shaking their heads at the eccentricity of their troop commander.

The remainder of the day was taken up by routine patrolling of the area, which I managed to avoid, and some low-level investigating of any unsearched local buildings. By now I was pretty confident that any remaining Iraqi soldiers would either have given themselves up or fled the area, so I joined in with the building searches, hopeful of liberating a little of Iraq's wealth for myself. It was clear that the majority of dwellings had housed soldiers at some point – there was a remarkable number of abandoned uniforms and items of equipment, not to mention ammunition. Unhappily, in terms of booty, the only thing I discovered was a wad of local banknotes, all sporting Saddam's sombre face, nominally of quite high value but now utterly worthless. I pocketed them anyway – one never knows when these things will come in handy for bartering, especially when dealing with the yanks.

Night fell swiftly and I made my way back to my shell-scrape, determined to get some much-needed sleep. Throughout the night US aircraft clattered overhead occasionally, and flashes and bangs lit up the horizon to the northwest, but the action was miles away from us and was therefore easily ignored. Somewhere around 3 a.m. I was woken unnecessarily by one of the Marines, worried about a build-up of vehicle movement on the main road. As far as I was concerned this was nothing to do with us and certainly not an adequate reason for waking me, so I bawled him out in spectacular fashion and went back to sleep. No-one else bothered to disturb me that night and I arose the next morning feeling thoroughly refreshed.

My third day in Iraq was largely uneventful and I spent most of it loafing around avoiding work, which was remarkably easy to do, since I was studiously ignoring the radio and almost no-one in the chain of command knew my exact location. The Brigade Commander, happy that Al Faw was now secure, wasted no time in taking the fight to the Iraqis. J Company's snipers continued to report occasional tank and artillery movement to their north and QDG had come across several large-scale Iraqi formations in the course of their recces. Rather than allowing the enemy time to regroup, the Brigade was pushing forward as fast as it could. Helicopters buzzed endlessly overhead and the road was thick with vehicles as 40 Commando increased the momentum of their push northwest towards Basra. Much as the Marines of 42 had been cock-a-hoop when we departed Kuwait, the men of 40 Commando were buzzing with anticipation as they left Al Faw. Convoys of Pinzgauers and Land Rovers crawled past J Company's positions, all crammed with men, equipment and weaponry. Ahead of them lay around 30 miles of unknown territory, thick with Iraqi troops and armour. Behind them they left a somewhat dejected company group, which remained to take care of Al Faw town, and the whole of 42 Commando, most of whom were also hoping for a move north as quickly as possible. Frankly, the previous couple of days had given me enough bragging material for several months of drinking in the Cavalry Club and I was entirely happy to watch someone else marching off to war instead of me. I hunkered down in my sleeping bag that evening a happy man – with a bit of luck and a following wind, 40 Commando would be in Basra inside a week, and then we could all go home.

Shortly before midnight, for the second night in a row, I was shaken awake by one of the Marines. Not happy, I demanded to know what the devil he was doing. The answer could not have been better.

"We're moving, Sir. Everyone has to make their way to the LS."

"Moving?" I spluttered. "Moving where?"

"We're going back to Kuwait, Sir," he told me, and was gone.

Perhaps it was the lack of sleep, or perhaps just wild optimism, but I was unable to stop my imagination running wild with thoughts of hot showers, decent food, a good night's sleep, and a rapid return to Blighty. Frankly, I should have known better.

NOTES

1 A handful of men within 42 Commando had also seen service in the Falklands War 21 years earlier. Uniquely, Colours Sergeant (later Warrant Officer) John "Ginge" Davidson served with the Reconnaissance Troop of 45 Commando in the South Atlantic and as a sniper with the Reconnaissance Troop of 42 Commando in the Gulf.
2 The sacking of the US Marine Corps helicopter squadrons was eventually reported in the British press and CO 42 Commando was quoted as saying the US aircrews had "bottled out". The press coverage caused a political furore – but since the comments were factually accurate and had the support of many senior British officers, no action was taken.
3 "Jundi": soldier (Arabic).
4 The Battle of the Marshes, fought largely on the Al Faw Peninsular, was one of the major actions of the Iran-Iraq war and is estimated to have cost the lives of 10,000 men.
5 Bodies collected by 3 Commando Brigade were indeed buried on the Al Faw peninsular to avoid a health hazard. The graves were marked and, under the auspices of the Red Crescent, they were exhumed a day or two later and given a formal Muslim burial.
6 Many of the Iraqi soldiers in the predominantly Shia south-east of the country had been drafted in from Sunni regions further north and were distrusted by the local populace, who quickly disassociated themselves from the fighters once the war began.

6

Back to Kuwait. This was amazing, unexpected, and excellent news. I had no idea what had precipitated it but if I had met the man responsible for the decision I would have kissed him. All around in the darkness was the quiet sound of rustling kit as the Marines stowed away their belongings in their bergens. I could even see the silhouettes of one of two keen souls standing on the track, rucksacks packed, waiting to go. I was up and out of my sleeping bag in seconds, delighted to be heading away from Iraq and back to somewhere I could get a hot shower and a cooked meal. My spirits sagged somewhat as I wrestled my bergen onto my back and realised the landing site was a good couple of miles away – no great distance, but a veritable marathon when carrying a small house on one's back, and all the more so since my feet had still not fully recovered from the pounding they had taken on our arrival. Annoyingly, there was no sign of either the truck or the taxi that the Marines had so diligently liberated, so there was no alternative to walking. Still, a few blisters and an aching back seemed a relatively small price to pay for safe deliverance from a war zone, so I braced myself for the long walk to the helicopters. After a few minutes, the whole troop formed up on the road and the long trek began. Happily, fortune smiled down on me once again and transport then arrived, in the form of an ancient, dilapidated flatbed van, which had been commandeered by 2 Troop. It was already crammed with Marines, but they promised to return and pick us up, so I stopped walking at once, plonked myself on my bergen and wasted no time in demanding a cup of tea from the man nearest me.

True to their word, the van was indeed sent back for us and we piled into it with gusto. It was only just big enough to hold everybody so I shouldered my way past the Marines and climbed into the cab beside the driver. Let the enlisted men fight it out for a space in the back, I thought to myself, it's only fitting that the officers ride in the front. In any case I wanted to have my seat secured lest anyone start any of that old-fashioned nonsense about allowing the more junior ranks onboard first. I wasn't walking a step further than I had to, and that was all there was to it. Eventually, with some ingenious use of straps and karabiners, the bergens were fastened to the outside while the men squeezed together in the back. Before we set off the driver hopped out to give a brief on the finer mechanical details of his vehicle.

"There's no brakes and the horn doesn't work. So if anyone gets in the way, shout at the buggers to move, or I'll run 'em over," he explained to the merriment of his passengers, before hopping back into the cab and starting the engine.

In the event, the van was only allowed to travel as far as the road junction at which we had been mortared on our arrival in Iraq, less than half the distance to the helicopter landing site. The rest of the journey was undertaken on foot, not my preferred method of travel but one I undertook willingly in the knowledge that a flight to safety awaited at the end of it. The landing site was back on the crater-pitted mud flats, about half a mile south west of where we had arrived just a few days earlier. Despite the bitter cold that night, the salt-crusted clay was not quite firm enough to support my weight and gave way with each step, allowing the cloying mud to gather around my boots as I walked. By the time I reached the designated rendezvous point my shoulder muscles were on fire and I was in a muck sweat. Unhappily there was a considerable wait for the helicopters to arrive, during which time the wind cut straight through my damp clothes, leaving me shivering like a schoolboy on a December rugby pitch. Fortunately my sniper colleagues were on hand, trading unlikely stories of shooting Iraqi soldiers at inconceivable distances and passing round steaming mugs of tea, which I unashamedly cadged from them whilst attempting to hide my hypothermic shivering. In the lee of an earth wall, a long line of stoves flickered, heating countless ration packs and mugs of tea and hot chocolate as J Company waited for its pick-up. As dawn broke, the Marines bantered among themselves, trading tales of firefights and narrow escapes, of wounded Iraqis and multiple surrenders, and of where we might be heading next. I had given no thought to this topic, happy enough in the knowledge that I was returning to the relative calm of Kuwait. Buoyed by their successes on the Al Faw peninsular, the boys were as eager as ever to take the fight to the Iraqis and were fervently hoping Kuwait was nothing more than a brief stopover prior to the next phase of the war. I kept my own aspirations firmly to myself.

    Then, from the south, silhouetted against the early morning sky, several Chinook helicopters appeared, filling the air with the din of beating rotor blades. In seconds, stoves were extinguished, kit packed away, and the Marines trotted out onto the mudflats. The pilots brought their steeds in fast, banking hard to sit them down as close to us as possible. I felt the blast of downwash and looked up to see the visor-wearing spectre of a helicopter door gunner peering down at me over the top of a huge rotary cannon. The machine swung rapidly round and set itself down in the mud, tail-ramp already open. I wasted no time in scrambling to my feet and clambering aboard, savouring the warm blast of exhaust on my face and the smell of aviation fuel in my nostrils, which I always find unexpectedly reassuring. Within seconds everyone was onboard and the helicopter was airborne again. The flight was remarkably short and before I knew it, we were back on terra firma inside Kuwait.

    Any hopes I had of a comfortable airbase with an officers' mess and some decent tucker were swiftly dashed. I exited the Chinook, blinking in the bright morning sunlight, to be confronted by one of the bleakest patches of desert I have ever seen – it was even more featureless than Camp Gibraltar. Brilliant yellow sand stretched to the horizon in all directions, interrupted only by dozens of vehicles and tents, and countless men digging shell scrapes in the soft sand. This, it transpired, was TAA Viking, the place from which 40 Commando had launched their assault a few days earlier.[1] Now, however, it was home to 42 Commando in its entirety, since the trucks and other heavy equipment had been brought up by road from Camp Gib. Self-evidently, Viking was nothing more than a staging post before our next foray into Iraq. I scuffed my feet through the sand, feeling a certain sense of inevitability about my plight. I had always known that thoughts of an early return home were absurdly optimistic (it's a facet of my yellow-livered character always to hope for an easy route out of a tight spot) but nonetheless the reality of a prolonged stay in the Gulf weighed heavily on my mind. I focused instead on digging my shell-scrape as rapidly as possible, with the express intent of climbing into it and sleeping away the day under the warm desert sun. Within minutes I had a workable hole in the ground, so I patted down the sides, dragged my bergen and webbing inside, unrolled my sleeping mat, lay down and pulled my sunhat over my face. I remember indulging in a somewhat confused fantasy in which the lovely Charlotte performed a series of unspeakable sexual acts whilst simultaneously plying me with gin and tonic, before sleep overtook me and I dropped into a blissful slumber.

A short time later I was awoken unceremoniously by a boot kicking me gently in the ribs. Peering out from under my sunhat, I was confronted by OC J Company.

"Time for us to say goodbye, Harry," he intoned. "Your services are requested by M Company."

"The miserable sods – I've only just got my head down," I replied, somewhat testily. "Tell them to wait. I shall join them later."

"No danger of that," laughed my tormentor. "They're saddling up for a move right now, and you need to be with them. I suggest you get a move on or you may have a long walk in front of you."

"A move where?" I enquired, clinging vainly to the hope of a return to civilisation.

"Umm Qasr," came the crushing reply.

The little port town of Umm Qasr had been targeted by coalition planners in the early phases of the deployment back in Kuwait. It was of strategic importance not just to the military but also to the allied PR campaign, since a deep-water harbour was necessary in order to bring in ships laden with humanitarian aid. Looking at the situation cynically (which I usually do), the invading Americans and Brits needed to be seen to be helping the local civilians as much as possible, if only to assuage the growing groundswell of anti-war public opinion back home. The required volumes of food, clean water and medical supplies were huge and getting shipping lanes open into Iraq was therefore a big priority. The mission to take the town had been assigned to a battalion of US Marines, but evidently something had gone awry, since they were about to be displaced by the Royal Marines. I had an immediate feeling of dread. (Months later I learned that the move into Umm Qasr was indeed politically driven: the failure of the U.S. Marines to take the town had caused considerable embarrassment at senior level, primarily because it meant the supply ship HMS Sir Galahad could not embark at the port and its cargo of humanitarian aid was therefore sitting uselessly at sea, rather than undergoing a stage-managed delivery in front of the world's press. I am reliably informed that the decision to bin the U.S. 15 Marine Expeditionary Unit in favour of the Royal Marines was taken jointly by Blair and Bush, eager as always to achieve a positive sound bite irrespective of the consequences.)

Far from being concerned at the scale of the task in front of them, the men of M Company were grinning like Cheshire cats. They had watched in quiet frustration as J Company led the charge onto the Al Faw and now it was their turn to be in pole position.² Unhappily for me, the CO had switched most of the commando's assets to the company group, including the snipers, UMST, and yours truly. God alone knows why he thought my knowledge of armoured manoeuvre might be useful in an urban assault, but there was no arguing with the decision, so I piled my kit onto the roof of a BV and climbed into the back.³ The vehicle bounced its way across the desert sand and joined the back of a lengthy convoy making its way onto a road which led northwest into Iraq. The Marines onboard opened the side windows of the BV and I watched the world go by – miles and miles of empty desert, sand and rocks bleached yellow-white by the incessant glare of the sun, with just the occasional stunted thorn bush to break up the monotony of the landscape.

The first sign that we were nearing the Iraqi border came in the form of recently-dropped litter. Scattered across the desert were thousands of small leaflets exhorting Iraqis soldiers to surrender and promising them fair treatment at the hands of the coalition. They had been dropped in their millions from allied aircraft in the days before the war and many had evidently succumbed to the desert winds and found their way back into Kuwait. Moments later the convoy ground to a halt as the lead vehicles encountered the border post, which was manned by US troops. There followed a brief exchange before we were ushered over the border and, less than eight hours after leaving the place, I found myself back in Iraq.

Immediately beyond the border lay the old United Nations peacekeepers' camp, built after the first Gulf War to facilitate patrolling of the demilitarised zone between Iraq and Kuwait. The convoy swung in through the gates of the camp to be greeted by a handful of redneck halfwits from the US Marines, sporting bandannas and ragged green t-shirts with the sleeves torn off. They looked for all the world like badly dressed extras from a cheap Hollywood Vietnam movie.

"Hey man, welcome to i-raq!" hollered a nearby imbecile, brandishing a machine-gun and a belt of ammunition.

"Go and fuck yourself," replied the Marine sitting next to

me, with venom. I couldn't have put it better myself. The Americans, looking visibly crestfallen, sloped off into some nearby buildings as their British counterparts de-bussed.

The UN camp, formerly a relatively pleasant spot in an unpleasant part of the world, had suffered at the hands of the Americans. Many of the buildings had been wholly or partly destroyed by shelling, their roofs and walls reduced to a tangle of bent girders and torn sheets of corrugated steel. The water and power supplies were destroyed, shell craters pitted the open areas, and much of the camp was covered in debris and broken glass. Worse, in the three days of their occupation, the US Marines had failed to dig any latrines and almost every building had been used as toilet. Flies buzzed constantly and the stench of faeces was everywhere. But there was no time for me to work out how best to avoid taking part in the inevitable clean-up, since I was faced by a much more pressing problem. With no ceremony, no recce, and no time for any sort of meaningful briefing from the yanks (not that they would have been capable of providing one – I gathered afterwards that three days in Umm Qasr had turned the battalion commander into a gibbering buffoon; the hapless creature was on the verge of a nervous breakdown), the company commander set about giving his orders for an advance on the town.

As a gaggle of officers and NCOs formed around the rear of his vehicle, OC M Company waved them into silence and held out his map in front of him.

"Right fellas, time is pressing on, the CO wants this town taken by nightfall, so let's not have any mincing around," was his opening gambit. I felt my bowels loosen as he continued. "We're going in on foot, supported by our BV-mounted HMGs and Milans." Using a biro, he outlined the proposed route on his map. "We'll move north from here, then west through the town via this main street. The boys will need to fan out into the side streets, and the snipers will be mobile on quad bikes, moving to our flanks to provide additional cover wherever they can." At this point I found myself hyperventilating with anxiety. I had been mixed up in some pretty poorly planned ventures in my time, including some fearfully ill thought-out jobs in Sierra Leone and Afghanistan, but nothing on this scale. Without the benefit of even a helicopter recce, M Company was about to conduct an assault on an enemy-held town which had bogged down an entire battalion of United States Marines for three days. It didn't seem to faze the company commander one bit though.

"The US Marines have been hit by sniper fire from numerous buildings," he continued, worsening my panic attack with every word. "This is Northern Ireland routine, plain and simple. Hard-targeting through the streets, fire positions on every corner, mutual support." My vision began to blur as the fog of panic closed around me. Then he softened up somewhat, adding, "Don't forget the locals though. They've probably had a shocking time with the yanks. Make sure the lads take stacks of biscuits and nutty with them and dole it out to the kids. Right, any questions?"[4]

There was a brief pause before someone asked, "What happens if they open up on us?"

OC M Company looked at him disdainfully as if he'd been personally affronted. "Then we sort it out the old fashioned way," was his curt reply. "Kick the door down, get stuck in, slot anyone with a weapon, and move on. They'll soon get the message. We move out in fifteen minutes."

With that, the NCOs and officers scuttled back to their waiting charges, eager to pass on the brief that would see us trekking into Umm Qasr unprotected and on foot. I said a quiet prayer and devoted the time to dousing my rifle liberally with oil, on the premise that I might soon need it to work.

By mid-afternoon, the whole of M Company and attached ranks, including one Capt. H Flashman of the Queen's Royal Hussars, was patrolling warily north from the UN camp. A mile or so away to the east lay the docks, out of sight from our low-lying position. Securing them was the underlying priority, but there was little point even approaching the port while a town of several thousand inhabitants lay hostile on the doorstep. Wasteland stretched either side of the road for a short distance, until we came to the first shanty-style houses to our west, squalid little mud-brick residences with tin roofs and broken windows and doors. At first glance the place looked unoccupied but on closer inspection I could make out the occasional face peering anxiously at us from behind steel doors or through filth-encrusted windows. No-one ventured out to greet us and even the dogs were silent, so the company passed on without stopping.

At the top of the road, some half a mile from the camp, was a relatively smart-looking hotel, standing proud in walled grounds adorned with little marble statues and well-tended palm trees. The lawns looked a little shabby and the façade could have used a coat of paint, but the overall impression was that, in its heyday, it must have been the destination of choice for visiting ships' captains and the like. It would soon become home to elements of 3 Commando Brigade Headquarters, but for now the place was abandoned to the elements so we passed without stopping. The road into Umm Qasr turned west and a smattering of houses began to appear on either side, generally single-story dwellings half-hidden behind robust-looking walls and wrought-iron gates. A mile or two later the buildings became smaller and more condensed as we entered Umm Qasr proper. The road surface became pitted and potholed, while most of the side roads were barely metalled at all. Rubbish was everywhere, discarded plastic bags clinging to every bit of foliage and broken glass crunching underfoot. Fetid puddles of oily water lay by the roadside and my nostrils were assaulted by the occasional stench of raw sewage. (I'm sure the tree-huggers will say the state of town was caused by the biting economic sanctions, but personally I point the finger of blame squarely at the locals – the idle buggers don't even bother burning their rubbish, they just chuck it out of the front door.) The local populace was more in evidence here, perhaps emboldened by their increased numbers. Women and children peered through gaps in wooden fences and round the side of steel gates and doors, while some of the local men were confident enough simply to stand in groups at the side of the road and watch as we passed. A sort of Mexican stand-off ensued, with neither side seemingly willing to break the silence. Then a couple of the Marines peeled off to a flank, offering boiled sweets to a handful of children hiding in a school-yard behind a low brick wall. Bewildered and not a little frightened, they hesitated before taking up the offering, then shot grateful smiles in our direction before running off, shouting to their friends. Within minutes, children were appearing in the street in their dozens, in some cases forcibly shoved towards us by their parents. Soldiers dug in their pockets and pouches, and Umm Qasr was awash with sweets and biscuits in minutes.

I began to relax, which is never a clever thing to do in hostile territory, and I paid the price almost immediately. A short, burly man came barging out of his house, kicking aside the kids who were clustered around me begging for sweets, and began haranguing me at the top of his voice. Bald as a coot, sporting a huge moustache and wearing the traditional Arab garb in a garish lilac colour, he was livid in the extreme. Fortunately my Arabic was up to the job, for I found it pretty straightforward to understand what he was saying.

"You, you are an officer, yes?" he demanded of me, pointing at my rank slides. "Why you bomb this town?! Why?! Many people now dead! My cousin, my uncle, their family, all dead! You Americans, why you keep bombing my town? Eh!?"

I drew myself up to my full height, looked down my nose at him, and replied with utmost sincerity, "My friend, I am *not* an American." He looked quizzical at this and was about to say something, but I waved him silent. "I am British. We are all British. The Americans have gone." This was not strictly true, since they were still loading up their vehicles back at the UN camp, but it made little difference since they would certainly not be re-visiting Umm Qasr.

"But why you bomb this town?" repeated my assailant at the top of his voice.

"Neh!" I replied. "We have not bombed anywhere *sadiq*,[5] we have only just arrived."

He looked at me unbelievingly and said slowly, "You, your friends, these soldiers, they are not Americans?"

I expectorated loudly and spat angrily on the ground – Arabs love a bit of theatre. "We are not American!" I stated with passion. "We are British. We are happy to be here. And if you behave well towards us, there will be no trouble."

"Where are the Americans?" he asked, still not quite believing me.

"Gone," was my monosyllabic reply. "And they will not be back."

This was evidently too much for him, for he reverted to type and began to assail me once again about his lost cousin and uncle. I clapped my hand on his shoulder to shut him up.

"*Sadiq*, I am truly sorry for your uncle and your cousin. But that is over now. No more bombing – as long as there is no trouble in the town."

At this he even smiled for a second, paused, then suddenly thrust out his hand in friendship, which I shook despite myself. He introduced himself as Sameer, then turned towards a group of local men that had formed a little distance behind him. "Then you are welcome," he announced at the top of his voice, grinning. "Very welcome. But no more bombing, eh?" He winked and gestured to his colleagues to come and meet me, which they did, albeit cautiously. A remarkably orderly queue formed, each one of them waiting in turn to shake me by the hand and mutter words of welcome in Arabic. Despite the exponential increase in the chance of contracting mange, I did my duty and thanked each one of them for the friendly welcome. In my experience, it often pays to keep the locals onside and I was taking no chances.

In the course of conversation, my burly accuser described himself as a businessman, though he declined to say what line of business he was in. Judging by the reaction of his colleagues to his presence, he was held in high regard locally and could therefore be a useful ally should things turn ugly. He invited me into his house for a cup of tea, which, not wanting to be separated from the Marines, I declined, whereupon he handed me a cigarette. I'm more of a cigar man as a rule, but in the circumstances I thought it might be inappropriate to ask for a Monte Cristo, so I accepted. As expected, the tobacco was utterly rancid – it was all I could do to stop myself coughing like a first-time schoolboy smoker. Hiding my discomfort I puffed away like a trooper, happy to be exchanging pleasantries rather than high-velocity rounds, which had seemed a distinct possibility when we exited the camp.

Time marched on. Unhappily for me, so did M Company. Before I knew it I was entirely alone, oblivious to the fact that the Marines had disappeared into the town centre without me. In fact it was one of the local men who pointed this out to me, with a wry grin on his face. I forced a grin back at him, shrugged my shoulders as nonchalantly as was possible in the circumstances and quietly finished smoking my cigarette. Eventually, with a growing sense of unease, I said my goodbyes and extracted myself from the group, then hurried down the main street hoping that nothing sinister occurred before I caught up with the Marines. Happily it didn't – unless you count being mobbed by dozens of children demanding sweets.

By the time I rejoined M Company they were about halfway down Umm Qasr's main street. There were less civilians here, since most of the housing was set back from the main road, but plenty of people still came out to observe our arrival in the town. The road opened out into a broad boulevard, bounded on either side by wide stretches of unkempt scrub, dotted with birch trees. The Marines weaved between the trees, emerging frequently to dart onto the road and hand over yet more sweets to any awaiting children.

Just to the south of the main street lay the local Ba'ath Party headquarters building, which it was felt was as likely as anywhere to house jundies. A large, imposing place, its grim façade was set back among the trees, ringed by a wire-topped brick wall. I kept my distance from the place and hid in a small culvert behind some birch trees as a section of men was sent forward to search it. There followed a brief interlude as they broke into the building – which wasn't easy, since the windows were barred and the steel doors had been bolted and padlocked. Unhappily for the Ba'athists, Royal Marines seem to have a penchant for breaking and entering, and the padlocks were smashed off in seconds. A few shots rang out as the interior of the offices were systematically cleared, but no Iraqis were found within and the boys returned from the depths of the building, squinting their eyes against the afternoon sunshine, empty handed.

We reached the end of the main street shortly before the sun hit the horizon, whereupon the company turned about and began heading for home. I was as amazed as anyone by this unlikely turn of events – we had marched into the heart of the town to a friendly greeting by the locals, without a single shot being fired in anger. I discovered later that our US colleagues had never ventured out of their armoured vehicles, hence the bewilderment of the Iraqis to see us patrolling on foot. The bombing which they were so upset about had been a disproportionate response by the Americans to small-arms fire and, with no-one on the ground to direct the incoming air-strikes, it had inevitably been horribly inaccurate. Those same Iraqis who engaged the Americans with their AK47s had taken a long, hard look at the newly-arrived Brits and sensibly decided that caution was the better part of valour. Silent or not, the fact remained that the town was still crawling with jundies, so I kept my wits about me on the return journey to the UN camp. Like the outbound journey it passed off peacefully and we were back inside the wire shortly after dusk. Umm Qasr had fallen to M Company with barely a murmur, and no-one was more relieved than me. To the great amusement of everyone present, the company commander memorably remarked during the ensuing evening brief that he had suffered harder nights out in Plymouth.

By the time we returned to the camp, the rest of 42 Commando had taken up residence and the place was a hive of activity. The last of the yanks had disappeared, tails between their legs, in the direction of Kuwait, leaving acres of derelict, unhygienic accommodation for us to choose from. Commando Headquarters was housed in one of the camp's larger buildings which had suffered only minor damage during the bombardment. J Company and L Company had found accommodation blocks near the centre of the camp, while M Company and J Company squeezed into a series of portakabin-style buildings alongside.

No accommodation had been set aside for the attached ranks and it was a case of every man for himself to secure the best of the remaining facilities. As you have probably gathered, every man for himself is a game I excel at, and it was only a short time before I discovered a plum accommodation block, largely unscathed by shelling, featuring not just a bed but a large, American-style refrigerator. The place was occupied by some enlisted ranks from the motor transport section, who I took great pleasure in evicting before going in search of some clement company, in the form of the combat camera team, with whom to share my new-found luxury abode. I eventually found them having a row with various members of Recce Troop over a dust-filled hovel with no windows, so it gave me great pleasure to invite them into my new home and thereby ensure I had the benefit of their company – not to mention the inside line on a lot of good gossip from Brigade Headquarters – for the foreseeable. Would you credit it, by the time we got back to my new home, several more Marines were in the process of moving in. The impertinent devils had even pushed my bergen to one side in their rush to ensconce themselves in the bedroom. I spent a gratifying thirty seconds venting my spleen and threatening to charge every man among them, before they dragged their belongings back through the door and scuttled off from whence they came. It was that kind of night – little more than anarchy, where the victor took the spoils and the devil took the hindmost. And if you did discover something of value, it paid to keep a tight grip on it, lest another roving party attempted to liberate it for themselves.

Their old home may have been a dust-filled dump, but in it the combat camera boys had discovered a stash of food – proper tucker from a grocery, mark you, infinitely better stuff than tinned rations – which they had diligently taken with them as they exited the building. As a result we treated ourselves to a slap-up dinner of spaghetti bolognaise (although the sauce had a slightly odd taste, being made from a couple of tins of ham, since there wasn't any beef). Under any other circumstances I would have thought it relatively meagre fare, but compared with boil-in-the-bag rations it felt like an evening at Simpsons in the Strand.

As we finished eating, the door crashed open and in strode the Battle Group Engineering Officer, whom I had first bumped into at Junior Staff College a couple of years earlier. He was a larger than life figure who, coming from good stock and being fairly able to handle a horse, was utterly wasted on the Royal Engineers; he self-evidently should have been a cavalry officer. Barrel-chested and with an ebullient personality to match, he was seldom without an idea for starting mischief, or at least an anecdote of previous illicit derring-do. On this occasion he was sporting an ear-to-ear grin and clutching an armful of parcels and letters from the UK.

"Evening chaps," boomed the BGE. "Didn't know where to find you, so I headed straight for the smartest looking building." He cast his eyes around the room, which was dimly lit by a couple of candles and a collection of head-torches. "I wasn't far wrong either, from the looks of it. This is a bloody palace compared with our grot."

"It's performance-related," I told him, with a straight face. "I'd offer you a seat but we don't have any. You can sit on a bergen if you wish."

He drew up a rucksack, dished out several letters, and then produced a half-pint bottle of whisky from his coat pocket. He was pretty liberal with the stuff, but then he could afford to be, since his father was sending him a parcel on a twice-weekly basis (the whisky being decanted into plastic ginger beer bottles in order to get past the screening processes of the British Forces Postal Service). It was just as well, since between us we disposed of the entire contents in a matter of minutes.

The conversation flowed as merrily as the whisky, with my Engineer chum and me exchanging anecdotes from Staff College (which under any other circumstances would have been crushingly dull; I can only think that the anarchy of war had made us nostalgic for the predictable tedium of Shrivenham) and the combat camera crew bemoaning the fact that our easy entry into Umm Qasr meant there hadn't been any firefights for them to film. Still without the benefit of a decent night's sleep since the invasion began, I quickly felt the pangs of fatigue creeping up behind my eyes and began contemplating a retreat to my newly-acquired bed, when suddenly we heard the crash of a huge explosion, the building shook, windows rattled, and the roof tiles lifted momentarily and dropped back into place with a bang.

"Shave a dog's head!" exclaimed the BGE, plagiarising a expression recently coined by the ever-inventive Ops Officer. "What in the blue blazes was that?"

"Buggered if I know Sir," answered the matelot cameraman, "But I'd suggest that, as Engineering Officer, you might want to report to the Ops Room and find out."

"Point taken," came the answer, and he exited the room at speed.

I prayed to the gods of cowardice and longevity that it wasn't the start of a bombardment. My prayers were evidently answered; in the minutes that followed the silence of the night was broken only by dogs barking in the distance and the sounds of the occasional vehicle entering or exiting the camp. Working on the assumption that being fast asleep and (apparently) ignorant of any threat to the camp might reduce my chances of getting dragged into any shenanigans, I wasted no time in sliding into my sleeping bag and stretching out on the mattress. I was asleep in seconds.

I was awakened the next morning by the BGE, still as exuberant about life as he had been the night before. The explosion, he informed me, was a Silkworm missile landing a short distance from the camp.[6] It had exploded harmlessly in the desert, which was bloody lucky considering there was a large military establishment, not to mention a decent-sized town, within a few hundred metres. News imparted, he shot off in search of his engineering brethren to brief them on the day's work.

I mooched over to the Ops Room for the morning brief, hoping to avoid any form of duties. The camp, even in its bombed-out state, was a far more pleasant environment than the town, and the thought of a quiet day soaking up the sun and devouring some more half-decent food, was a compelling one. Inevitably, such plans were scotched the moment the Commanding Officer opened his mouth.

"Congrats to OC M Company on yesterday's efforts," he began. "We've got this place in our grasp now, we need to make sure we keep it so. Our main efforts are therefore humanitarian aid, coupled with ensuring the security of the town. The place is presumably still crawling with Iraqi troops and Ba'ath party members, so let's set about rounding them up."

The remainder of his orders were taken up with the specifics of how these tasks were to be achieved. Now that the town was deemed safe, the ITN camera crew had been brought up from Kuwait and were eager to get some shots of Marines patrolling the streets. Food and water would be distributed to the populace by Marines operating from trucks driven up from Kuwait. Meanwhile, J Company was tasked with mounting lengthy patrols through the town and searching any unoccupied buildings that might be housing recalcitrant jundies. I slouched discreetly at the back of the orders group hoping, as usual, to avoid work and, as was fast becoming the norm on this deployment, failed.

"Flash," said the CO almost as an afterthought, glancing in my direction, "there's no point in you sitting around camp scratching your arse. The guys on the ground can always use a little extra experience, and I know you've served in Northern Ireland, so you can join in with J Company's patrol routine. Enjoy."

If he had had an axe to grind with me, he couldn't have done it any better. But what made the CO's final remark so galling was that he actually meant it. As far as he was concerned, probably the toughest thing about being in command was the lack of time spent on the ground, sticking it to Johnny Foreigner. He actually envied blokes setting out on patrol, and doubtless would have traded places with me in a heartbeat, the bloody lunatic. I did my best to look stoical and determined and hoped my silence lent me a false air of confidence which would disguise the mild hysteria which was enveloping me.

The first patrol left the camp on foot a couple of hours later, with yours truly tagged on at the back. I was getting heartily sick of being sent on every mission the Commando undertook, especially since my blistered feet were in need of some quiet recovery time, but it didn't do to complain, not in 42 Commando anyway, so I suffered in silence. Umm Qasr didn't look any better second time around, it was still a squalid little town with filth everywhere I looked. I mooched along at the back, mind in neutral, wondering how long it would be before I was reunited with my bed and how many, if any, jundies we would encounter before then. The patrol took the same route I had travelled before, turning left in front of the hotel grounds and winding its way down the long main street. Asides from the empty Ba'ath Party building, there were also a couple of schools and several industrial units which lay idle, many of which would be ideal refuges for frightened Iraqi soldiers. Several of them would be searched during the course of the day and at least one of the section commanders in the patrol had already expressed a hope that some of the jundies came out fighting.

Halfway down the main street I was greeted by the grinning

face of Sameer, my assailant of the day before, now apparently my best friend. He came barrelling over, gesticulating wildly and salaaming in quick-fire Arabic, which rather alarmed the Marines adjacent to me. I waved them away, explaining that Sameer was a local contact whom I needed to speak with for intelligence reasons. They did as they were bid and my new-found buddy, as expected, invited me into his house for a cup of tea. His gang of consorts was nowhere to be seen and anyway my feet were in agony, so I gladly accepted and slid through the door as the patrol disappeared up the street.

My broken Arabic was barely enough to understand him at first, but I have a way with languages and within a few minutes we were conversing reasonably easily. Sameer's house was fairly basic in layout but it was at least clean, and his sofa was an extremely comfortable, well-worn leather number, presumably imported in the days before economic sanctions. I slumped into it and he squatted on the floor, cross legged. He bellowed a series of commands over his shoulder and then turned to face me so the conversation could begin in earnest. How many of us were there? How long would it be before Saddam was toppled? How long would we stay for? Did we know there were lots of fighters (foreign fighters, he called them, in reference to the fact that they were Sunni rather than Shia Muslims) still hiding in the town? What about the Ba'ath Party people, what did we propose to do with them? ("You think you are in control of the town, but you are not, the Ba'ath Party people are still in control here, you know?") I answered his questions as best I could, which by and large meant a series of thinly-disguised "I don't know" replies. Still, he seemed satisfied enough and I guessed that his standing in the community would be even higher now that he could boast of having entertained a British officer in his house.

Our chit-chat was interrupted by a swish of the curtains separating the lounge from the kitchen. The recipient of Sameer's commands was his wife, a plump little woman who greeted me with a wry smile despite having her head bowed in the traditional manner. She carried an enormous tray of tea and cakes, which was all rather English in nature – and I did them proud by tucking in as if I hadn't eaten for a week. The food tasted all the better knowing that the patrol I was purportedly in was currently kicking down doors, risking life and limb in pursuit of enemy soldiers.

Sameer's wife retreated to the safety of the kitchen and our conversation continued with the revelation that Sameer was a taxi driver. To be more precise, he was the owner of a taxi firm, which employed most of the individuals I had met the previous day. Every cloud has its silver lining – in Sameer's case the imposition of economic sanctions had resulted in the closure of Umm Qasr's school, gifting him a monopoly on taxi rides to and from the school in Basra for those parents who could afford it. As one of the bigger employers in the town, he was looked up to by most people and tolerated by the Ba'ath party henchmen, who he disliked with a passion – although he was wise enough not to broadcast his opinions too widely among his countrymen for fear of retribution. To me though he was most forthcoming and wasted no time informing me of the whereabouts of several leading Ba'ath party members, including his next door neighbour.

I lost track of time during the conversation, though it certainly went on for long enough for me to amply fill my belly. Eventually Sameer's wife called through from the kitchen to tell us that the patrol was once again passing the house, this time on its way back to the UN camp. I said my farewells, thanked them both profusely for providing such excellent tucker, and tagged quietly onto the end of the patrol as it made its way down the street. The Marines were in high spirits, having rounded up several Iraqi soldiers, two of whom had been hiding, ironically, in the abandoned school buildings. The boys were also sporting all manner of Iraqi ordnance – mainly Russian hand grenades and rocket-propelled grenades, scores of which had been handed over by the local kids. Apparently the little buggers had dug up several ammunition caches, the contents of which they had surrendered in exchange for biscuits and sweets.

Back at camp, the evening brief brought a change of tack. No longer would 42 Commando be content to allow Ba'ath party members to co-exist in the town. The CO now wanted complete control, and to that end a series of night raids on known addresses was announced. M Company would lead the way and the first series of raids would take place in the small hours of the following day. Like an idiot I volunteered my list of Ba'ath party members, most of which tallied neatly with the targeting matrix prepared by the intelligence cell; Sameer's list included a couple of new names but the rest they already knew about. I found this somewhat disappointing but the intelligence chaps were really quite excited about it, since it corroborated their own information and demonstrated the reliability of their source. The contribution was enough to earn a chuck-up from the CO.

"I don't know how you manage it – two days in the town and already you're a mine of useful information, practically a one-man intelligence cell, eh?" he laughed out loud. "Bloody good effort, Harry, bloody good effort. Of course, it would be wholly unfair not to allow you to be there at the finish, so make sure you team up with M Company for tonight's job, eh? Good man." I could have kicked myself for being so utterly stupid; I should have guessed that the information might lead to me being sent on another foolhardy mission into the town, and yet I had failed to keep my mouth shut. The result was an invitation to spend the night rampaging through the streets with a load of bloodthirsty louts, rather than tucked up in bed where I belonged. I choked back my disappointment and endeavoured to apply a façade of enthusiasm for the job in hand, leaving the CO grinning like a Cheshire cat and muttering about the extraordinary nature of his attached ranks.

It turned out that the intelligence cell's source was a local imam, a rotund little man who was instantly nicknamed the "spherical clerical". Tubby he may have been, but he was also bold (or daft) enough to accompany M Company that night in order to finger the Ba'ath party hoods during the arrest operation and thereby ensure that no-one untoward was bundled off to the prisoner handing centre. The intelligence cell boys were so concerned about him being identified and assassinated that they dressed him in British military kit complete with helmet, shamagh and goggles. We bounced out of the camp in a series of four-ton trucks and Land Rovers at around 2.30 a.m., the boys once again alive with nervous energy and me once again with a dry mouth and intestines churning.

Most of the addresses due a visit were clustered in a relatively affluent area of downtown Umm Qasr ("relative" being the salient term here, since the whole town was an armpit as far as I could make out). The streets were quietly cordoned off by the Marines – an easy job to do at three in the morning, since the place was utterly deserted. Then, with a silent nod of his head, the spherical clerical confirmed the first address to be visited, and the silence was abruptly shattered as a team of Marines sledge-hammered the door open and burst inside. A commotion stared inside as the family leapt out of their various beds to find out what was going on. Women and children began wailing, and several male voices could be heard shouting in panicky Arabic. Minutes passed and the place became quieter, before the door burst open again and a pair of scruffy looking men, probably in their late thirties, were thrust out into the cold night air, looking bewildered and more than a little frightened, and simultaneously comical adorned in only their stripy nightshirts. The imam looked at them briefly through his grubby goggles, nodded, whispered something to one of the int. cell guys, whereupon the pair of them were plasticuffed and bundled into the back of a waiting truck.

Without hesitation the entry team and surrounding entourage quickly moved down the street to the next house on the visit list. One or two curious neighbours, awoken by the commotion in the first address, poked their noses out from their front doors to see what the fuss was about. The Marines were in no mood to tolerate spectators though and the doors were swiftly slammed shut, much to the chagrin of the surprised occupants.

More sledge-hammering ensued and the entry team burst into a second house. This time the occupant was bundled out even more quickly, leaving a multitude of wailing women in his wake. Unshaven and a little older than the first two, he was immediately fingered by the waiting cleric and shoved unceremoniously onboard the four-ton truck. The entry team also emerged clutching a brace of rifles and a quantity of ammunition which our captive had hidden under his bed. Evidently caution had proved the greater part of valour and he had elected not to use it.

Several more houses were visited in quick succession, each yielding its frightened occupants into the glare of Land Rover headlights and thence into the back of the truck. Several more weapons were seized by the Marines, who were evidently enjoying the whole occasion. Their morale rose even further when the occupant of one house, a ruthless fellow according to Sameer, who was greatly feared in the local community, emptied his bladder in fear and was bundled into the truck with his nightshirt sopping wet.

For my part, I used the pretext of increasing the security of the prisoners to hop aboard the truck and join the pair of Marines standing guard. This had the dual benefits of saving my aching feet from further walking and allowing me to vent my frustration on the Ba'ath party hoods by administering a swift kick in the ribs to any who looked like misbehaving. The Marines frowned on this sort of behaviour but I had endured plenty of privations over the previous days, so I brushed off their protestations and spent a thoroughly enjoyable hour or so thrashing the daylights out of Umm Qasr's political heavies. It was quite a cathartic experience, I don't mind telling you, and my morale was much improved by the time the night was over.

The following morning I was met by an exuberant BGE who told me that the RFA Sir Galahad had finally docked at Umm

Qasr port.[7] I was non-plussed by his enthusiasm for this event, until he reminded me that there was a bar onboard and she would therefore be carrying a quantity of beer. Without further ado we jumped in his Land Rover and sped off towards the docks.

The grey hulk of the Galahad was the only vessel in sight, which was unsurprising since the coast and approaches to the port had been mined by the Iraqi forces. The mine clearance operation had been carried out largely by a specialist contingent of Australian troops, some of whom were in evidence when we arrived. Festooned with state-of-the-art equipment and natty little American rifles with optical sights, they looked just like a Special Forces team. I sauntered over for a chat while the BGE practically sprinted up the gangplank in search of the ship's purser and his supply of booze. I caught the back end of a conversation in which a pair of Aussies were debating the number of troops contributed by each country in the coalition.

"We've got to be one of the bigger ones," stated one of their number.

"No bloody way," countered his colleague. "We're a poxy couple of thousand. I bet the Brits have got a lot more than that."

At this point I entered the fray and was invited to comment. "There are about 42,000 British servicemen in the Gulf," I told them. (The figures had been widely reported in the press prior to our departure from Kuwait.) "And there are about 250,000 Americans."

"Bloody hell, we might as well have stayed at home," he retorted, crestfallen.

I would cheerfully have carried on the conversation with him but for the fact that one of their colleagues was approaching and my attention was distracted, primarily because she was an extremely attractive young filly, hair tied back in a bun, and a curvy figure still discernible beneath her baggy desert camouflage. Her Australian comrades were still engrossed in conversation about troop numbers and paid her no heed, so I stepped forward and introduced myself.

"G'day Harry," she responded, squeezing my hand for all it was worth. "I'm Michelle. It's good to finally meet the Marines."

"My dear, I can assure you that I am *not* in the Marines," I said, laying on the charm for all I was worth. "I am a cavalry officer, merely attached to the Marines for the duration."

"Jeez, cavalry huh?" she said breathlessly, looking up at me with wide brown eyes. "I hope you don't mind me saying, but you sound pretty posh."

"Oh, I'm not sure I qualify as posh," I chuckled. "Perhaps well-bred is a better description. Say, have you been aboard the Galahad yet?"

She hadn't, so I wasted no time whisking her up the gangplank, crisply returning the salute from the sentry at the top, and turning aft. Years earlier, I had suffered the misfortune of spending several days at sea onboard an RFA, most of which I spent throwing up over the side as the flat-bottomed barge wallowed in heavy seas. As a result of that passage I knew that several guest cabins were located in a little-visited area near the stern. It took less than a minute to navigate to our destination and, as expected, the cabins were empty and we didn't encounter another soul. As the saying goes, there are only two certainties in life: death and Australians, and young Michelle proved to be no exception. The cabin door clicked shut behind us and, God bless her, the little Aussie harlot leapt on top of me as if there was no tomorrow. For several wonderful minutes I forgot all about the war as we coupled like stoats, despite the somewhat restrictive nature of Sir Galahad's bunk beds. The unexpectedness of the encounter – not to mention Michelle's marvellously lithe physique – made the whole experience all the more enjoyable, and it was with a broad grin on my face and morale fully restored that I shoved the little hussy back down the gangplank half an hour later.

In the depths of the ship I discovered the BGE in heated

conversation with the purser, a jovial fellow who was more than happy to sell us his beer, but who was marginally taken aback by the quantity we wished to purchase – all of it.

"I think there are about 1,400 cans left," he said, peering into the stockroom.

"That's fine," came the booming reply. "We'll take the lot."

The purser seemed mildly disbelieving about this, but the BGE was adamant.

"Cleared it with the CO," he said, grinning. "A couple of cans per man should make for a decent barbecue, don't you reckon?"

It was the first I had heard of it, but the BGE quickly enlarged, explaining that he had contacted an old business chum in Kuwait, who was shipping sufficient meat and potatoes to Umm Qasr to facilitate a slap-up barbecue for all 766 blokes in the unit. Subject to the town being quiet and the continuation of normal patrol routines, the CO was happy to allow a spot of al fresco dining – the men had earned a break and they would certainly enjoy a couple of cold sherbets. Unable to rope any sailors into doing our spadework, I was forced to manhandle best part of a thousand cans of beer into the back of the BGE's Land Rover, much to the amusement of the onlooking Australians.

That evening's barbecue made an uplifting change from endless boil-in-the-bag rations and was therefore an enormous hit with the boys. I wolfed down a hefty steak sandwich and retired to my room, where I had taken the liberty of stashing several dozen cans of beer in the fridge. The combat camera team joined me a short time later and we proceeded to get famously drunk. Bloated with beer, still on a high from my earlier Australian conquest, I eventually collapsed into bed, sated, sometime after midnight. By any standards it had been a good day. Had I known of the horrors that lay ahead, the smile would have been wiped off my face in seconds.

NOTES

1. TAA: Tactical Assembly Area.
2. Flashman is being a little generous to J Company. In fact elements of 40 Commando were the first to land on the Al Faw, arriving some six or seven hours ahead of 42 Commando because of the delays caused by the problems with the U.S. helicopters.
3. BV: a tracked over-snow vehicle originally procured by the Royal Marines for use in the arctic, but which has proved itself unexpectedly adept in all manner of environments, including the desert.
4. Nutty: sweets, chocolate.
5. Sadiq: friend (Arabic).
6. Silkworm: an anti-ship missile made by the Chinese.
7. RFA: Royal Fleet Auxiliary – a support ship. Flashman's mention of mines is correct: the arrival of the Sir Galahad was delayed by a day or more because of the need to clear the shipping lane immediately outside the port.

7

Royally hungover, I awoke the morning after the barbecue with a shocking pain behind my eyes and my tongue stuck firmly to the roof of my mouth. A fistful of aspirin eventually fixed the former, and the application of hot coffee, courtesy of the ever-helpful combat camera boys, fixed the latter. Nevertheless I was still at a fairly low ebb as I made my way to the morning briefing.

Instead of being allowed into the briefing room, I found my way barred by the adjutant. A stickler for discipline (like most adjutants), I couldn't quite fathom him out – he seemed amiable enough yet there was sometimes an air of cynicism about him, which made me wonder whether he had seen through my bluff façade to the quaking coward underneath. I still hadn't quite forgiven him for sticking me onboard the lead flight of helicopters out of Kuwait; less than a week later, he was about to deal me an even worse hand.

"Ah, Harry, a word," he began. A sense of foreboding crept over me and I wondered for a moment if this was going to be a ticking-off for pinching a case of beer and getting drunk the previous evening. As it turned out, it was infinitely worse than any reprimand.

"We got a signal last night from Brigade," he continued, ominously. "As you know, 40 Commando is working its way northwest from Al Faw to Basra."

I knew this all too well – I had watched their convoys

passing my position only a few days earlier.

"Well they've been having quite a time of it. Word is they've run into a stack of Iraqi armour south east of Basra." I could see immediately where this was heading and I didn't like it above half, I don't mind telling you.

"Of course they're dealing with it just fine, but the chaps in Brigade Headquarters thought that a bit of armoured expertise might help their cause – might enable them to second guess what the jundies will do with their tanks before they actually do it. At first there was no-one available, until some bright spark thought of you."

I wasn't sure whether it was my hangover or simply a rush of adrenaline, but I suddenly wanted to throw up. Choking back the bile, I spluttered, "A novel idea, but I assure you I am plenty busy enough with 42 Commando. It surely wouldn't do just to punt me across to another unit . . ."

"Decision already made, Flashy," he interjected. "Not worth protesting now. I suggest you get your bergen packed – an escort party from BRF is on its way and they'll be ready to leave at 0900." And with that the cold-hearted bastard strolled off to the morning briefing, leaving me shivering in the frigid morning air.

It took only a few minutes to shove my limited belongings into my bergen and prepare to depart from my luxury accommodation. The combat camera boys, normally among the more sensible souls in the unit, proved themselves to be every bit as insane as their Royal Marines colleagues by being transparently envious of my situation.

"40 Commando's been having proper fire-fights," commented the cameraman. "I bet their combat camera team has got some cracking footage. Wish we were going with you."

I didn't humour this nonsense with an answer, focusing instead on dousing my rifle liberally with oil. I had last cleaned it before we entered Umm Qasr on the premise that it might be needed. Given the situation 40 Commando were in, it now seemed a racing certainty.

As promised, my escort was ready and waiting by 9 a.m. Two BRF Land Rovers awaited, each one complimented by a driver and a machine-gunner, all of whom had been assigned to get me safely to 40 Commando's position.

"This could be an interestin' ride," commented one of the drivers, a cockney, as I climbed into his vehicle. "Keep your eyes open an' start bleedin' yellin' if you see anything dodgy." I assured him I would do just that.

"I wouldn't worry too much, Sir," he grinned at me. "Since you're the VIP, the other 'Rover is going point. If we get ambushed, they'll cop it first."

His words were cold comfort and I could feel my heart pounding as we left the relative calm of the UN camp.

A few miles north of Umm Qasr lay the little town of Umm Khayyal, a low-rise, mud-brick affair standing rather pointlessly in the desert. J Company had moved into the town a day or two earlier and had been conducting aggressive patrolling ever since, as a result of which the road was deemed relatively safe. Nevertheless I remained on my guard – the area was still a tinderbox and it wouldn't surprise me at all if the locals turned nasty. But instead of being met by hoards of stone-throwing Iraqis, I was stunned to witness a football match taking place between the men of J Company and a local team which was being cheered on by most of the town's population. Evidently no strangers to competitive football, the Iraqis scored two goals in the time it took us to drive past; the Marines were evidently taking a pasting.[1] The rest of Umm Khayyal passed by in a blur and we quickly left the town, speeding east on the desert highway.

From Umm Khayyal our route took us through an area in which there had been only sporadic patrolling by the Brits – mainly 7 Armoured Brigade, but with occasional aggressive actions from 16 Air Assault Brigade as well. The odd British smash-and-grab raid may have put the willies up the Iraqis but it certainly didn't mean the area was safe, so I checked that the magazine was firmly housed on my rifle and gripped it tightly as the Land Rover hummed along the road. At first there was no sign of life bar the occasional curious-looking civilian standing on the roadside but as the miles passed evidence of battle became gradually more visible – Iraqi tanks and APCs lay burnt out on the roadside, some practically sawn in half by the cannon fire from A10 aircraft; others with gaping holes in the side where they had been hit by our own Challenger tanks. Jundie corpses were visible in several wrecks and a couple of the vehicles were still smouldering, so I knew the fighting had been very recent. Far more worrying than the destroyed tanks was the sound of gunfire that could occasionally be heard above the hum of the Land Rover tyres. It was impossible to tell exactly how distant it was, but there could be no doubting that fierce fighting was taking place in the date palms to our north.

Eventually the lead Land Rover turned north along a dirt road leading towards the Shatt-al-Arab river. Thankfully the rough surface didn't slow down the vehicles much, and we jolted our way across the potholes at speed. Any confidence I had that speed would keep us safe was dispelled in an instant when we ran into an Iraqi ambush. The air erupted in a cacophony of sound as bullets ripped overhead and into the vehicles. I threw myself into the foot-well, while my driver remained cool as a cucumber, navigating along the track without a hint of fear. In an instant the machine-gunner, standing in the rear of the Land Rover, let fly with a deafening burst of fire. Tracer rounds flew into the undergrowth, while hot brass cases and links from the ammunition belt cascaded into the belly of the vehicle, many spewing into the front and thence onto me in the foot-well. I yelped in pain as a burning cartridge dropped down the back of my neck, and struggled back onto my seat in time to witness a brace of Iraqis being cut down by the machine-gun fire – and good bloody riddance too, I remember thinking to myself. Several other Iraqi troops were visible and for a moment the adrenaline of battle got the better of me. Foolishly forgetting the perilous situation I was in, I jumped onto the seat and started blasting away with my rifle. In truth, I had assumed the worst was over – most of the Iraqis who had opened fire on us had been slain by the machine-gunner, and I made the naïve misjudgement of assuming the rest would flee. I realised the enormity of my mistake when a rocket-propelled grenade flew across our bows, missing the vehicle by inches. The air was once again filled with roaring as a second rocket was launched. This one was better aimed and rapidly found its mark – me. The RPG smashed into my webbing pouches but, presumably because of the soft fabric surface, miraculously failed to detonate. Instead, the warhead ricocheted off, mercifully flying skyward away from the Land Rover. The impact was like a kick in the guts and I was knocked off my feet, screaming, ending up gasping for air on the floor of the Land Rover. For a brief moment the sound of bullets ceased and all I could hear was the din of the engine as we continued to tear along the track. Then the machine-gun began firing again and I realised with a growing sense of horror that far from being out of danger, the Land Rover had slid to a halt and the Iraqis were shooting at us again. AK47 fire began thumping into the undergrowth either side of us, and then I heard the awful smack-smack-smack of bullets striking the vehicle as the jundies improved their aim. Fuelled by the need to flee the scene, I grabbed the dashboard and hauled myself up and out of the foot-well once again. The situation was grim: the Land Rover had careered off the track, presumably because the driver had been ducking the incoming RPG and rifle fire instead of keeping his eyes on the road, and we were wedged in a shallow ditch. Above me the machine-gun was still blasting away, while the driver was frantically wrestling with the gear lever in an attempt to reverse out and get us moving again. Less than 100 yards from the track I could make out the silhouettes of a dozen or more Iraqi troops, all clad in black combat fatigues, blazing away with their Kalashnikovs as they advanced towards the stricken vehicle.

My instinct for self-preservation took over and I was on the verge of leaping out of the vehicle and making a run for it when our cockney driver glanced up at me and yelled, "Come on Sir, get some bleedin' rounds down! The fackin' jundies'll be on top of us in a moment!"

I realised in an instant that he was right, the black-clad devils were approaching fast and despite the best efforts of the machine-gunner they were still getting nearer to the vehicle with every passing moment. I jumped onto my seat and began firing my rifle for all I was worth. I hit a couple of the buggers too, which given the state of my nerves was remarkable – I was shaking like a leaf. Then with a jolt the Land Rover wheels finally gained some traction and we jumped backwards onto the track. Simultaneously I felt an incredible thump in my chest and was blown backwards out of the cab, landing on my back in the undergrowth.

"Christ, I've been shot," I remember thinking to myself, "I can't breathe. I'm bloody dying." Sobbing with self pity I closed my eyes and waited for the end, only to be rudely awoken by a punch on the arm and a scream of cockney abuse.

"Bleedin' 'ell, Sir, try and stick wiv the agenda will ya?" I opened my eyes, fully expecting to see myself soaked in blood with my innards spread all over the floor. To my surprise there was no sign of any injury, with the exception of sharp pain in my sternum and a bruised backside from where I had fallen from the Land Rover. The only evidence of my being shot was a small hole in the centre of my body armour, where an AK47 bullet had struck the ceramic breastplate – which fortuitously was designed to stop just such a projectile.[2] I felt myself being pulled towards the vehicle and realised that the driver had a hold of my smock and, with near-superhuman strength, was dragging me back into the cab. I scrambled to my feet and clambered in, enabling him to leap back into his own seat. Above us the machine-gunner was still blasting away – God alone knows how he wasn't shot during the melee – but for all his efforts, the Iraqis had closed to within yards of the vehicle. Then with a crunch of gears we were off, careering away down the track and out of danger. Bullets cracked overhead and one or two thumped into the back of our fleeing vehicle, then we rounded a bend, the Iraqis disappeared from view, firing ceased and we were safe, at least for the moment.

For a few moments there was silence, save for the grinding of the engine and tyres, then the driver and machine-gunner burst into fits of laughter. I failed to see anything remotely funny about the situation but joined in anyway, once more play-acting the devil-may-care Flashy rather than the terrified wreck I had been a just a few short minutes earlier.

"Bleedin' jundies couldn't hit a barn door at twenty paces," laughed the driver.

"Aye, well, thank God for that!" came the reply from the back, "If they knew what they were doing, I don't think any of us would still be here."

They continued chuckling about our narrow escape most of the way to our destination.

The track wound its way through a maze of fields and canals and the scenery became increasingly lush and fertile as we approached the river. Suddenly, without warning, the driver of the first vehicle slammed on his brakes and turned left onto a small track, little more than a couple of muddy ruts in the ground. We followed close behind and I could quickly make out several troop positions partially hidden in the undergrowth. Ahead of us the ground opened out into a flat mud-plain, crisscrossed by tracks and drainage canals. A series of buildings was visible in the distance, although I couldn't ascertain what their purpose was or whether they were occupied.

"Is this it?" I demanded.

"Yeah, welcome to 40 Commando," answered the driver, and with that we slid to a halt.

A couple of Marines appeared alongside the vehicle, apparently members of the Brigade Recce Force, since they evidently knew my driver and machine-gunner.

"Captain Flashman, is it?" asked one.

"Absolutely," I answered. "D'you know where I can find the CO?"

"The CO?" he looked quizzically at me. "I don't think you'll find him here, Sir. He's a few miles behind us. This is D-company, the lead element of 40 Commando. It'll be the company commander you want. He's off to a flank with one of the anti-tank teams at the moment but he's due back here any minute."

The lead element of 40 Commando. The words echoed uncomfortably around my head. I was exactly, precisely, in the one place I least wanted to be – at the very spearhead of the British assault, with absolutely no method of escape.

At that moment the air was filled with the crack of high-velocity rounds. I threw myself on the ground and scrabbled into a position of safety behind the Land Rover's rear wheel. On looking up I discovered, rather embarrassingly, that I was the only person present who had sought cover – the remainder of the men had not bothered moving.

"Don't worry about it, Sir," said one of the Marines as I got to my feet. "Everyone does that when they first arrive. The jundie snipers are useless – they never hit anything. You'll get used to it."

As if to prove the point, another couple of bullets flew uselessly overhead. I ducked instinctively and was far from certain that I would ever be able to stop myself from doing so – the cowardly instincts in me are much too strong for stiff-upper-lipped heroics. In the distance I could hear the staccato bursts of machine-gun fire and the occasional crump of high explosive anti-tank rounds exploding. A battle was being fought, and it wasn't far away either.

"Ah, you must be the infamous Harry Flashman," came a voice from behind me. I turned to meet the company commander, a warlike individual sporting chest webbing, camouflage face paint and a huge grin. "I hope you're looking forward to a spot of tank-killing. There are dozens of the wretched things around here."

I seized his outstretched hand like a drowning man. The Marines ahead of us might be engaged in a battle, but I maintained a quiet hope that the company commander would stay far enough behind the front line to remain safe. I fully intended to stay with him.

"The CO tells me you've spent more time with Brigade than most of the Marines," he joked. "I'm not quite sure how you're supposed to assist us, but anything you can do to help clobber these armoured units would be appreciated."

I made all the right noises, endeavouring to come across in a quietly confident let's-give-these-chaps-what's-coming-to-them manner, since this was evidently what he was expecting. Many of the Iraqi commanders – the senior ones at least – had been trained at Sandhurst in the late eighties. Some of their more experienced armoured corps officers had even attended Staff College, in Camberley as it was then, so it was a fair guess that their armoured doctrine would look a lot like our own. In my opinion it was also probable that Johnny Foreigner would do his best to emulate the Brits but not quite get it right – these chaps always seem to lack the killer instinct when it comes to the crunch. I commented as much to the company commander who seemed unsurprised – apparently 40 Commando had been advancing quicker than the Iraqis could fall back, meaning the enemy was in total disarray and unable to form a cohesive counterattack. The result was easy pickings for D-company's anti-tank crews and for the helicopter gunships that continued to prowl overhead. Another burst of fire rang out as we talked, but the icy bastard didn't even flinch.

"Anyhow, enough small talk. On with the war!" declared the company commander, signalling an end to our conversation. "We're pushing on this afternoon and I need to give a set of orders to the troop commanders. No rest for the wicked," he chortled. "You might as well sit in on the briefing – it'll give you a good idea of the current situation."

The current situation turned out to be far from good. Since leaving Al Faw town, 40 Commando had smashed its way across 30 miles of broken country, encountering numerous mechanised and armoured enemy formations en route, plus a fair number of supporting arms, artillery batteries and infantry. Considering the Commando Group was in essence an enlarged battalion – albeit a rather well-trained and equipped one – it was remarkable how far and how quickly they had advanced against such prolific opposition. But success had come at a price. Forced to pull back or be destroyed, many mobile Iraqi troops had retreated in the direction of Basra. Those that failed to move quickly enough had, by and large, been destroyed, but there were plenty of escapees who were now compressed into just a few square miles of countryside. The result was a significant build-up of Iraqi troops and armour immediately to our front, which would have to be destroyed if the Commando was to break through to Basra. With a sinking feeling I realised I had joined the unit immediately prior to a pitched battle. The troop commanders had their blood up, the company commander was raring to go, and I knew enough about the CO to know that having gained this much momentum, there would be no waiting for reinforcements. Instead it would be on-on, all the way to bloody Baghdad if he got his way, and the devil himself could take care of anything that stood in his path. And toiling in their wake, trying desperately to keep himself out of mortal danger, would be one Captain H Flashman QRH.

I have served with a multitude of different regiments and units over the years and in all that time I have never seen one with morale as high as 40 Commando's that week. Time and again they had proved themselves the better of their enemy and the bloodthirsty buggers were lusting for more. Unhappily for me, it looked as if they were about to get exactly what they wished for. The OC's orders were for an advance to contact – an inglorious military expression which means we don't know exactly where the enemy is, so we'll advance until someone starts shooting at us. In my humble opinion it was little more than suicide, but I kept my jangling nerves under control by telling myself that I would be firmly ensconced in Company Headquarters and therefore hopefully far enough behind the front line to be safe, all things being relative. But even that morsel of comfort was taken away when the OC introduced me to his subalterns.

"Chaps, meet Captain Flashman. He's from the Hussars, attached to the Brigade to provide us with a bit of much-need know-how on armoured warfare. He'll give our lead elements a steer on where to deploy our anti-armour assets." My blood ran cold. "Frankly there's no point in him being anywhere but up front, since that's where he can be of most use, so he'll be chopped around between the various troops depending on who is confronted by the biggest armoured threat."

My circumstances had been unenviable beforehand, but at this proclamation I almost emptied my bowels where I sat. The OC barely drew breath however, moving on to point out likely Iraqi positions on a series of maps and aerial photographs. His impatient young charges hung on every word, each one eager to make their mark on the war and no doubt hoping for the lion's share of the action. For my part, I sat in silence, wracking my brains as to how I could extricate myself from the situation. If I could only get a message back to 42 Commando, perhaps I could engineer a recall to Umm Qasr. It was a tantalising thought but there was no obvious mechanism for carrying it out and no time either, since 40 Commando's advance was scheduled to begin in just a couple of hours.

By the time the orders had finished I had descended into a fit of depression. Unable to make good my escape, I focused instead on filling my belly. The men of D-company proved as adept as any at rustling up hot drinks from nowhere, and I took full advantage by shamelessly scrounging both tea and boil-in-the-bag rations, which were available in abundance. I cleaned my rifle too, conscious that I would probably be forced to rely upon it again before the day was done.

A short time before the advance was due to begin I managed to lighten my load by clipping my bergen to the outside of one of D-company's Pinzgauers.[3] Everyone else did likewise, so that by the time we moved off the vehicles were barely visible, festooned under dozens of packs. I reluctantly took my place with the lead troop, sticking to the troop sergeant like glue, since he came across as a sensible soul who was likely to remain out of harm's way. I made a point of distancing myself from the troop commander who was bounding around like a hyperactive spaniel and seemed just the sort of chap to run into trouble.

The country to our front was wide open, consisting of tracts of unkempt farmland interspersed with occasional shrubs and thickets. To the north, nearer the river, palm trees were visible and underfoot the going was difficult due to the multitude of irrigation channels. Away from the river the ground was considerably firmer, making for easier patrolling for which I was grateful since my feet were still a little sore from all the miles I had covered with 42 Commando. Vehicle-mounted Milan crews buzzed around to our flanks, busily looking for enemy vehicles to engage, while the bulk of troops moved on foot, advancing inexorably toward the distant buildings. For some unknown reason the sniper fire had halted – I guessed that wherever the sniper was hidden, he didn't much fancy the thought of facing down a company of testosterone-charged bootnecks. Either that, or our movement had simply taken us out of his field of view. Whatever the reason, I was grateful for the respite, even if it was likely to be short lived.

Our advance continued unhindered for some time and I began to wonder if we were experiencing a re-run of the Umm Qasr walkover. No jundies were visible and there was no sign of movement up ahead. I knew that other companies were also advancing, out of sight on either flank, but since I could hear no firing I reasoned that they too must be having an easy time of it. But the troop sergeant alongside me looked far from relaxed. Given the days of constant action D-company had endured, this was unsurprising, but his tense expression had a marked effect on me and I kept my wits about me. Then, on the horizon, a glimmer of movement caught my eye. I'm not normally one for scaremongering but I was devilish nervous so I turned to point it out to the chaps nearest to me, when a horrifying ripping sound filled the air as a tank shell tore overhead. I threw myself onto the floor and immediately realised just how exposed I was lying out in the open, away from any decent cover. Machine-gun rounds began cracking all around, some throwing up dirt to my front and others smashing into the undergrowth a few dozen yards away. I screamed and buried my head in my arms, fully expecting to die in a hail of bullets. But the burst of fire was short lived and when I looked up I could make a drainage ditch about twenty yards ahead of me, which I wriggled towards it for all I was worth. The more observant or quick-witted Marines had sprinted into it the moment the shells had started flying and were therefore safely out of the line of fire. Only a small number of us had been stranded out in the open, and I didn't plan to be there long. More tank shells whistled overhead, exploding in the vegetation a couple of hundred metres behind me. As if to spur my progress bullets hammered into the earth just a few feet to my left, their customary supersonic crack leaving my ears ringing. I yelped and crawled instinctively away, moving ever faster towards the ditch, into which I eventually slithered gasping for breath, much like a fox going to earth and, I imagine, with a similar sense of relief.

"I thought you were a goner out there," commented a Marine as I collapsed at his feet at the bottom of the ditch. "It's a bloody miracle you weren't hit. I dunno why you didn't just jump in here when it started."

"Damned impertinence!" I exclaimed, but the rebuttal was lost in the crash of an artillery barrage immediately to our front. The enemy gunners had found their range and shells began to pound our position. I buried myself in the bottom of the ditch, chest heaving, listening to the sound of battle unfolding above me. It had taken a few long minutes, but the heavy weapons systems of 40 Commando were now in full voice. Between the exploding artillery shells I could hear the thump of heavy machine-guns clearly audible in the distance, and the occasional earth-shaking explosion meant the Milan launchers were busy too. During a momentary lull in the shelling I stood up in a low crouch and peered over the top of the ditch. I could see now that the Iraqis I had initially spotted were a tank crew. The tank itself was mostly hidden from view inside a large culvert, though its main gun and co-axial machine-gun were pointing ominously in our direction. The Iraqis, at least as far as I could see, had not left their vehicle. This was surely a mistake, as the open landscape meant they were exposed on several sides. Their immobility was the polar opposite of the Marines, whose aggressive advance was clearly visible. Pinzgauers and Land Rovers darted around, their crews blasting away with whatever weapon system was available to them. But the tank wasn't the only threat, since the landscape had come alive with pockets of Iraqi infantry firing AK47s and rocket-propelled grenades for all they were worth. Their rifle fire seemed woefully inaccurate but the RPGs were better aimed and posed a genuine threat to 40 Commando's open-topped vehicles.

Rifle bullets were clipping over our heads from several directions and the grim reality dawned that we were almost surrounded by the enemy. The ditch seemed secure enough as long as one kept one's head down – and I was certainly doing that – but my Royal Marine colleagues seemed far from happy to remain static. The troop commander was out of sight, somewhere in cover on our right flank, but his voice could be heard loud and clear over the radio, urging his men to locate the nearest pockets of enemy and report back to him as soon as possible. To my mind the obvious response to this demand would have been to feign radio failure and remain silent. But the section commander to my left had other ideas and immediately radioed back to say that he had sighted a small group of three or four enemy in a copse some distance to his left. The reply was swift and unequivocal: he was to remain in place until an HMG was brought to bear, then to mount an immediate assault with all the troops available – meaning the eight men of his section, plus the troop sergeant and yours truly.

Artillery and mortar rounds crashed all around and an eternity passed until a small convoy of Pinzgauers came up behind us.

The HMG crew in the lead vehicle wasted no time opening fire on the Iraqi position to our left, leaving the way open for an assault. The section commander gave the order to advance and the Marines began vaulting out of the ditch in their eagerness to close with the enemy.

"It's suicide – come back you bloody fools!" I screamed, but my cry was lost in another shattering explosion. The Iraqi gunners' aim had improved; the earth bank of the drainage ditch gave way, chunks of red hot shrapnel whistled past my ears and I was showered with mud and stones. The explosion knocked me unconscious and, when I came round, I found myself flat on my back in the bottom of the trench. Dazed and half deaf, I picked myself up to discover I was alone – the Marines had vanished immediately before the artillery struck and were already closing fast on the Iraqi position. I had seconds to get out before the next Iraqi barrage crashed down, and I wasn't about to waste them. I scrambled out of the ditch and sprinted after my colleagues with a speed born of sheer ruddy terror. All around me were the sights and smells of battle: bullets cracked left, right, overhead; mortar bombs whistled through the air, exploding nearby; smoke obscured the view across the muddy ground; the smell of cordite was everywhere. Despite it all the Marines maintained their mechanistic, irrepressible advance, sprinting forward in short bounds, taking advantage of every scrap of cover, all the time pumping rifle fire into the enemy position. The .50-calibre heavy machine-guns kept up their pounding of the Iraqis too, spraying chunks of earth and splinters of wood from the undergrowth. The Iraqis were far from done though, and AK47 fire continued to come at us in bursts from positions hidden deep within the thicket of trees. Rocket-propelled grenades screeched out of the woods and across our front, evidently aimed at the vehicles to our flank, but it was to no avail – the Marines reached the trees without losing a single casualty (which was little short of a miracle) and the vicious bastards were mixing it with the terrified Iraqis within seconds. A tiny white flag appeared from a trench to my front but it was far too late, a grenade had already been posted into the position from a passing fire-team and the hapless occupants were blown to smithereens a second later. Theirs was the first trench I came to and despite the blood and human debris scattered around it I dived inside as if my life depended on it.

Over the radio, somewhat unexpectedly, came the voice of the troop commander urging his men on – he had brought up the rest of the troop and the section assault had become a full-blown troop attack, which was no bad thing given the number of Iraqis concealed in the woods. Then the realisation dawned that they would be coming up behind us, and any uncleared positions would be subject to more grenade posting. I looked behind me in the nick of time – a pair of Marines was metres away, rifles in the shoulder, scanning the area for signs of moving enemy. A stand-off ensued during which I stood like a rabbit in the headlights while they checked me out via their telescopic sights. Fortunately the instinct of self-preservation was by this stage stronger than ever, so I wasted no time in dropping my rifle and raising my hands above my head. Eventually they recognised me for who I was and continued on their way with a cheery wave, kicking the Iraqi corpses to ensure they were dead as they went.

As the Marines swept through the trees, I caught sight of more of our vehicles bouncing along a rough track beyond the trees. The Pinzgauer carrying our bergens brought up the rear, lurching its way along a track, jolting over the heavily potholed surface. As it approached the thicket of trees I caught a glimpse of movement off to a flank and immediately knew what was going to happen. The assaulting Marines had not yet reached the far edge of the woods and the Iraqis stationed there took full advantage of the slow-moving target, unleashing several RPGs simultaneously. The rockets flew into the hapless vehicle but to my utter disbelief there was no ensuing fireball – the soft surface of the bergens presumably failed to trigger the warheads – and the Pinzgauer continued to lurch along the track unhindered. Another rocket screamed out of the woods and connected with the driver, knocking him bodily from his seat and out onto the track, but once again it failed to detonate. Finally, a warhead connected with a solid surface on the vehicle and the resultant explosion threw pieces of vehicle and equipment – *my* equipment – in all directions. I assumed the driver had copped it in the blast, but to my amazement he picked himself up off the floor and, seemingly unharmed, sprinted off towards his colleagues before the jundies had the chance to take another pot-shot at him. It was probably the most miraculous escape I have ever witnessed; he should undoubtedly have been killed several times over. Within seconds the assaulting Marines overran the Iraqi trenches and the RPGs were silenced forever. But this was cold comfort to me, since the contents of my bergen – my entire worldly possessions for the duration of the war in Iraq – had already been blown to smithereens.

Then, from behind me, I heard the unmistakable chock-chock-chock of helicopter gunships approaching. A brace of the sinister looking machines flew directly overhead, the leading aircraft spewing fire from its rotary cannon onto a line of Iraqi trenches before banking sharply and turning away to the south. The second gunship slowed just momentarily to release its cargo of missiles before also banking away to the south. The massive ensuing explosion produced a pall of black smoke to our front and left the area relatively quiet – small arms fire could still be heard in the distance, but nobody was firing in the foreground.

"Hoofing!" commented the Marine standing next to me. "I can't see the jundies getting up after that little lot."[4]

He was right, too, the earth culvert and the tank within it had been reduced to a blackened, burning mass. Nothing stirred after the gunships departed, which was a tremendous relief – as far as I was concerned, a toasted Iraqi was far preferable to one who was shooting at me.

We waited in the woods for best part of an hour, half expecting firing to begin again. But the area immediately to our front remained silent, the Iraqis having succumbed either to the attentions of the gunships or to the assault troops of 40 Commando. Those Iraqis fortunate enough to have survived the onslaught were stripped of their weapons and bundled away to the rear to be carted back to the prisoner handing centre in 4-tonne trucks. Eventually the radio crackled into life and the order was passed to continue the advance. By now every Iraqi south of Basra must have heard our approach, which could weigh in our favour if they decided to scarper or seriously count against us if they planned to avenge their fallen comrades. Disconsolately I dragged my mud-covered self out of the woods and took my place at the rear of the troop, emerging from the trees alongside the troop sergeant. The pace seemed notably slower now, which didn't surprise me one jot since the lead men were becoming more wary with every step. Bursts of small-arms fire still sounded to our north, which did nothing to calm my nerves, and the sweat trickled down my back as the bright sunshine baked the earth under our feet.

The buildings which had been mere specks on the horizon when we set off eventually loomed into view ahead of us. They looked to be houses of some description, elevated on stilts presumably to keep them dry in the event of the mudflats flooding. There was no obvious sign of movement therein but nevertheless I deliberately slowed my pace as we approached, keen to keep as much distance between the objective and me until someone declared the place safe. Following my narrow escape just a short time earlier I also kept half an eye open for a suitable bolthole in the event of bullets flying. Once again, my instinct for self-preservation proved invaluable, as a silhouette was spotted in an upstairs window of the farthest house and the Marines let fly with everything they'd got. Thankfully, the response from the Iraqis wasn't aimed in my direction, although this didn't stop me leaping like a frightened stag into a gully that ran alongside the track, from where I observed the Marines smashing their way into the nearest residence. The bloodthirsty blighters were inside within seconds

– I could see their silhouettes flitting across the windows as they cleared the rooms inside. The Iraqi fighters put up a stiff resistance though and the noise of heavier-calibre fire emanating from their AK47s could be heard constantly. A few stray bullets punched out of the wooden walls and flew in my direction, ensuring I didn't raise my head above the top of the gully – not that I needed any reminding. My nerves, already frayed from earlier encounters, were at breaking strain and there was no way I was going anywhere near a punch-up between a houseful of recalcitrant Iraqis and two dozen Marines baying for blood. Instead I crouched in the bottom of the ditch, waiting for a sign the area was safe. Eventually I saw a party of Marines being dispatched to the next house, which I took to mean the first building had been declared safe. However, the jundies holed up in the second house were no less stubborn, so the fighting continued unabated. After a few more minutes cowering in my ditch I witnessed several Iraqis running from the building under a white flag, jabbering away in frightened Arabic until a couple of the bootnecks got hold of them and forced them to the ground. The bullets stopped flying altogether shortly afterwards so, after a prudent pause to ensure this wasn't merely a lull in the fighting, I climbed back onto the track and scuttled into the nearest house.

The interior was as dank and gloomy as the exterior; mingling with the acrid cordite smoke was a musty, stale smell which told me the place had been uninhabited for some time. Stray items of grubby furniture were dotted around and rubbish was scattered on the floor. The place had a somewhat ominous air about it and I felt instinctively unsafe there. I have learned from bitter experience to trust such intuitive feelings, so I began to search for an escape route in case the situation became ugly. I walked through to the back of the house and made a mental not of a north-facing rear door which had been conveniently left unlocked. Upstairs, I found the troop commander and troop sergeant deep in conversation about the viability of remaining in the house and using it as a patrol base.

"What do you think Sir – are we vulnerable to Iraqi tanks if we stay here?" asked the troop sergeant.

"Not especially," I replied, conscious that for the first time since the war began I was actually doing my job and offering advice on armoured movements. "If I were an Iraqi tank commander, I wouldn't fancy my chances manoeuvring a T55 over the mudflats, there'd be too much risk of getting bogged down. So they'll probably stick to roads and tracks, which makes them vulnerable to anti-armour ambush. I'd say the threat is pretty limited really."

"So should we stay here, or push on?" asked the fresh-faced troop commander.

I had done quite enough pushing on for one day so my answer was forthright.

"Stay right here," I countenanced, solemnly. "You've got a good base with enough elevation to see much of the surrounding country. There are no obvious objectives to your – our – front and there ain't much daylight left. If I were you I'd get on the net to the company commander and tell him you're done for the day."

He did too, and I almost fainted with relief when he got the necessary authority for us to stay put for the night. My heart was still trip-hammering from all the earlier adrenaline and I was becoming increasingly desperate to get some rest. News of our stay came as an obvious disappointment to several of the Marines, who were once again keen to be pressing on – their eagerness to risk their lives in armed combat never ceased to amaze me.

I made my way downstairs, keen to find somewhere quiet to get some undisturbed shut-eye. There were plenty of quiet corners but most of the house was filthy and I didn't fancy waking up with lice, so I poked around, opening doors and peering into every nook and cranny in the hope of finding a suitable spot for a nap. Just as I was resigning myself to the probability of sleeping in filth, the wall of the house exploded into a hail of splinters, pieces of wood flying towards me amidst the cacophony of noise associated with being on the wrong end of a Kalashnikov. A large timber splinter caught me square on the thigh, embedding itself in my flesh and causing me a great deal of pain. I howled and collapsed onto the floor clutching my wounded leg. It was as well that I did, since the next burst of fire came hot on the heels of the first, smashing through the wall and showering me with more fragments of the building. To be entirely honest, I'm not sure why I acted as I then did, I can only assume I suffered some sort of nervous breakdown. Under attack again, in agony due to my injured leg, something inside me snapped. Despite the flying bullets, I jumped to my feet and sprinted out of the rear door of the house, limbs flailing, screaming in abject terror. I had no idea where I was going and frankly I didn't care – anywhere was better than being besieged in a filth-ridden cesspit with a bunch of psychotic maniacs. As I exited the building I was vaguely aware of fire coming from the upstairs windows, which I remember thinking was a little odd, since the enemy assault was clearly on the other side of the house. But the Marines could have been shooting clay pigeons for all I cared – I could see the outline of the date palms to the north and in my panic-fuelled insanity I was intent on reaching them. I didn't get more than 50 yards before fate conspired against me, in the form of a length of barbed wire concealed in the muddy earth. I caught the toe of my boot in a loop of the stuff and crashed to the ground face first, knocking the wind out of my lungs. My fist was still firmly clenched around the pistol-grip of my rifle and when my muscles clenched as I hit the deck I inadvertently snatched at the trigger. Without even being aware of it I had instinctively taken the safety catch off my rifle when the building came under fire. Worse, at some point during the day I had evidently knocked the change lever from single-shot to automatic. The result was an unintentional burst of a dozen rounds or more – not much more than a single second's worth, though it seemed an eternity at the time – before I managed to release the action and stop firing. Given that the rifle was trapped underneath me I was devilish lucky not to blow my head off – but fortunately I kept my chin up and the rounds shot straight out from underneath me, flying towards the date palms in a deafening roar. Once my own rifle fell silent I expected relative calm to descend, but instead I became terrifyingly aware that bullets were flying all around. With abject horror I realised that I was just yards from a series of well-hidden Iraqi trenches which had gone unnoticed when the Marines assaulted the building. A number of the incumbent Fedayeen had snuck out of the position and were attacking the Marines from a flank – which accounted for the rounds flying through the east-facing wall – while the rest were providing covering fire from their trenches.[5] My panic-fuelled flight to safety had horribly backfired: instead of being away from this madness and concealed in the palm trees I was completely exposed, visible for all the world to see, an obvious target on the bare earth. A braver man might have continued forward to engage the enemy, but I had no such combative instincts. Instead, I cradled my head in my hands and sobbed tears of self-pity while awaiting the bullet that would finish it all. I cursed the Marines, the Iraqis, the CO, Tony Blair – anyone, in fact, who had even a modicum of responsibility for my current plight. Bullets cracked past my ears on both sides and battle raged over my head for several endless minutes, before the firing slowed to an occasional single shot, and I realised with incredulity that I was entirely unharmed. Caution remained the better part of valour though, so I made no attempt to move until the area had lain silent for some time. Eventually, satisfied that the worst danger had passed, I gingerly lifted my head and took stock of the situation. Before I could move, I was grabbed under both arms and dragged unceremoniously into the house by a brace of Marines.

"What the devil . . ." I spluttered.

"Don't speak, Sir," answered one. "Save your breath."

I began to protest but my rescuers were convinced that I was fatally wounded and would have none of it. I was rushed into the house and laid down on a foam sleeping mat, all the time being told to conserve my strength and, in a faux-reassuring tone, that everything would be okay. Well, I'm not immune to a spot of pampering and I would have made more of it if there had been anything actually wrong with me. But given that I had just produced a spectacular negligent discharge, and given that I was essentially unhurt, albeit very shaken up and with a throbbing pain in my leg, I reasoned that I was in deep enough trouble without being caught play-acting or faking injury, so I opted to come clean sooner rather than later.

"Look, chaps, I appreciate the effort," I stuttered in a faltering voice, wondering what they must be thinking of an officer who not only fled the scene of battle but who also lost control of his weapon in the process, "but really, I'm not hurt. Well, asides from my leg of course..." I allowed my voice to trail off, hoping to leverage the sympathy vote in order to ward off their inevitable anger.

"Are you sure, Sir?" asked one of them, jamming two fingers into my throat, presumably to take my pulse. "Only there's claret all over your face and you look to be in a bit of a state."

I reached up and gingerly touched my forehead. To my surprise he was right, my fingers came away sticky with blood.

"Well I don't know what the cause of that is, but I promise you it ain't a bullet wound," I told my audience. Truth be told, I suspected I had gashed my forehead on a piece of barbed wire as I fell, though I couldn't be sure. Whatever the cause, it looked a lot worse than it was - I couldn't feel any pain at all. In contrast, my thigh, with the shard of wood still embedded, was throbbing like the blazes.

Just then the troop sergeant appeared, pushing aside one of the Marines to get a better look at me. I held my breath, waiting for wrath of a veteran NCO to fall on me, knowing he had seen me for the coward I really was. Instead, he bent down and squeezed my arm, exclaiming, "Bloody hell, Sir, that was the bravest thing I've ever seen. We had the situation in hand you know, there was really no need to conduct a one-man assault on the jundie trenches."

"What the..." I was about to ask what the devil he was talking about, but stopped myself. Suddenly I realised how different my 'assault' must have looked from his perspective. A fire-fight had broken out, the house was under attack from two sides, and out of the building, howling like a banshee, comes one of his number who sprints towards the enemy trenches before diving to the ground in order to engage the Iraqis at close range. I must have given the appearance of a fanatic hell-bent on making himself a martyr.

"Well, yes, I suppose it may have looked a tad rash," I muttered, manfully. "But y'know, in the heat of battle, well, instinct just takes over..." I stopped and stared purposefully into the middle distance as if mulling the possible consequences of my actions. What was actually going through my mind was an overpowering sense of relief. First off, I was still alive and not too badly hurt - although the stabbing pain in my leg still persisted. Second, my attempt to desert in the face of the enemy, coupled with some astonishingly amateurish conduct, had been perceived as heroism and if anything my reputation, which by rights should have been in tatters, stood to be significantly enhanced by the day's events. I could have wept with relief. Instead, I glanced up at my audience and said, "I say, d'you think the company medic could take a look at my leg?"

A pair of Marines scuttled off to fetch the medic while the troop sergeant peered at the blood-stained front of my desert trousers, cautiously lifting the fabric away from the skin around the hole where the sliver of wood had penetrated. Shortly afterward the medic arrived and the subsequent inspection of my right thigh did nothing to offer me any comfort. The piece of wood, a wedge-shaped shard around an inch in length, was embedded in my thigh muscle, around nine inches north of my kneecap. The flesh around the entry wound was badly swollen and the area drenched in blood. The medic seemed quite sanguine about the whole affair though – I suppose after a week of fierce fighting he had seen a lot worse.

"No probs," he said, grinning at me. "Obviously we need to get it out pronto before septicaemia sets in. But it looks as if I can get hold of it, so I don't think we'll have a problem."

Despite my protestations about being taken to the Regimental Aid Post, he began to douse my leg with iodine. The inky brown liquid seeped into the wound and I squealed with pain.

"That stuff always hurts," grinned my tormentor, before unclipping a pair of fold-away pliers from his belt in order to take hold of the offending item. The extraction was every bit as painful as the iodine, but at least it was over quickly. The medic brandished the offending item in the jaws of his pliers, threw it to one side and proceeded to make me wriggle in agony as he opened up the wound to make sure no debris remained inside.

Once the area was cleaned to his satisfaction he produced a needle and thread and began to close the punctured skin. I continued to thrash around like an epileptic, because the heartless bastard hadn't bothered with an anaesthetic.

After an eternity of stitching and sewing he finally doused the area with antiseptic powder and dressed it with a spotless white bandage.

"I think we're done, Sir," he proclaimed at last, pulling my filthy, blood-encrusted trouser leg down over the pristine bandage. And with that he disappeared, leaving me sprawled on the sleeping mat, alone.

My mind was still racing from the roller-coaster ride of the day's events but beneath the adrenaline-fuelled high I knew I was dog tired, so I lay back on the sleeping mat and closed my eyes. Relieved and amazed to be still alive, I felt sleep wash over me – even the residual pain in my right thigh failed to keep me awake for more than a few moments.

I was rudely awoken sometime in the early hours by a Marine shaking me by the shoulders. Freezing cold from a night spent without a sleeping bag, I sat upright cursing, fully intent on seeing out the rest of the night without getting embroiled in any more idiocy with D-company.

"The company commander is asking for you," said the Marine.

I was incensed. "Then tell him to come and find me," I answered frostily. "Is he not aware I have an injured leg?"

"He's only next door, Sir," answered the Marine awkwardly. "I think he wants to chat to you about our next move."

"For God's sake!" I exclaimed, clambering to my feet. "Why are you lunatics in such a rush all the time?"

He didn't bother responding to this but scuttled rapidly away, leaving me hobbling stiffly towards the doorway.

I found the company commander poring over a map of the area with two of his troop commanders. My nerves were still fragile from the previous day's activity and I was far from sure I could endure another advance to contact so soon. I braced myself for the news, all the time trying to work out how I could possibly avoid being dragged into the melee.

"Harry!" he exclaimed. Then, less enthusiastically, "Bloody hell, you look a mess. You feeling okay?"

"No, by George, I am not," I told him bluntly. "I am pretty damned far from okay, if you must know. My leg is hurting like the blazes, I'm freezing cold, my equipment has been scattered across most of southern Iraq, and now I am being deprived of sleep. What do you want?"

"Er, actually old man, I got you up to tell you we're getting rid of you." I looked warily at him and waited for more. "Apparently 42 Commando want you back," he added. "Mind you, after a day or two with us, I should think that's a good thing – any more heroics and I think we'd be sending you home in a box." The subalterns chortled obediently at his bonhomie and even I cracked into a grin. All things considered, Umm Qasr was like a holiday camp compared with the horror of 40 Commando's assault and the thought of returning there was, in the circumstances, the best possible news I could have wished for.

"BRF will take you back to Umm Qasr," he added. "They'll be here in a few minutes."

The first fingers of dawn were brightening the eastern horizon by the time the Land Rovers arrived. Unburdened by a rucksack I hobbled out of the house and we sped off, engines grinding noisily as the tyres struggled to grip the loose surface. My driver was a cheery soul, regaling me with tales of recent firefights and narrow escapes involving the cavalrymen of QDG. It had surprised me that I hadn't clapped eyes on their armoured recce vehicles during my time with 40 Commando, but evidently they had been keeping themselves busy elsewhere, seeking out Iraqi formations all the way from Al Faw to Basra and beyond.[6] Damned fine chaps, the Queen's Dragoon Guards, even if they are Welsh.

By the time we reached the metalled road, daylight was upon us and I was able to get a better look at the surrounding countryside. If the previous day had been turgid for me, it had evidently been a darned sight worse for the enemy. A few burned-out tanks had been visible on the roadside on my inward journey, but now they were everywhere. Many vehicles were still smouldering, the corpses of their former occupants often lying nearby, thrown from the vehicle by the massive force of the missile strikes. Dead infantry soldiers could be seen lying next to their trenches. The blackened hulks of armoured personnel carriers and transport trucks lined the side of the road – they had been shoved aside by our advancing Challenger tanks – and dismembered artillery pieces and 4x4s lay nearby, equally silent. It was an eerie scene, made more so because the two Land Rovers were the only things moving in the still landscape. I kept my wits about me though, and I was grateful that the machine-gunners in both Land Rovers did likewise. Thankfully the journey was uneventful and we arrived back at Umm Qasr unhindered, in time for me to scrounge a quick cup of tea from the chief clerk prior to the morning brief.

NOTES

1. J Company lost 7-1, but the match served its purpose in calming relations between the locals and the Marines.
2. During the course of the war, several men of 40 Commando escaped death or serious injury when bullets struck the breastplate of their body armour, a seemingly remarkable occurrence since the breast plate is relatively small (roughly A5 in size).
3. Pinzgauer: a versatile, open-topped 4x4.
4. Hoofing: excellent or outstanding (Royal Marines slang).
5. Fedayeen: extremist Iraqi troops, highly loyal to Saddam Hussein.
6. The QDG acquitted themselves with such courage on the Al Faw peninsular and beyond that the Brigade Commander took the unprecedented step of issuing every man a commando flash (badge) to be worn on the sleeve of their smocks and nicknaming them the "Royal Marines Light Horse".

8

In my delight at escaping the horrors of 40 Commando's assault I entirely forgot about my bedraggled appearance. Dried mud and blood streaked my face, my clothes were torn and filthy, and the white of a bandage was plainly visible through the gash in my right trouser leg. On top of all this I was limping like a cripple, since my leg had seized up in the night and was causing me a good deal of discomfort. The result was a great deal of curiosity within 42 Commando Headquarters as to what I had been up to. But before I had even begun to wax lyrical about my derring-do, I was seized by the Ops Officer and dragged off into a briefing with OC L Company.

"Harry, sorry to jump this on you when you've only just returned." He grinned unapologetically. "We've been tasked with an urgent mission and I need to get you guys on the road as quickly as possible."

My heart sank. After the bloody inferno of the past 24 hours I had fully expected at least a full day to get some rest and sort out my equipment, most of which lay scattered in the dirt back on the Al Faw. Instead, here I was, about to be thrust headlong into another episode of madness. I began to yearn wistfully for a night curled up in my bed, and felt a lump forming in my throat. But of course I said nothing, and the Ops Officer continued with his briefing.

"Here's where the problem lies," he explained, pointing at a map pinned to the wall. "The Al Faw peninsula is away to our east, we're here in Umm Qasr, and 40 Commando has cleared most of the route to our north towards Basra. But there remains a bloody great area of marshland and waterways to the northeast which is completely insecure. No-one else has got the manpower to clear it, which is why it's fallen to us. With a little help from our friends in 539, of course."[1]

I could see an immediate flaw in his plan: namely, me. "Look here," I interjected. "I can see why you need to clear this area, but it's a job for you boating types. What good is an armoured specialist in an area of marshes, eh?" I chortled at the obvious logic, but the Ops Officer looked unfazed.

"Two points," he replied. "First, the Iraqis don't just use tanks, they use all kinds of Russian armour, and a good deal of it is amphibious. Think of all those BTRs and BMPs they've got. Those things would be ideal in the marshes."[2] My heart sank. "Second, and more to the point, a little bird tells me you were involved in raiding operations in the Congo a few years back, and we could use a little first hand experience, if you catch my drift." He held up his hand to stop me objecting. "I'm afraid there's no arguing Harry, the decision has been made."

These "riverine" operations, as they were described, involved the clearing of huge tracts of marshland crisscrossed by dozens of canals, dykes and narrow waterways that riddled the low-lying land on the south side of the Al Faw peninsula. The whole area was a maze of tracks and waterways, punctuated with tiny settlements and solitary thatched fishing huts. Line-of-sight would inevitably be difficult from small boats because of the endless reed-beds which lined the riverbanks and obscured the view of the land beyond. It was no place to hide a large formation of troops, but determined pockets of enemy could remain hidden in there for months. (They'd probably develop trench foot, mind you.) It was also ideal landscape for mounting ambushes on easy targets – like difficult-to-miss boatloads of Royal Marines. It's an understatement to say I wasn't keen to join the party, but there was no moving the Ops Officer, so I kept my thoughts to myself and he pressed on with the brief.

"We've outflanked this whole area," he continued, gesticulating to the map. He was right too: 40 Commando were situated to the north and east, and 42 Commando held the towns of Umm Qasr and now Umm Khayyal to the immediate west and northwest of the marshes. "But as long as it remains unsecured it represents a weakness – a potential threat – to our supply routes along the north side of Al Faw and into Umm Qasr itself. There's no easy way to do this, so we're going to send multiple simultaneous patrols through the waterways to flush out anything – or anyone – hiding in there." He paused for breath while staring impassively at me, then added as an afterthought, "You'll have air cover, of course!"

The transport for the entire company was due to depart later in the day, so I had a little time to eat fistfuls of painkillers (my leg was still throbbing like the blazes) and to wash myself liberally with bottled water. I would have given my eye teeth for a hot shower (not to mention a decent night's sleep), but the water was at least clean and I felt a darn sight better just for clearing the mud and grime off my carcass. Feeling somewhat more human I set off to acquire a new set of equipment to replace my previous set which remained scattered over the Al Faw peninsula. Thankfully the QM had sufficient spares of everything to replace not just my bergen but also everything inside it, so within a couple of hours I was transformed from a bedraggled wretch in torn clothing to a dapper young fellow sporting entirely new equipment and smelling faintly of shampoo. Quite the dandy, all things considered. I didn't have long to enjoy my improved wellbeing though: as I packed the contents of my Bergen a line of 4-tonne trucks drew up outside and the men of L Company began to clamber onboard.

By the time the wheels started rolling the sun was at its zenith and I was damp with sweat before we left the camp. A few miles of dust and dirt and my pristine clothing was as squalid as that of the Marines sitting alongside me. I gripped my rifle between my knees and endeavoured to maintain a look of steely focus. Inside I was mentally wondering where the trucks would stop and whether it would be possible for me to make a break for the Kuwaiti border. I didn't have long to ponder the idea. The wagons jolted to a halt and I peered cautiously out through a gap in the canvas sides. We were at the end of a small metalled road, at the foot of which was a concrete slipway into a murky estuary. To our south lay the KAA waterway, which stretched into the distance and ultimately led out into the Gulf. To our north lay nothing but marshland — albeit with a bloody great river running through it.[3] And immediately in front of us was a gathering of small, high-speed boats: the rigid raiders so beloved of the Marines. A brace of larger landing craft stood stationary in the water some distance offshore, but it was clear from the gesticulations of the raider coxswains that we were not destined to go anywhere near them. The prospect of being shot at whilst in a small boat was evidently very appealing to the Marines of L Company, and their eight-man sections barged past me in their hurry to board the waiting craft. Hastily shouted commands mixed with the ominous rattle of belts of ammunition being loaded into the breaches of waiting machine-guns and the clack-clack of rifles being loaded and cocked.

    L Company's commander was a bear of a man who, judging by his size and predilection for crucifying himself on the unit's only rowing machine, had probably spent more of his university days out on the river than in the bar. Despite this obvious shortcoming he was certainly popular among his boys, most of whom seemed to consider him a relatively safe pair of hands and a cool head in a crisis. His saving grace, at least as far as I was concerned, was that he was the only OC of a fighting company who had not succumbed to a Mountain Leaders' course. Given the near-suicidal tendencies of the MLs, that fact alone was almost a cause for celebration. Nevertheless he was obviously spoiling for a fight and there was no getting away from the hard fact that we were destined for a waterborne assault against an invisible enemy, probably outgunned, and certainly very vulnerable. Just the kind of situation in which the Marines revel, and which I revile. Still, there was no use arguing, so I threw my pristine new bergen into the bottom of the raiding craft and followed the OC aboard. The engine revved for a moment then we drifted silently away from the shore into the middle of a small flotilla which floated patiently as the last boats were loaded. After a short pause the OC gave the "go" signal over the radio and a cacophony of engine noise filled the air as we sped off along the river.

The raiders formed a tight arrowhead formation in the wide expanse of the estuary, with our little vessel somewhere near the centre – not a bad place to be, I thought to myself. The craft were thrown from side to side as we negotiated the twists and turns in the river, bumping and dipping as we crossed the wakes of the leading boats at speed. To our front I could see several British helicopters patrolling the area, doubtless looking for targets for us to engage. The number of raiding craft looked fairly impressive and I had high hopes that the sheer volume of noise might frighten off any Iraqi troops. But then the river began to narrow, and small groups of raiding craft peeled away from the back of the formation to explore smaller tributaries and channels on either side of the main waterway. The main body of the flotilla slowed to a leisurely plod to allow these foolhardy explorers time to catch up. It was hugely disconcerting. Even moving slowly, the noise of our engines rang out over the flat marshlands, eliminating any possibility of surprising the enemy, and our pedestrian progress made us virtual sitting ducks. The OC didn't seem unduly fazed though. Instead he nonchalantly chattered into his radio, presumably keeping in touch with the recce parties exploring the side channels. It was impossible to eavesdrop on the conversation over the throbbing of the engines, so I settled back into my seat, gripped my rifle tightly, and scanned the reed-beds in the hope of spotting something that might trigger our retreat. But there was nothing to be seen, just endless reeds waving gently in the morning breeze, and certainly no sign of jundies plotting my destruction. The warmth of the sun made itself felt through my windproof clothes and, combined with the gently hypnotic slap-slap-slap of water against the hull of the boat, it conspired to make me feel distinctly drowsy. My fingers gradually loosened their grip on my rifle and my head began to nod with the rhythm of the boat as my thoughts drifted away from the job in hand. All in all, Iraq wasn't such a terrible place to be, I thought to myself. The Al Faw had been rough but I'd survived. And here, on the water, with the sun beaming down, life was pretty civilised really. Nothing much to worry about . . . my eyelids closed and I began to doze.

My catnap was cut short by the simultaneous roaring overhead of a Lynx helicopter and a burst of static and furious chatter over the OC's radio. Commands were hastily shouted and our coxswain glanced behind him before opening the throttles, whereupon the rigid raider leapt forward like a greyhound from a trap. Some of our number were still absent, having not yet returned from the tributaries to our rear, but whatever lay ahead, we weren't waiting for them. I crouched down, clinging onto the side of the boat for dear life as we bounced over the wash of the other craft. I caught an occasional glimpse of the Lynx helicopter to our front – which was now accompanied by another smaller helicopter – flying low over the marshes and seemingly doing their utmost not to remain static for a moment. Everything smacked of an imminent engagement with the enemy and I felt the bile rising in my throat once more. The helicopters began firing on targets to our front – I could see spent rounds and link falling from the machine-gun in the doorway of the Lynx – and I realised that we were seconds from joining the firefight.

Right on cue, the air all around us was filled with the staccato crack of high-velocity bullets – not just the discharge from one or two riflemen, but the concerted firepower from several belt-fed weapons. Worse, the rounds were not just coming from one direction, but from two very different sources. We were caught in the crossfire between Iraqi troops in the marshes and a beach party from 539 which was blasting away with a GMPG from a bend in the river almost a kilometre away. The coxswain slewed the raider from side to side, presumably in an attempt to dodge the incoming rounds – a complete waste of time – and several bullets thudded into the fibreglass hull as he did so, smashing lumps out of the boat and sending me into a blind panic. I ducked beneath the gunwale and clung on as the boat bounced its way across to the left hand bank of the river, momentarily escaping from the line of fire. Helicopters continued to roar overhead, door-gunners blasting away at targets hidden in the reeds. With a whoosh and an almighty bang a Lynx discharged a TOW missile, before wheeling sharply south and tearing away over the horizon.[4] The coxswain was shouting into his radio and gesticulating at the rearmost boats to cross to our side of the river before they rounded the bend. One or two took heed; the rest scuttled across soon enough when the bullets started flying again. With the engine noise more subdued I overheard the OC bellowing into his radio and realised with growing dread that he was ordering his troops to assault the beach in front of us. Engines revved once more and the flotilla leapt forward, Marines blasting away with their rifles and machine-guns as we went. The machine-gunner in the bow of our boat let fly with several long bursts, showering me with hot cartridge cases, but I was too terrified to care. With every second we were getting closer to the enemy and the boat was becoming a bigger target for their rocket propelled grenades and AK47s to hit. Bullets began thumping overhead and I had an overwhelming sense of impending doom. But fate was to lend a hand. The raider zigzagged left, right, left as the coxswain attempted to dodge the incoming fire. Other coxswains were doing the same, doubtless attempting to make life difficult for anyone aiming an RPG at us. We swerved left, the boat next to us swerved right, there was an almighty bang as the two hulls collided, I failed to hang onto the gunwale and in a split second I found myself free falling into the river. We were travelling at a good 30 knots and the water hit me like a sledgehammer. I suspect I blacked out, thankfully only for a moment, for the water was chillier than I had expected and it brought me to my senses pretty sharpish. My webbing pouches rapidly filled with water, but for a few moments they retained a modest buoyancy and I was able to grab a lungful of air, glancing behind me to ensure I wasn't about to be run over. I thanked my stars that the raiding craft had all safely passed me, and thanked them again as I realised I was only yards from the nearest reed bed. I swam to it like a man possessed – my rifle was still slung across my chest and my equipment was dragging me down with every stroke – but with a strength born from the prospect of drowning I reached the reeds in the nick of time. I sobbed for breath, clutching at the roots and mud, desperately seeking some purchase for my feet. There was none – the riverbanks were false, made up only of huge floating reed mats. After an almighty struggle I was able to force my way between the reeds, where I wedged my torso such that I no longer had to kick my legs to stay afloat. I was utterly trapped, unable to make headway into the cover afforded by the reeds, and equally unable to swim the 400 yards or so to the nearest stretch of dry land. I consoled myself with the thought that that same dry land was currently the setting for a battle between the Iraqi army and the bloodthirsty louts of L Company, which was clearly visible across the water. It was certainly no place for a panic-stricken cavalry officer. No, the only thing to do was wait and hope I wasn't forgotten in the melee. Stray bullets whistled overhead as the helicopters made frequent passes over the troops, machine-guns blazing once more. L Company were all ashore though, and from the look of things the Iraqis were taking a proper pasting. They were clearly on the retreat, having disappeared from the beach itself and melted back into the reeds beyond. The Marines of L Company continued to blast away but I thought it was unlikely that they would pursue the jundies into the undergrowth – it was impossible to see more than a couple of yards and maintaining control would have been all but impossible. As the firing slowed I began hollering for someone to come and rescue me, but my cries weren't heard and I was all but impossible to spot, half immersed in water and jammed between the reeds. I waved an arm and shouted myself hoarse for a couple of minutes but there was no sign that I had been either heard or seen. Every time I wriggled or waved I slid further into the muddy water, so I quickly accepted that it was futile and focused on staying motionless in the hope of not keeping at least part of my torso above the waterline. On the beach, it appeared the firefight was finally petering out, so I was optimistic that a search party would be despatched before too long.

The company commander eventually called a re-org and groups of Marines made their way out of the reeds and onto the beach. Sensibly, they chose not to congregate in one area but pushed out to the left and right, spreading themselves thinly across the length of the river front. Off to the right, out of sight of L Company, I caught sight of a group of men forming up in a small area of beach hidden behind a thicket of reeds. At first I assumed it was simply a group of Marines which had become separated whilst in the reed beds. But even from several hundred yards away there was something odd looking about them. I began screaming at the top of my voice, trying desperately to sound a warning, but like my earlier shouting it went unheard. In any event it would have been too late. I watched in horror as the Iraqis launched their counter-attack.

A roar carried across the water as an RPG was launched at the company headquarters. Kalashnikov fire was suddenly all around, dirt and water spraying up as the bullets flew into the mud amongst the Marines. The beach erupted into mayhem, with men yelling commands and blowing whistles. The Iraqis were counter-attacking in force, and no-one had seen them coming. The company signaller was frantically bellowing into his mic in an attempt to get the helicopters back into action. But L Company wasn't waiting for air cover. With remarkable tenacity the boys surged into the undergrowth, firing bursts from their rifles as they went. A pocket of Iraqi infantry was rapidly located on the left flank, and it disappeared in the fireball created by a phosphorous grenade, which brought a huge cheer from the beach and simultaneously set fire to a large area of reed bed. The jundies weren't finished though and rockets continued to whistle through the air, accompanied by the thump-thump-thump of machine-gun rounds. I watched in morbid fascination and prayed that the Marines would prevail – I didn't much fancy the prospect of being taken prisoner by this invisible enemy, or worse, being left to freeze to death in the frigid river. The battle continued to rage for some time, but the prospect of more white phosphorous forced the Iraqis backwards and the return of the Lynx and its rotary cannon was the final nail in the coffin of their assault. Thus it was a triumphant band of Marines that traipsed out of the bushes onto the beach, smothered in mud and twigs but grinning from ear to ear and chattering with adrenaline-fuelled energy, much to the annoyance of the Sergeant Major. The company commander wasted no time in extracting his men and they boarded the waiting raiding craft in a hurry. They would have to drive past my position so I wriggled myself into a position where I could best attract their attention. Then, to my abject horror, the flotilla of boats turned sharply away and set off north, upstream. I screamed my lungs out, horrified at the prospect of being abandoned, but of course no-one heard and the boats disappeared from view in a matter of seconds. I even thought of firing my rifle to attract their attention – always assuming it would still work after the soaking it had received – but decided it might invoke the wrong kind of response. Instead I just clung to the reeds, shivering and wondering when they might return.

The day dragged on interminably. Try as I might, I couldn't haul myself out of the water – the reeds wouldn't support my weight, so I had no choice but to remain half submerged. I wasn't prepared to abandon my equipment and swim for it, not with half the Iraqi army crawling around in the undergrowth. So I stayed put, and became gradually colder as the day wore on. The reeds waved lazily overhead in the light breeze, conspiring to prevent the sun from warming me up, until by mid-afternoon I was halfway to hypothermia. The cold stiffened my limbs and my gammy leg began to ache like the blazes. As the sun began to drop towards the horizon I had the awful notion that the boats might have used another channel to return to the KAA. It was entirely possible that no-one was coming to rescue me. I became hysterical with panic. Once night fell the temperature would plummet and I would surely die of exposure. It was too awful to contemplate. My teeth began to chatter and I shook dramatically, though I'm not sure whether it was through cold or fear. Probably both. How did I end up in these awful situations? Why me? I was destined to die alone, freezing or drowning in a muddy hellhole. It was quite feasible that my body would never be recovered – it would simply slide into the water and disappear forever. And I had no-one to blame but myself. If only I had held onto the boat properly. If only the bloody coxswain had done his job properly. If only . . . I was close to tears when I finally heard the hum of a raider engine approaching. The noise grew ever louder – not one raider, but several. They were returning! My spirits soared. I elbowed aside the reeds, thereby making myself slightly more visible from the water. The roar of the engines continued to build and I raised an arm in readiness to wave. Then they appeared – three raiding craft from the south, skipping over the water at maximum speed. I screamed my lungs out and waved frantically as they zoomed by, but in vain. I was neither seen nor heard. Instead of L Company returning south, these boats were the earlier recce parties, now trying to catch up the main body of the company group. The wash they created was immense and frigid water flooded over me in multiple waves. I clung to the reeds, frantically trying to pull myself higher out of the water, but to no avail. The waves subsided and I was once again half submerged, lying prone in the mud and slime. I confess I began to sob.

Dusk had fallen by the time I heard the raiding craft returning. I frantically pulled my torch from my webbing pouches, only to discover that the wretched thing had drowned and was no use whatsoever. I threw it disconsolately into the channel and began waving like fury as the boats approached. But once again, my hopes were dashed. Even if they had been able to hear my screams above the roar of the engines I would have been damned difficult to spot. In any case, unbeknown to me, the company had spent much of the afternoon shooting up various pockets of Iraqi fugitives, nerves were frayed, and the coxswains were piloting the flotilla out of the marshes at best speed – just as I would have done in their shoes. The boats zoomed by without slowing even a fraction. The sun had already dipped below the horizon and I was alone for the night. It was barely 24 hours since I had survived the inferno of 40 Commando's assault on the Al Faw – how cruel, then, to escape almost unscathed only to end up drowned, alone, freezing in a brackish bog.

That night was perhaps the longest I have endured – and there have been a few, I don't mind telling you. Without the warmth of the sun the temperature dropped rapidly. Throughout the night, as my senses became less and less functional, bursts of tracer fire lit up the sky to the north and east, helicopters could be heard in the distance, and there was the occasional crump-crump-crump of mortar bombs landing near Umm Qasr. I couldn't tell whether they were ours or theirs – not that it made any difference. The noise of fighting died away in the early hours and without its welcome distraction I began to hallucinate. The night was pitch dark – there was no moon and the light cast from the stars was only enough to illuminate the nearby water's edge, no more. Delirious from cold and fatigue, my vision distorted everything around me. Screaming faces emerged from the reeds, Iraqi boatmen slid by silently, old crones peered at me from the water, and – by far the worst – I even imagined my old headmaster shaking his head disapprovingly at me as I lay in the mud. How I didn't go stark staring mad I shall never know. But eventually the pitch black of the eastern horizon began to turn an inky blue and the first fingers of dawn crept over the marshland. I was utterly exhausted from fending off the cold but slipping into unconsciousness would allow my body to succumb to hypothermia, so I forced myself to stay awake just a little longer. Surely, now that day was breaking, a search party would be sent for me.

Before the sun had climbed over the horizon, the beating of rotor blades filled the air and a Gazelle helicopter passed overhead, flying slowly, clearly looking for something – or someone. I rolled onto my side, ignoring the freezing water which ran down the inside of my smock, and began waving frantically. The helicopter continued its passage north, slowly disappearing out of sight over the endless reeds. But less than five minutes later it was back, this time travelling even more deliberately. I began to wave once more and this time I was spotted. The aircraft hovered overhead and the co-pilot waved back, whereupon it banked sharply to the south and disappeared at speed. A further half hour's shivering ensued before the silence was again fractured by rigid raider engines. The helo crew had done their stuff – the coxswains had been given my exact location. As the boats rounded the bend they cut their throttles and drifted over to me. A brace of Marines dragged me from the frigid water and I was dumped unceremoniously in the bottom of a rigid raider, much to the mirth of all present. The raiding craft shot off downriver while some kindly soul threw a dry smock over me, despite which I shivered uncontrollably all the way to our pick-up point.

Back at the UN camp I was bundled off to see the doc, who prescribed hot drinks and a full day of rest. I could have kissed him. I changed into a dry set of combats, contemplated collapsing into bed, but instead decided to vent my spleen at OC L Company before the day grew much older. I found him inside the Ops Room.

"Ah, Flashy, I was wondering where you'd got to," he laughed. "Nice day for a swim – surprised none of the boys jumped in with you."

"You bloody madman – I could have drowned out there!" I shouted.

He clapped me on the back and replied, "Ah well, you look okay to me. Sorry it took us so long to find you. There was plenty of scrapping further north, and I'm afraid I had to focus on the job at hand. You must have been half frozen last night. Still, no hard feelings – at least you're back with us now." I did my best to look reproachful and stalked off to bed. Bloody Marines – far too busy getting themselves into trouble to worry about the likes of me. I wriggled into my sleeping bag and passed out.

NOTES

1 539 Assault Squadron, an amphibious boat group utilising all manner of small vessels from landing craft to hovercraft.
2 BTR – wheeled armoured personnel carrier; BMP – tracked armoured personnel carrier. Most Russian vehicles dating from the Cold War were routinely fitted with propellers and capable of swimming.
3 The KAA to which Flashman refers is the Khawr Abd Allah, while the river onto which the operation launched was the Khawr Az Zubayr.
4 TOW: tube-launched, optically sighted, wire guided.

9

I awoke just after dawn, stiff as a board and still smelling faintly of river water, but nonetheless content to be alive and in a relatively safe place. The UN camp was already a hive of activity, with Marines scurrying around, engines revving, and the general hubbub of a busy military workplace. After a quick strip wash, shave, and a cup of hot coffee, I felt almost human again, and wandered over to the Headquarters building prior to the morning briefing. The place was already full of eager young officers and NCOs, itching to find out what was on the agenda for the day.

    I responded to the inevitable questions by waxing lyrical about my amphibious heroics of the previous day, but before I could get properly into my stride the adjutant cut short my monologue and called the morning briefing to order. The usual G1 and G2 issues were rattled through with no small degree of haste, before the CO stood up to lead the G3 items. This in itself was a pretty good indicator that something sinister was about to be announced, but as usual I failed to see it coming, my mind being too busy working on embellishments to my story rather than concentrating on the briefing. I soon started to pay attention when he began gesticulating towards a white board on which a large operations diagram had been drawn in bright green ink. The name at the top of the board stood out in bold capitals: BASRA. With a sinking feeling I realised that the reason for my recall was not to spend a few quiet nights in Umm Qasr, but to be part of another episode of collective madness.

The CO's diagram, which he had cobbled together with the help of the Adjutant and Ops Officer, was a masterpiece of Staff College-style conceptual thinking. The more I stared at it, the more agitated I became – these theoretical plans seem fine on paper if you're the kind of chap who gets excited by that sort of thing, but in practise I prefer a more simplistic plan that's easier to adjust if Johnny Foreigner starts gaining the upper hand. On the sketch map, three large areas of land were highlighted: Basra city centre, the suburbs to the south, and the date palm plantations and suburbs to the east. Across each section was written a single word: Find, Fix, Strike. (For the uninitiated, these are the three principle offensive military activities as defined by the boffins at Shrivenham. The Flashy version of Find-Fix-Strike is Find-Run-Hide, from which you can deduce that I was gravely concerned by the CO's outline plan.) The explanation was given that 40 Commando, who were already approaching the eastern suburbs of Basra, would fix the enemy in that location. BRF would soon be engaged to the south of the town in an attempt to find the enemy strongholds, which would then be neutralised by airstrikes or by the gunners of 29 Commando Artillery, all of which would leave the way open for an assault on the town centre by 42 Commando, supported by the Challenger tanks of 7 Armoured Brigade. With typical bootneck enthusiasm the entire staff was chomping at the bit within seconds, with yours truly joining in the hoo-har for all I was worth – I had nothing to lose and by this stage I had fully realised the futility of attempting to resist the collective fervour of two dozen Marine officers scenting blood.

Plans were spelled out for the entire Commando Group to depart Umm Qasr by the end of the day, handing over the camp to the sappers and loggies who were already running the port. The overnight move would take us north to a staging post a short distance south of Basra itself, where the assault troops would join forces with a couple of squadrons of Challengers for the final push into the town.

"We'll be needing your armoured liaison skills more than ever, Flash," remarked the CO halfway through his briefing. "You'd better get yourself patched up and ready for action," he added.

I knew better than to contest the decision. Gammy leg or not, I would be riding in the vanguard, once again at the pointy end of proceedings rather than down the back where I belonged. It put me in a proper funk for the rest of the day, much of which I spent washing the grime from my tired carcass with countless bottles of mineral water, which were now being shipped to us in ever more liberal quantities.

Having cleaned my body, if not my clothes, I made a foray to the QM's department and was re-equipped with the basic accoutrements of soldiering, including a new rucksack, sleeping bag, spare set of camouflage clothing, and even a set of mess tins. Meanwhile, the camp erupted in a hubbub of activity as equipment was stowed, weapons cleaned, vehicles prepared, and 42 Commando prepared for battle yet again. The prize – Basra – served to focus the minds of all involved and morale, which had begun to ebb slightly as work in Umm Qasr became more mundane, shot up once again. I whiled away a pleasant couple of hours on my bed, trying not think about the inevitability of once more putting myself in mortal danger. I found Charlotte Woodstock to be a good source of distraction, so I focused instead on fantasising over what I would do to her when – if – I got home. The combat camera team was as enthusiastic about the move as everyone else in the Commando Group, but they did at least provide an endless stream of tea and coffee throughout the day.

By late afternoon the UN Camp looked an entirely different place. Equipment was stowed away, offices cleared, rooms emptied, and vehicles lined up in neat rows awaiting the move north. Anything remotely useful was pilfered and packed in the vehicles; since most of the men were travelling in the back of 4-tonne trucks, the camp was systematically stripped of soft furnishings in order to create makeshift mattresses. I couldn't face the thought of spending an entire night in the company of the officers on the Headquarters staff, whose boundless energy and enthusiasm I found a constant drain, so I sought out the BGE – who was no less enthusiastic about the prospect of a punch-up but could at least partake in a meaningful conversation about fox-hunting – and clambered into the back of his truck.

"I hope you haven't come empty-handed," he commented. "There's a cab fare to pay here, Harry, and I'll accept any gifts you can rustle up."

"I've nothing to offer but my wit and repartee," I countered. "Although I have brought my mattress so at least the ride will be a bit less uncomfortable."

"Good man," grinned the BGE, then added, "By the way, I hope you don't mind sharing the wagon with a load of RCKs. The consolation is that if they go off, I guarantee you won't feel a thing."[1]

The thought of dying in a massive accidental explosion was far from comforting but plastic explosive is pretty stable stuff and anyway I had nowhere else to travel, so I tossed in my mattress and struggled up over the tailgate, cursing my sore leg, which seemed to be getting worse rather than better.

"Leg giving you gip, is it?" enquired the BGE, his voice full of insincerity. "I have just the medicine." And with that he produced a half-pint plastic bottle full of scotch which we began drinking before the convoy had even left the camp. I expected it to be a long, hard night and I suspect for the drivers it was. For my part, the whisky numbed the pain in my leg and I passed out, sandwiched between the tailgate of the truck and the hard cases of the RCKs, only to awake when the convoy stopped shortly after first light the following morning.

In the faint morning light, I could see that the entire convoy was precariously exposed, stationary on a thin metalled road which snaked its way across seemingly endless mudflats. The halted vehicles posed an obvious target to enemy gunners so I wandered up the line to find the reason for the delay. It transpired it was one of the attached American soldiers who had caused the problem, by spectacularly falling out of his Humvee.

Apparently the chap was the vehicle's machine-gunner, perched high on a sling seat poking out of a cupola above the cab. The night's journey had proved too much for him and he had succumbed to sleep just as dawn was breaking, thereby toppling from his vehicle, injuring himself quite severely in the process. Clearly it wasn't the finest hour for the US Marines – they've no bloody stamina, these Yanks; I put it down to the lack of a decent public school education – and his colleagues were busily assuring their British colleagues that it wouldn't happen again, while our medics cared for their crippled comrade. Eventually he was either patched up or shipped out (I never found out which) and the convoy started rolling again.

Our temporary destination was only a short distance further along the road. The roar of tank engines greeted us as we rolled into the car park of an abandoned university campus. The place was already a hive of activity so I elected to stay in the truck where I hoped I would remain undiscovered and ignored. My relaxed state was soon ended by an immense crash of artillery, at which point I practically shat myself and dived over the tailgate in a desperate attempt to seek shelter. I needn't have worried: rather embarrassingly the crash was caused by outgoing artillery shells from a gun-line concealed behind a nearby wall – infinitely preferable to incoming fire, but it gave me a heck of a start nevertheless. I berated myself for failing to spot the difference, but under the circumstances I would have jumped at the sound of a kindergarten cap-gun and in any case half of the Marines made the same mistake, so at least my embarrassment was diluted somewhat.

The artillery fire may have been harmless – although I'm sure it felt very different on the receiving end – but my exit from the truck had been spotted by OC M Company, who trotted over to inform me that he was once again leading the charge into an enemy-held town and just like last time, I had the privilege of accompanying him.

"Stacks of supporting armour this time, which is a bonus," he quipped. "Obviously none of our wagons are armoured though, so you'll just have to risk it in a BV. We're not due to move out until late afternoon – I'll be giving a set of orders in the lecture theatre at 1400. See you there." He shot me a wink and disappeared.

I had attended several exercises in which the orders had been given in a lecture theatre – usually at establishments like Sandhurst or Shrivenham, where the instructors monitored every word – but never a live operation. There was a sort of dark irony about the prospect of receiving orders in such a clinical environment. At least, that's what I assumed until I strolled over to the lecture theatre later in the morning, to discover that it was a dusty flea-pit, in darkness save for the light creeping in from the fire exit doors, inhabited by numerous sleeping Marines and several thousand mosquitoes, as a result of which I didn't stay more than a few seconds, and even that was enough for me to get bitten several times.

I spent much of the rest of the morning exploring the university campus. A once-proud series of modern buildings, the place had been reduced to dereliction by either the exiting Iraqis or the incoming Brits, or both. Doors were broken, shattered glass lay everywhere, furniture was typically missing or broken, and none of the classrooms looked as if they had been used in months. There was nothing remotely useful left to pilfer, in fact the only thing of interest I stumbled across was an entire classroom full of enormous hand-painted anti-American propaganda posters. Either the students were all passionately pro-Saddam and anti-Western, or the curriculum left a lot to be desired, for although all the posters were unique pieces, the themes running through them were constant and highly inflammatory.

As I climbed the floors of the building I was able to get a better view of the surrounding countryside. Away to the southeast, the sky was darkened by plumes of smoke from several burning oil wells, which made the stark sunshine seem all the brighter in the foreground. The countryside to the south and west was largely flat and featureless, crisscrossed by ribbons of tarmac elevated above the flood plains. And to the north, plainly visible, lay the city of Basra. Thin columns of smoke and dust were visible outside the city centre, evidence that our artillery and air assets had not been lying idle. The university site was several miles from the town so it was impossible to pick out specific landmarks, but I could see the gentle curve of the Shat-al-Arab river and the lush greenery that marked the limits of the eastern suburbs – the point to which 40 Commando were already advancing. The scale of the town was immediately apparent: Basra is a fully-fledged city. If the jundies chose to dig their heels in, we could be embroiled in street fighting for weeks. I shivered and scuttled down the stairs, eager to cadge a much-needed cup of tea before the impending orders group.

Without electric lighting the theatre was too dark to give orders, so OC M Company made do in the lobby. There was no seating and the floor was covered with broken glass, so we stood together in a huddle and listened as he rattled through the details. If his orders for the entry into Umm Qasr had been brief, these were not much more expansive. The upshot of the plan was that we would drive headlong into the centre of Basra, flanked on all sides by APCs and main battle tanks from 7 Armoured Brigade, and seize a series of key crossroads and bridges over the river. Simultaneously J Company would seize the huge presidential palace, which lay just to the east of the town centre, while K Company would come up behind us, sweeping through the southern suburbs. There was very little intelligence about how many enemy troops were located in the town, and even less about where they were likely to be holed up. The threat of ambush was highlighted several times, as was the possibility of de-bussing from the vehicles in order to assault enemy positions on foot. I stood in silence, suffering heart palpitations and chewing my fingernails to the quick. Entering Basra with my cavalry colleagues in a Challenger tank would have been frightening enough, but the idea of offering myself up as a target in a soft-skinned vehicle had my sphincter twitching in terror. No-one else gave the slightest hint of apprehension though so I kept my thoughts to myself.

"We'll be rolling in alongside a load of tanks and APCs," stated the OC matter-of-factly. "Flashy – where is he?" He spotted me lurking in a corner. "Ah, there you are. If we get into a punch-up on the way in, we'll need your input as to how we can deploy the tanks to help sort it out, okay?" I nodded weakly. "There's a space in the BV behind mine. Stick to me like glue, yeah?"

My throat was dry but I managed to grunt an acknowledgement, and the conversation moved swiftly on to air cover.

An hour after receiving our orders, the BVs and Pinzgauers of M Company began to shake out into a long line outside the university campus. Equally visible and much more impressive were the Challenger tanks and Warrior armoured fighting vehicles of 7 Armoured Brigade, whose massive diesel engines spewed fumes into the air as they jockeyed into position. As instructed I climbed reluctantly into one of the lead vehicles; if it had been down to me I would have been as near the back as possible, but that option had been quashed. No, it was once-more-unto-the-breach-dear-friends for old Flashy, all smiles and bravado, with nary a soul knowing that I was practically vomiting bile at the thought of the peril that lay ahead.

Eventually the BV lurched forward, rubber tracks squeaking on the hot road surface, and we were under way. The Marines in the vehicle wedged open the back door to allow the air to circulate, affording me a first-class view of the enormous convoy which stretched out behind us. The first miles were unremarkable, as we plodded steadily through the barren landscape south of the town. Then, as Basra drew nearer, brown turned to green and a series of small fields and allotments bounded the road on either side. Small dwellings became visible, rapidly followed by larger houses and then streets and cul-de-sacs as we entered the southern suburbs. I braced myself, gripping my rifle across my knees. But instead of being met by bullets and bombs, I was stunned to see groups of civilians waving at us and smiling. As the journey progressed, the groups turned to crowds until, by the time we entered the town centre, the streets were lined with people clapping and cheering our arrival. Children waved tiny home-made Union Flags and Stars & Stripes while their parents applauded and waved to us. All in all it was a very different reception to the one I had been expecting and I'm sure I was more delighted than anyone. I leant out of the open window of the BV and waved back to the crowd, happy to play the role of Flashman the Liberator – just as long as I didn't have to do any fighting of course.

By early evening we arrived at a large roundabout in the middle of town and our lead vehicles juddered to a halt. First out, despite the obvious risk of snipers from all the surrounding high-rise buildings, were the ITN boys, who rapidly set up a satellite antenna and, despite the incessant clucking of their media minder, were broadcasting news of our arrival to the world within seconds. The OC was also in evidence, wielding a map and pointing to a series of road junctions and nearby buildings. The ground shook beneath my feet as a pair of tanks rolled up alongside, then they were gone, screeching round the corner and tearing lumps out of the tarmac with their tracks as they went. It was a sight that would have made any jundie think twice before starting any trouble, and it made me feel a darn sight better about the situation. I sauntered over to the OC, who was busily directing his men to various strategic points in the vicinity.

"Harry, let me give you a quick heads-up," he said. "The building to our front will be my headquarters." He pointed to a sizeable four-story building that was still being constructed. The walls were incomplete and wooden scaffolding shrouded large parts of the façade. It stood on muddy wasteland behind a brick wall, beyond which several constructors' portakabins had been erected. "We've a couple of checkpoints down the road opposite the hospital." The hospital was a substantial, modern-looking multi-storey building which dominated the local landscape, complete with armies of doctors and nurses coming and going through the front doors and a line of ambulances parked outside. "The rest of the blokes are pushing out towards the river and the main road junctions, where they'll set up VCPs overnight."[2] He jabbed at the map with a biro. "I'd like you to make your way to this junction, just on the far side of the river, and team up with the VCP there. The tankies will have several of their vehicles up there too, plus another two stationed just across the river in front of the hospital, here," he pointed on the map once more. "If anything kicks off in the night, you're to take charge of the local armoured assets and sort it out, okay? Don't bother getting authority from up the chain – we've already got it. But if the place is quiet you can let the tankies go about their business as usual." I nodded in acquiescence and he was gone, striding off to find some other hapless individual who looked in need of further employment.

I cut across the wasteland outside the construction site that was now the Company Headquarters, hoping to cadge a lift across the bridge from one of the many vehicles outside. Annoyingly most of them were busy finding parking spots so I continued on foot, eager to get away from the nearby buildings, which had still not been searched for jundies. The ground floor of the Headquarters was getting the most attention, since the solid brick walls offered no obvious entry points and the steel doors were all locked and bolted. Groups of Marines began sledgehammering the doors, but they were quarter-inch thick steel plate and not likely to budge in a hurry.

"I say! Need a hand?" I didn't need to look to know the voice belonged to one of the young tank commanders – the public school accent rather gave the game away. The Marines were quick enough to accept the offer and stepped smartly aside as he ordered the driver to reverse. With a blast of diesel fumes the tank lurched backwards and smashed straight through the wall. Gears crunched and it jolted forward, masonry and plaster dust crashing over the hull as it exited the building. Marines swarmed through the hole in the wall and emerged triumphant on the first floor a couple of minutes later, grinning from ear to ear. The rest of the building was searched in minutes and with no sign of any enemy soldiers the Company Commander wasted no time in moving in.

I left them to it and walked across the bridge to join the squad of chaps at the VCP on the far side – which in reality simply consisted of their BV parked diagonally across the road to block one and half lanes of traffic. Efficient as ever, the Marines had already spread out away from the vehicle and were stopping and searching the few civilian cars and pickups that passed. Warrior armoured vehicles rumbled past several times during the course of the evening, accompanied by a brace of tanks and, somewhat unexpectedly, a Challenger recovery vehicle, sporting a large St Andrews Cross and a crew grinning from ear to ear.[3] For the most part the evening was remarkably quiet – evidently most Iraqis had chosen to stay indoors, an eminently sensible decision in the circumstances.

Shortly after nightfall a small number of civilians began to file past the checkpoint, making a beeline for the river front road. They disappeared out of sight around a bend, and reappeared thirty or so minutes later, clutching all manner of possessions including mirrors, cabinets, clocks, and even a wardrobe. The looting had begun. As with most cities, river front properties were the most sought after and in Basra they all belonged to the Ba'ath Party faithful. These people had held on to the last, toughing out a series of hit-and-run raids that had been mounted by 7 Armoured Brigade and elements of 16 Air Assault Brigade over the previous days. But confronted by the full-scale arrival of the Commandos and their armoured brethren, none of whom showed any sign of leaving, the Ba'athists scarpered, leaving their fabulously well-appointed residences defenceless. Basra's unwashed masses, persecuted for almost 30 years, moved quicker than a swarm of locusts. The more industrious looters worked through the night, purloining as many valuables as they could carry – I saw one chap struggling along the road with an entire double bed balanced precariously on his head. But the best trophy of the night went to a tiny, middle-aged women dressed entirely in black, who emerged carrying an enormous cut-glass chandelier. The thing was taller than she was, forcing her to carry it with her arms outstretched above her head. It obviously weighed a good deal too, for she had to stop and rest every twenty yards or so.

Unhappily, not all of the night's arrivals were so benign. A small hardcore of stay-behind loyalists mounted a series of raids on checkpoints around the city. Most of these were simple affairs, in which an apparently unarmed civilian swiftly produced a Kalashnikov from under his robes and opened fire on a VCP. The Marines were alert to the threat and, perhaps by dint of looking like the murderous devils they were, attracted very little of this sort of attention, but the APC crews were less lucky and took several casualties during the night. It wasn't just rifle-wielding maniacs I fretted about though, since the radio buzzed constantly with alerts of suicide bombers roaming the area with pounds of plastic explosive hidden beneath their clothes. During the course of a sleepless night we were indeed approached by one such fellow, though it fortuitously turned out that he was far from eager to meet his maker. Walking slowly and deliberately, he attracted the suspicion of the Marines long before he reached the VCP. As they moved to stop him, he opened his robes, revealing an array of explosives strapped across his midriff. The next thing he knew he was on the floor with a mouthful of dirt and his front teeth missing as the VCP team jumped him before he could detonate the charge. It turned out that the chap was anything but a volunteer and had been forced into the role of suicide bomber by the local Saddam loyalists, who had kidnapped his wife and family and threatened to execute them if he didn't comply. Evidently even this threat wasn't enough for him though, and he got cold feet as he approached the checkpoint. It gave me an awful start, I don't mind telling you, and I spent the rest of the night all a-jitter, sheltering in the lee of the BV whenever anyone approached.

Word of the free-for-all spread fast and as dawn broke the

streets came alive with hundreds and hundreds of eager treasure-seekers all looking for their little slice of the bounty. Marines and tanks moved onto the river front road to maintain some semblance of order, but the situation was already descending into anarchy. As the richer pickings were snapped up the vultures became more and more aggressive, tearing asunder anything that could physically be moved or broken. Windows and doors were smashed, fittings torn down, vehicles burned – the happy-go-lucky night-time scenes were consigned to history as the mood began to turn sour. The Marines moved in to stop the worst of the violence but they were faced with an overwhelming task, since literally thousands of people were now openly stealing anything that wasn't nailed down. I held back – an angry mob is never an easy thing to control, as I found to my cost in Sierra Leone a few years back – and anyway I had more than a little sympathy with Basra's citizens, reasoning that if I had been repressed for three decades, I would probably enjoy a little light vandalism too. Sensibly, the Marines decided that houses that were apparently abandoned and which therefore presumably belonged to the Ba'ath Party were fair game, and let the looters have a free rein. But they drew the line at properties that were obviously nothing to do with the old regime, physically ejecting looters from shops and restaurants and even firing warning shots on a few occasions. Sometime before noon a flotilla of small civilian boats sped across from the north side of the river and moored up alongside the riverbank footpath. The occupants jumped out and stormed into the nearest properties, many of which were inhabited by terrified civilians, all doing their best to hang onto their possessions in the face of rising lawlessness. For the Marines, many of whom were – unbelievably – aggrieved at the lack of a fire-fight on the way into Basra, this was a golden opportunity to put on a show of force. Warning shots cracked overhead, forcing the raiders back onto their boats. Those who had already entered nearby properties scuttled out, keen not to miss the boat ride home. The Marines fired more and more warning shots ever closer to the looters, who by now were in full flight. Many still refused to drop their booty though, so the men of M Company increased the pressure still further. I watched as a large Arab man struggled across the road clutching a stack of plates he had pilfered from a nearby restaurant. A rifle cracked and the crockery exploded in his hands as the bullet struck home. The looter collapsed onto the floor screaming in fright, while the M Company boys and I collapsed in fits of laughter.

Around lunchtime another suicide-bomber warning was broadcast over the radio. This time the suspect was thought to be driving a pickup truck full of explosives, which he apparently intended to crash into one of our checkpoints. At the time the warning was given, unseen by any of our troops, a local thief, presumably somewhat carried away by the looting fever which had gripped the town, was in the process of stealing a pickup from the hospital car park just south of the bridge on which I was stationed. Seconds after the warning was given, he crashed the pickup through the hospital gates and screeched out onto the road, heading directly towards a brace of tanks parked on the roadside. The Marines didn't hesitate for a second and within a matter of moments the pickup was riddled with bullet holes fired by anyone who could get a clean shot. The chaps at my checkpoint poured fire into the hapless vehicle, much to the surprise of a local pensioner who was busy pedalling his bicycle across the bridge at the time. Tracer rounds flew past him on both sides but he continued pedalling unfazed and even waved cheerily to us as he passed the checkpoint a short time later. The boys in the Company Headquarters also let fly, including at least one heavy machine-gun crew whose armour-piercing incendiary rounds not only punched holes in the pickup truck but also set it on fire. The vehicle swerved from side to side and eventually ground to a halt. After a pause of a few seconds, the driver's door swung open and the occupant, evidently not in the best of health, collapsed onto the road and began to crawl towards the hospital. The HMG and small-arms fire had taken their toll though: one of his arms had been blown off and his torso was riddled with holes. Gallons of blood poured out of him onto the road, and the world's most unlucky car thief died just a few feet from the burning pickup.

It was long past any civilised lunchtime – needless to say, the Marines were so preoccupied with their VCPs and anti-looting patrols that they hadn't stopped for food – so with belly grumbling I made my way on foot back across the bridge to M Company headquarters. The building site in which the headquarters was housed was an absolute death trap, which no doubt appealed to the Mountain-Leader OC. Rickety wooden scaffolding covered part of it, there were no walls, and the stairwells consisted of flat slabs of concrete with a mesh of steel reinforcing rods thrown perilously on top. I was delighted to see that the Challenger crews had chosen the surrounding area as a tank park, so I sauntered over and spent an enjoyable few moments cadging not just a cup of tea but also a hot lunch from one of the troop commanders. Despite their self-evident differing mentalities the Marines and tank crews were getting along famously, which was fine by me since, as the liaison officer, I would take much of the responsibility for the state of working relations. In fact it was more a case of symbiosis for the purpose of self-preservation: while the tanks had a menacing and almost omnipotent presence, their crews, when not hunkered down inside, were extremely vulnerable to small arms fire. The Marines, on the other hand, were past-masters at dealing with small-arms fire, but liked the kudos that came from having 75 tons of rolling steel on hand whenever the locals got a little feisty. The roles were so different that there was no competition between the two, and the result was a working camaraderie that one seldom sees outside of wartime – and a marvellous opportunity for me to take credit where none was due. (Needless to say I made mention of it frequently during the following month when I knew the CO would be writing my end-of-tour report, but the old bastard never mentioned it once.)

My arrival at the Company Headquarters coincided with the news that we were to be replaced by another company and withdrawn from the city. Good news indeed, made better by our destination, which was the palace, successfully seized by J Company the previous evening. The place erupted into a frenzy of packing and equipment stowage as the Marines scrambled into the vehicles, eager to get to the palace and do a spot of looting of their own. A convoy of vehicles quickly formed and within minutes we were rolling east along a road parallel to the river.

Saddam's palace looked impressive enough from a distance but on closer inspection was disappointingly lacking in opulence. Situated in expansive grounds, it consisted of a series of ornate buildings backing onto the Shat-al-Arab river and a plethora of smaller, less impressive buildings set back from the river, which I could only assume had been designed to house servants. The most impressive structure – essentially the centre of mass of the whole palace complex – was a huge marble-fronted affair, complete with gigantic stone pillars either side of the front door. Inside, grandiose marble staircases ascended from a huge, airy entrance lobby to a series of enormous, bare bedrooms. (Needless to say, the CO had adopted this building as his Headquarters. For all its ostentatious gaudiness, in my opinion it was much more becoming of a battle group commander than the 1970s dross back at Bickleigh.) The whole area was surrounded by lawns – mostly unkempt – punctuated by a series of ornamental lakes and crisscrossed by roads and bridges. With very few exceptions, the interior of most of the buildings was unfinished – many had no electrical wiring and were lacking in even rudimentary plumbing. By the time I arrived any loose fittings and furnishings had been purloined by the magpies of J Company, leaving the place even more bereft of creature comforts. J Company themselves had moved into an adjacent building, almost as flamboyant as the Headquarters palace, the rear of which featured a huge marble balcony jutting out over the Shat-al-Arab. In the water beneath the balcony was a tangle of barbed wire and steel pickets, designed to prevent riverboats from approaching the palace. Preventing Marines from swimming is broadly similar to keeping a Labrador retriever out of water – impossible. The more adventurous souls within J Company had discovered that the barbed wire entanglement could be cleared with a running jump from the balcony and several dozen men were happily swimming in the river below, enjoying a respite from the incessant heat of the afternoon sun, despite the best exhortations of the adjutant for them to get back onto dry land.

Beyond J Company's temporary home lay another palatial building, largely unoccupied. I explored its many empty rooms before discovering my old chums from the combat camera team ensconced in an upstairs bedroom – which of course was lacking a bed, or any other furniture come to that. Somewhat larger than a squash court, and with high ceilings to match, the room had the advantage of marble walls and shuttered windows, which meant it was pleasantly cool despite the 40°+C temperature outside. Inevitably a stove was already lit and I rapidly accepted their offer of tea. I dragged my belongings up the stairs, lay myself down on a sleeping mat and immediately drifted off to sleep.

A half-decent night's sleep did me the power of good and I awoke feeling if not optimistic about my situation, at least not as gloomy as I had been the previous days. After all, we had taken Basra without too much fuss, I had avoided further injury, my leg was on the mend, and I had set up home in a palace. All in all, things could have been worse. I set off for a stroll around the grounds, keen to get my bearings and avoid the headquarters staff for as long as possible. Turning away from the Commando Headquarters, I followed the road across a small bridge. A small distance away I spotted K Company's vehicles parked neatly outside yet another impressive-looking marble edifice, and BRF's Land Rovers could be seen coming and going from outside a smaller, less ostentatious building further away still. I strolled on, alone in my thoughts, until I was rudely interrupted by the roar of an engine and the squealing of tyres as the BGE's quad bike slid to a halt alongside me.

"Harry! What brings you down this way?" He didn't wait for a response but simply shouted at me to get onboard so he could give me a lift to his 'office'. There was no pillion seat so I perched atop the steel luggage rack on the back and the bike took off underneath me like a scalded cat. Gears crunched and we gathered pace, stiffly ignoring the 10mph speed limit imposed on the camp by the RSM.

"I got it well over 50 yesterday night!" he yelled above the noise of the wind and engine, "and I reckon she'll do 60 if I start my run from one of the bridges. Trouble is, the bloody road's too short!" As if to illustrate the point he slammed on the brakes and we screeched to a halt outside an unremarkable-looking two-story building a short distance from the main gates to the palace grounds. The oblong block was constructed from concrete, though the front wall had been clad in black marble to give it a veneer of authority. The BGE vaulted from the bike and barged through the doors, evidently eager to show off his new quarters. Inside, it was plainly obvious why the engineers had commandeered this particular building: unlike the grandiose palaces to which the Marines had flocked, their abode was fully furnished. Carpeted hallways led to a series of small, comfortable rooms, complete with sofas, dining suites, beds – there were even little china vases on the bedside tables. After a night spent with nothing more than a finger-thick kip-mat between me and a bare marble floor, I wandered around in a state of ill-concealed envy.

"No idea how we'll get all the loot home," commented the BGE with a wry smile, "but I'm sure we'll manage it somehow."[4]

We whiled away much of the morning drinking coffee laced with scotch and enjoying the cool air that was afforded by the thick concrete walls. For much of the morning, K Company's vehicles rumbled past outside, closely followed by L Company as 42 Commando sent out numerous patrols in a futile effort to halt the looting. I stayed well away from the Headquarters, happy to take advantage of the Royal Engineers' hospitality and, more importantly, avoiding the possibility of being sent out on patrol.

By mid afternoon, some of the morning patrols returned to the palace, bringing with them stories of a town descending into chaos. The lawlessness had become so widespread that looters were openly walking into the hospital wards and helping themselves to medical paraphernalia, despite the pleas of the doctors that the equipment was not only in desperately short supply but also utterly valueless outside the hospital. Short of transport, the Marines ended up dispatching a handful of their number around the town in a borrowed ambulance from which they blared loudspeaker messages exhorting the citizens of Basra to stop looting the hospital for their own good. I have no idea whether it was effective but the novelty value of seeing an ambulance chock full of Marines and loudspeakers was enough to grab the attention of the locals, and the boys returned to base full of stories of high jinks with the ambulance drivers, who had clearly enjoyed their impromptu sightseeing tour.

The traffic in and out of the main gate was not exclusively military during that long, hot day in Basra. Civilian press vehicles began to arrive in ever-increasing numbers, many sporting satellite broadcast dishes on their roofs. Not officially attached to any military unit, most of these camera crews had taken a gamble and driven up from the Kuwaiti border unescorted as soon as they heard the city had fallen. In an attempt to avoid coalition fire many of their vehicles – mainly Toyota and Mitsubishi 4x4s – had identifying chevrons hastily painted onto the doors and bonnet, or simply stuck on with black masking tape. In every case the crews looked relieved to have made it unscathed through the insanity that was sweeping the town and to be safely behind the solid walls of the palace. They rapidly became even happier once it was made plain that there was accommodation for them (albeit a little spartan) and that the Marines were generous hosts who typically kept them supplied with ration pack meals and endless cups of tea.[5] The marble steps leading to the front doors of the palace became a regular backdrop for TV news bulletins over the ensuing days, and the men of 42 Commando became increasingly adept at creeping up behind the journalists and getting their faces broadcast on the evening news.

The following day was much the same, insofar as I managed to avoid any of the tedium of patrolling and spent most of my day in hiding with the Engineers. Basra was still in turmoil, although the worst of the looting was dying down, principally, I suspect, because there was nothing left to steal. Public disquiet was already slowly starting to gravitate towards the British troops, mainly because there was no-one else accountable within the town. The water supply was still not functioning properly, the electricity supply was non-existent, and law and order were completely absent, so it came as little surprise that the good people of Basra should demand a few improvements. In any event, I reasoned that I was much safer behind the wire in the camp than on patrol outside – an assumption that was well-founded, since hardliners were still mounting attacks on patrols and checkpoints throughout the town. The day brought more journalists to the palace and an influx of media "minders" from Brigade and Divisional Headquarters. Several of them were well known to me from earlier campaigns (I had served in Afghanistan and Sierra Leone with most of the Media Ops crews) so I wasted no time in cadging a drink from them. It is a truism that the people most likely to carry booze in a war zone are journalists – and if you aren't friendly with any of the journos, then their minders are almost as reliable. An old colleague from Kandahar days discreetly produced a half-decent bottle of malt from his bergen and as luck would have it, I had just received a parcel from Roddy Woodstock which included a brace of Cuban cigars. We agreed to meet on the palace roof that evening for a civilised drink and smoke away from prying eyes – not to mention the swarms of insects that gathered each evening near the banks of the river.

Everything else around the palace was being filmed so it

came as little surprise to see the TV cameras set up to record the CO's evening briefing. Rather than being held in the bare rooms of the palace, the meeting was held outside on the riverbank, presumably because it created a more atmospheric backdrop for the television pictures. It also meant I was eaten alive by mosquitoes, which did little to improve morale and simply sent me into a frenzy of silent hypochondria in which I pondered once again whether or not southern Iraq was a malarial zone. Thankfully the evening brief was uneventful; no-one so much as remarked on my absence during the day, and I managed to scuttle away before I got tasked with any suicide missions the following day. The only high note was provided by the BGE, who waited until the cameras were trained upon him before announcing, to the incredulity of all present, that his Engineers had discovered a Silkworm Missile launcher in the city centre. Realising it was a gag, the TV crews quickly panned over to the Ops Officer, who struggled to contain his mirth as the briefing continued. As the sun disappeared below the horizon the palace grounds were illuminated by several dozen floodlights as various TV crews prepared to broadcast their news bulletins home. Unlike the highly mobile ITN crew who had been with us since Kuwait, these chaps came equipped with all the paraphernalia of Broadcasting House, from floodlighting to large-scale cameras mounted on huge tripods and long booms carrying huge furry microphones. The resulting footage made a stark contrast from the fuzzy videophone broadcasts of 42's embedded journalists and the clean marble backdrop of the palace gave Iraq an improbably civilised feel to the viewers back home. At least, that's what they tell me – like everyone else present, I never got to see the footage.

   Briefing over, I clambered up a fire escape and onto the roof of my quarters, a peaceful spot looking out over the river and high enough to afford a pretty good view of much of the town. The Media Ops boys, not being needed at the CO's briefing, were already tucking into the scotch with some aplomb. Happily, the whisky was supplemented by several hip flasks of brandy and a small bottle of rum, so there was plenty of booze to go round. I puffed away merrily on one of Roddy's cigars – a Cohiba siglo No2, if memory serves – while we exchanged stories from the previous three weeks. In the background a small world-band radio was tuned to the BBC World Service and, in between my hammed-up tales of derring-do from the Al Faw, I caught snatches of news from elsewhere in the country. Baghdad had fallen that day – images of Saddam's statue being torn down were being shown repeatedly by every TV station – and there were further reports of Iraqi troops surrendering en masse to the north and east of the city. Then came the infamous "mission accomplished" broadcast by George W Bush, announcing the end of major combat operations. Cheers went up around the palace as the news was passed and, if they were anything like me, every man present started thinking of a return to Blighty. (If I'd known how long it was going to be before we were sent home I would have found the nearest logistician and spat in his eye, but there's no use crying over spilt milk, as they say.) The Media Ops boys and I raised a glass and toasted our success and, as if to crown the moment, a Royal Navy Sea King helicopter flew low overhead, firing anti-missile flares from its belly in an impromptu celebration. The pilot, evidently enjoying the moment, banked hard in front of the palace and the light from his flares was reflected by the river and lit up the marble walls of the palace quite spectacularly. The cheering grew all the louder, and I took advantage of the distraction to quietly quaff as much of the booze as I could while no-one was looking.

I intended to spend the following day – my last full day in Basra, as it turned out – avoiding work and enjoying myself with the Media Ops boys but, alas, it wasn't to be. Unlike the previous 48 hours I was spotted during the morning briefing by none other than the CO, and immediately put to work co-ordinating a weapons amnesty which he wanted publicised across the town.

"All these buggers have got firearms, Harry," he told me

earnestly. "If we get even a small number of them handed in, the streets will be a little safer for all of us. I know you've had experience of this sort of thing in the Balkans, so I'll leave it to you to get on with. Keep me posted of progress, yes?"

I had indeed had some experience of weapons amnesties, and very nearly lost my life when some idiot handed over an armed anti-personnel mine, but he wasn't to know that. I nodded with faux enthusiasm and he moved on to some other topic.

Thankfully, putting together a weapons amnesty was significantly easier than I had anticipated, largely due to the eagerness of the Marines for the task. Posters were knocked up in no time and distributed around town by the outgoing patrols. An enormous advertising hoarding – hand-drawn on the back of several map-sheets – was hung up outside the main gate. At my insistence, a large pit made of sandbags was constructed at the same point. I had no desire for anyone to bring any ordnance into the camp, especially not the kind of old, homespun or unstable explosives one finds in such countries, and this way they could be dropped in the pit and destroyed in situ if need be. In many ways, this was precisely the kind of work I excelled at, since it involved giving instructions to dozens of minions while doing precious little myself, and all without leaving the safe environs of the camp. By early afternoon the first weapons had been handed in (mostly Kalashnikov rifles and the like) and I was starting to feel a sense of genuine enthusiasm for the job. With some rapid success if was a fair bet that the amnesty would be widened and, with yours truly at its centre, it had the potential to keep me out of danger for several days at least. But all that changed midway through the afternoon when, with a rumble of tracks, several APCs from 7 Armoured Brigade rolled into the palace grounds. I wandered over to see whether I knew any of the occupants and as luck would have it, one of the officers who disembarked was an old chum from Sandhurst days, who immediately told me that Headquarters 7 Armoured Brigade was moving in, while 42 Commando was moving out, although he didn't know what our destination was to be. Armed with the news I strode across to the Headquarters building, royally annoyed that I was to be ousted from my relatively new home and the security afforded by the thick stone walls of the palace, presumably to be thrust back into the firing line in some other god-forsaken part of the country.

As with any impending move – and I have seen a few in my time – the Headquarters erupted into pandemonium. Radios chattered as the troops on patrol were brought back to base, space on vehicles was squabbled over, and I don't doubt that each man present was quietly wondering how they could smuggle back the various trophies they had purloined from the palace. Our destination, it transpired, was the oilfields west of Basra, near the small town of Rumaylah. This particularly bleak stretch of desert was punctuated by a series of oil pumping stations, or gas/oil separation plants (GOSPs) as they are known in the business. Formerly the home of elements of 16 Air Assault Brigade, 42 Commando was to take over the real estate the following morning. I spend a fretful last evening in the palace, feeling a sense of deep envy of my cavalry brethren and idly wondering if there was some mechanism by which I could conjure up a transfer to their Brigade. (In the event I'm jolly glad I didn't, since they ended up stuck in Iraq long after the Marines had departed.) The only thing I did manage to achieve was to divest myself of the weapons amnesty, which was picked up by some hapless Intelligence Corps staff officer who seemed utterly terrified at the safety and security implications it posed. I gave him a three-minute verbal brief on my progress to date, handed over what little paperwork there was, and left him sweating.

I arose early the following morning, keen to secure a seat in a vehicle while there were still some available. The Engineers' truck which had brought me to Basra was unavailable, mainly because it was jammed full of loot from the palace – the boys did their best to hide the trophies under drab green tarpaulins, but the game was rather given away by a huge roll of carpet and a sofa hanging over the tailgate. In the end I took up the offer of a lift from the Adjutant. Convoys always present attractive targets to insurgents but I reasoned that the Adjutant's was hardly likely to be the lead vehicle. Several Marines were also crammed into his BV, including a one who chose to stand on his seat, looking out of a cupola in the roof, from where he could scan the surrounding countryside with his rifle. It took an age for the convoy to form up, but eventually the lead vehicles began to move and we lurched into motion a few seconds later.

NOTES

1. RCK: Rapid Cratering Kit – a plastic explosive charge which blows a substantial hole in the road to create an instant obstacle for enemy vehicles.
2. VCP: Vehicle Checkpoint.
3. The Challenger recovery vehicle is essentially a Challenger tank hull minus the gunnery system, equipped with a huge bulldozer blade on the front and steel hawsers for towing stranded vehicles out of trouble.
4. A few trophies were taken from Saddam's palace, but shortage of space on the trucks meant most of the furnishings were left in situ.
5. The Marines' generosity was repaid with huge amounts of PR from the broadcast footage that followed the arrival of so many journalists. Most TV news channels carried pictures of 3 Commando Brigade almost exclusively – to the obvious chagrin of the Army units also involved in the war.

10

The road to Hell is paved with good ideas, so they say. I don't doubt it for a moment – I've borne the brunt of Lord-knows-how-many ill-conceived ideas in my time, the whole messy business in Iraq being just one of them. I can tell you something else from first-hand experience too: the road to Rumaylah is littered with potholes – or at least it was when I travelled along it. As the morning sun pushed the mercury well over the 40° mark we lurched and bounced through every damned pothole in Iraq, or that's how it felt inside the tin box of the BV. I gripped my rifle with my knees and tried to ignore the bruising of my buttocks by stuffing packet after packet of fruit biscuits into my face. The Adjutant, ever happy to be travelling headlong into unknown danger, whistled a cheery tune, while the Marines in the back kept a wary eye out of the grubby windows in case of trouble brewing. The early part of the move was spend crawling through the suburbs of the town, with yours truly making a spectacular hash of the map reading – largely, I suspect, because I was more focused on not spilling a cup of tea which was precariously balanced between my thighs. Fortunately, before it caused any significant problems, my appalling navigation was corrected by one of the Marines who had the foresight to bring with him a hand-held GPS system. Thankfully the navigation was only a belt-and-braces check (at the insistence of the Adjutant) since we were blindly following Recce Troop's vehicles in any case. It seemed they knew where they were going, since we negotiated dozens of road junctions and intersections without making a single error. (You may think this unsurprising, since it's the job of any reconnaissance troop to navigate through new territory, but you'd be amazed how often military pathfinder units stuff things up – especially when it's a hot environment and the pressure is on.) As Basra receded behind us the country changed to wide open desert, littered with the debris of fighting and the neglected remains of a crumbling oil infrastructure. Burned out vehicles lay in the sand, often with minefield warning signs posted nearby, while aged oil pipelines leaked pools of their sticky black cargo into the desert. The scene was an environmentalist's nightmare – made more so by the addition of hand-scribbled notices near the tank hulls warning visitors of depleted uranium in the vicinity, left over from the armour-piercing rounds fired by US aircraft. The convoy ploughed on through the heat of the day, following the long, straight desert roads for mile after mile; Rumaylah was further away than I had thought. But eventually a series of oil platforms became visible on the horizon, the road forked, and we drew up outside a large installation.

The place was much bigger than I had imagined – more like a small refinery than a simple separation plant (which goes to show how little I know about the oil industry). Storage tanks and pumps were connected by an incredibly complex lattice of pipe-work, all held together with a steel frame structure which soared fifty feet or more into the desert sky. The centrepiece was a huge chimney, at least 200 feet high, underneath which nestled a series of command and control buildings, most of which were used to house 42 Commando's Headquarters staff over the ensuing weeks. As the vehicles rattled into the compound it became rapidly clear that there were relatively few buildings compared to the number of people, so the scramble for accommodation ensued almost immediately. I managed to find a quiet spot in the corner of a large room that was full of racks of electronic switches and the like. The concrete walls and floor meant the place was cool and there were no windows, so the only light came via the open doors at either end. I unrolled my bedding and left my bergen on top to prevent the space being purloined by anyone else, then set off on a stroll around the real estate, keen to see what my new dwelling held in store.

The GOSP site was an oblong roughly 300 yards by 500 yards, a fact I ascertained by clambering up the steel staircase of the central chimney. (I had an ulterior motive for this laborious task, which was the optimistic hope that my mobile phone might get a signal from the top. It didn't, so I returned to earth out of breath and frustrated at my failure to send any more SMS smut to Charlotte W. The randy little slut would just have to wait a little longer for my attentions.) From the summit of the chimney it was easy to make sense of the maze of paths and walkways down below, and I could see that a large amount of the real estate was taken up by buildings apparently unconnected with the oil infrastructure. When I descended I discovered a huge amount of real estate devoted to maintenance – vast hangars full of all manner of mechanical equipment from lifting derricks to welding gear – and even a large laboratory, complete with Bunsen burners and hundreds of sealed jars of chemicals. The small amount of permanent accommodation – most of which had been rapidly seized by the Commando Planning Group – was augmented by numerous portakabin-style huts, all of which were falling down and not fit to house cattle. I poked around inside one or two of them and was surprised to find several ancient photographs of Japanese workers posing with their Iraqi colleagues, presumably taken back in the late 1980s before the imposition of economic sanctions. The place was filthy dirty and reeked appallingly, so I didn't investigate further but cut across the compound back to my quarters.

I turned in early that night – there was nothing to do to pass the time, and the interminable heat had left me fairly tuckered out. My room was dark and (relatively) cool, and I relished the thought of a decent night's sleep. Unhappily, Iraq's numerous pests had other ideas. The hum of mosquitoes was rapidly overshadowed by the scuttling of thousands of cockroach feet as the room came alive. I sat up, disgusted, and switched on my torch, at which the revolting creatures scattered towards the corners of the room – but not before I established that there were, literally, hundreds of them. I'm not a fan of creepy-crawlies in general, and cockroaches in particular make my blood run cold, so I de-camped onto the roof of the building and slept there for the ensuing weeks. It was, at times, windy, wet and inhospitable, but at least there were no bugs.

With little idea of the local area, the Commando quickly pushed out mobile patrols to establish the lie of the land. The fighting companies were all located in nearby GOSPs which gave us control of a wide area almost without leaving the plants. The outlying landscape, as far as one could see from the top of the chimney, was nothing more than barren desert, mile after mile of pale yellow sand which eventually merged into the heat haze of the horizon. The only colour in this bleak landscape was provided by the fertile green banks of a huge man-made waterway, which I think was a canal constructed to connect the Tigris with the Euphrates. Whatever its original purpose it was almost wholly disused by the time I arrived, save for a few native fishermen casting hand-made nets from dugout canoes – all very primitive and unexpectedly serene after the mayhem of Al Faw and Basra. They were friendly buggers too, and I whiled away many hours over the forthcoming weeks chinwagging with them and even casting the odd fishing line, all on the pretence of collecting intelligence for the Headquarters. Most of them were descended from the Marsh Arabs whose habitat had been eradicated by Saddam Hussein many years earlier – the canal was now the only habitable stretch of waterway on which a few families were still able to eek a living.[1] If I was expecting a hero's welcome from them I certainly didn't receive one; these were inward looking people who were justifiably disinterested by strangers, whatever their nationality. Getting rid of Saddam didn't matter a fig to them, since not even his departure could bring back their homeland. I knew what would matter to them though – fodder – so I brought it with me by the trailer load. Primitive they may have been but they weren't stupid, and after a couple of visits and several hours of enduring my broken Arabic, I found myself on friendly enough terms with several of the headmen.

But that was all in the future, and in any case the CO and his Headquarters staff were largely disinterested in the Marsh Arabs since they posed no noticeable threat to the coalition. The little town of Rumaylah, on the other hand, was a veritable hotbed of activity, although no-one could quite work out why. The HumInt Cell was busy talking to every man and his dog but no clear pattern seemed to be emerging, yet by all accounts the town was a tinderbox and the chaps returning from the place said the tension in the air was palpable.[2] Patrols were dispatched there almost by the hour and, inevitably, it was only a couple of days before I was sat at the CO's morning brief when some bright spark suggested I should join them so that my linguistic skills could be put to good use.

"Capital idea," agreed the old man, nodding wisely at whichever well-intentioned halfwit had made the suggestion. "Recce Troop is on its way into the town this afternoon," he added, gesturing towards the patrol roster which was pinned on the wall. "It makes perfect sense for you to join them, Captain Flashman."

I feigned excitement at the opportunity to get out of the compound and the Staff nodded their approval. The CO didn't pause for breath and the conversation moved on, leaving me sweating at the prospect of untold dangers ahead.

Thankfully, given the searing heat, at least the Recce Troop boys had the good sense to drive to Rumaylah (it was just over two miles) in Land Rovers rather than make their way on foot. However, like most Marines, given the choice they preferred to do business on foot, so we de-bussed just short of the town and began footslogging through the streets. Perspiration poured down my back, soaking my shirt and causing my webbing belt to start rubbing, while the pistol-grip of my rifle became slippery in my grasp. Unlike Umm Qasr or Basra the inhabitants of Rumaylah shied well away from us. No-one emerged from their doorway for a chat – even the local brats didn't beg from us, which was unheard of. The chaps grinned and waved at anyone who would look at them but it was to little avail – even the most amenable of the townsfolk would only shoot back the most fleeting smile before darting back indoors or ducking behind the curtains. Shifty buggers, these, I thought to myself, and it ain't because of anything the Brits have done, of that you can be certain. Someone was causing mischief among them – I just hoped that whoever it was, the Marines got hold of him while I was safely tucked away inside the wire of the compound.

I confess I spent most of that afternoon as nervous as a high-court judge in a West End brothel, and a lot less comfortable too. I had the unnerving feeling that our progress was being observed and spent much of the time looking warily about me, trying to catch a glimpse of fleeting silhouettes on rooftops or in alleyways. I saw absolutely nothing of note and it was only on the route back to the Land Rovers that I began to calm down, when shots were fired up ahead, I hit the deck like a sack of spuds, and the air was filled with the deafening crack of high-velocity rounds and the smell of cordite as the Marines engaged whatever threat had manifested itself. I wasn't remotely interested in closing with or killing the enemy, and spent the majority of the fire-fight curling into an ever tighter ball in a nearby doorway, almost puking with fear. I have never enjoyed the sensation of being shot at, and after the set-to on the Al Faw my nerves were in a parlous state. Fortunately nothing larger than an AK47 was trained upon us, and all the rounds that were fired in our direction went wide, but the experience did nothing for my nerves. From the speed they moved you never would have guessed that Recce Troop had been on their feet all afternoon (adrenaline is a great tonic) and they swept down the street like a well-oiled machine, leapfrogging from doorway to doorway, blasting away at likely targets, and generally frightening the living daylights out of anyone looking on. By the time they reached the edge of the town, with me panting breathlessly behind them, the enemy had vanished and the place fell silent again. We never did work out where the shots were fired from, so the brief journey back to the Headquarters was filled with wisecracks about the library window and the grassy knoll.

After the quiet of the previous few days the evening brief was once again humming with excitement at news of an engagement, however small. Recce Troop's commander gave a brief précis of the fire fight, such as it was, and the CO vowed to get to the bottom of whatever was happening in Rumaylah if it killed him. Frankly I wouldn't have minded if it did, since his demise would undoubtedly have improved the odds on my survival. In the meantime his dirty work was done for him by the Ops Officer, who took it upon himself to attach me to the HumInt Cell.

"They're overstretched already, Flash," he announced to me and the assembled masses. "You speak a bit of the lingo and we know you like gassing with the locals." There was dutiful chuckling at this from his peers. "You might as well get yourself onto the streets and see what info you can glean for us, yes?" There was no arguing with him so I sat nodding like an ass while the bile rose in my throat and the hair stood up on the back of my neck. The irony was not so much that I was once more being thrust into the thick of the action, but that the unapproachable bastard would cheerfully have gone in my place given half a chance. (Despite being only the same rank as me the Ops Officer was self-evidently the CO's right hand man and, by the latter stages of the war, was practically running 42 Commando's campaign unilaterally – albeit with the tacit blessing of the old man; the two of them made a fairly formidable double act.) There was no hope of persuading him to change his mind so I saved my breath and the conversation moved on to other topics.

The HumInt Cell was a ragtag little group of about half a dozen individuals, both regulars and reservists from several different regiments, who had been hastily cobbled together at the start of the campaign. Some were veterans with over 20 years' experience (most of it spent hiding behind garden walls in Belfast, I should imagine) and others were wet behind the ears with no campaign experience whatsoever, but with a good grasp of Arabic. Small and disparate the group may have been but there was little doubting that, ever since 42 Commando had arrived in Umm Qasr, they had been among the busiest souls in the battle group. Cajoling, persuading, bribing and I don't doubt threatening members of the local population, the HumInt boys had done us proud: it was they who had stumbled across the Spherical Clerical back in Umm Qasr; their sources had fingered dozens of Ba'ath Party activists both there and in Umm Khayyal; and they had done more than most in the struggle to keep Basra under control. As a result they were the darlings of the Headquarters and had a great deal of input into the conduct of operations. That was all very well but the very reason for this success was their work ethic, which to my eyes appeared to involve getting into danger at every possible opportunity, spending their time liaising with the most treacherous people imaginable with few weapons and even less back-up. As you can imagine, given the choice between idling my days away inside the camp or roaming the streets in search of elusive troublemakers, I wasn't exactly overjoyed at the prospect of my new posting. The move was not entirely without its compensations though: the Intelligence Corps has more than its fair share of women and I had spotted a couple of reasonably attractive young fillies enjoying the hospitality of the HumInt team on more than one occasion, presumably on some kind of attachment from Divisional Headquarters. I don't normally socialise with Int. Corps staffers – they're typically common as muck and have manners to match – but if the opportunity presented itself, I wouldn't say no to a quick roll in the hay. Under normal circumstances I wouldn't look twice at an enlisted Int. Corps bint, but these were not normal circs and anyway it would beat being shot at on the streets of Rumaylah. I made up my mind to have a crack at one or the other of them at the first opportunity.

In the meantime it was on, on, straight into the path of mortal danger. I was dispatched into the town with two other chaps for company, in search of, well, we weren't quite sure. Frankly I suspected that we were simply in search of anyone who would talk to us. Rumaylah was only a small place, but it had its share of teachers, doctors and the like, figures of some authority who are normally happy to espouse their views given half a chance. Not today though. The town was clammed up tight, most people seemed to be away from home or, more likely, they simply refused to answer the door. We had even come armed with a bribe: in return for a little information, the Assault Engineers were prepared to renovate the entire school. Since the place had evidently not seen a coat of paint in years, that seemed like a reasonable offer – but the head teacher feigned absence so we left empty handed. At least nobody shot at us as we departed, which was a blessed relief,

The HumInt boys presumably kept up their efforts for the next few days. I say "presumably" because I missed whatever action took place on account of contracting a particularly unpleasant gut infection. That evening I came down with a high fever, my bowels exploded in all directions, and I spend a deeply distressing night vomiting my guts out. I managed to avoid duties of any kind for the following three days and spent my time lying on a kip-mat sweating profusely and groaning whenever anyone approached. The bug had being doing the rounds ever since we left Kuwait so by the time we arrived in Rumaylah I was one of the few people not to have suffered its wrath. Sympathy was therefore minimal and I was largely left to my own devices for as long as it took to recover.

By the time I was back on my feet the Commando Group had grown restless. With the exception of Rumaylah, there was nothing but barren desert and GOSPs within 42's area of operations – not nearly enough work to occupy four companies of Marines. More than a week had passed since we arrived and the fighting companies took it in turns to patrol the town and spent the rest of their days whiling away the time sunbathing and doing endless physical exercise. The Headquarters was awash with Marines running around the perimeter fence or working out with weights which had been assembled from pieces of steel left lying around the camp. Thankfully the QDG boys were stationed close by and were less inclined to spend their time in fruitless physical labour. I spent several pleasant evenings with them and was delighted to receive an invitation to a midweek "hunt" which they had arranged. There were no foxes or hares to be had but nevertheless as night fell, the desert was illuminated by spotlights and we spent an entertaining couple of hours shooting up the local stray dog population. The mangy creatures proved very adept at avoiding incoming fire and were remarkably difficult to hit – but I dropped a couple nonetheless, which was more than the average tally. Unhappily, on returning to the GOSP I discovered that my QDG brethren had neglected to inform the Headquarters of this activity, and the Marines had been on high alert ever since the bullets started flying. After my explanation the CO seemed to think the whole episode was quite a hoot though, which was a blessed relief, since I was braced for an almighty bollocking (I suspect he was as bored as the rest of us and would probably have liked an invitation.)

Ever inventive, the Marines found numerous novel ways of entertaining themselves, the latest of which was a raft race on the nearby canal. Numerous teams from each of the companies and several from the Headquarters spent countless hours constructing their Heath Robinson craft, most of which could barely float at all. Oil drums, cable reels, water barrels, wooden planks and scaffolding poles were all commandeered and lashed together with miles of rope. On the allotted day, four-tonne trucks delivered the flotilla to the canal-side where the rafts were arranged in line abreast at the water's edge. OC J Company started the proceedings with a whistle blast and, much to the amusement of the watching Marsh Arabs, dozens of

Marines took to the water, paddling their rafts with shovels, home-made oars, and even their hands. Given the stifling heat – not to mention the Labrador-like instinct for getting wet that is possessed by all Royal Marines – a dip in the canal proved an overwhelming temptation for many. In several cases there wasn't sufficient room on the raft for all its occupants, so crew members simply swam alongside, or attempted to board other rafts. The entertaining scenes were made even more amusing when a convoy of vehicles from 16 Air Assault Brigade crossed a nearby road bridge. These poor souls were still being forced to wear body armour and helmets, while underneath them in the canal were dozens of Marines with nothing more to protect them than a pair of swimming trunks. Goodness knows what the Arabs made of it all.

I took advantage of the entertainment to stroll along the towpath and strike up a conversation with a group of dumbfounded local fishermen who were perched atop a low wall adjacent to the canal. They were a tad reticent to talk at first but my rapidly improving Arabic helped break the ice and within a few minutes we were chatting amiably enough. There was little point even trying to explain the frivolity taking place in the canal so I made a point of agreeing with them that anyone swimming therein must be barking mad, and doled out numerous fruit biscuits to reinforce the point. The conversation gave me a rapid insight into the mindset of these people: they weren't upset in the slightest by the arrival of the Brits – as long as they were left to live without interference they didn't much care who was running the country. I didn't outstay my welcome but made a point of memorising the name of the headman – Tariq – then waved them a cheery farewell as the Marines began exiting the water.

The next day I cadged a lift with an outgoing patrol and hopped out on the bridge in order to say hello to the Marsh Arabs once more. Unsurprisingly the same group of men were sitting quietly, chatting among themselves, smoking and generally whiling away the time, much as people with uncluttered lives do the world over. They invited me to join them and even produced a pot of tea, almost as if I had been expected. In return I produced biscuits by the dozen and the conversation flowed merrily. The fertile banks of the canal were festooned with green reeds and grasses, giving the place a distinctly European feel, while passing fishing boats added a feeling of quiet serenity. All in all it was a much more attractive spot than the dust bowl of the GOSP.

With relatively unchallenging conversation, improved scenery, and no-one around to foist work upon me, the canal-side proved a very convivial location in which to spend my days, especially as the hospitality of the locals grew with every visit. Justifying my constant absences was fairly easy, since each day I learnt a little more about the inhabitants of Rumaylah and its environs, information which I assiduously fed back to the HumInt Cell and the Headquarters staff each evening. In return for the local gossip I plied the fishing community with all manner of contraband from ration packs to cigarettes and even half a bottle of Scotch on one occasion – funny how religious objections disappear when the hard stuff is produced.

"Harry, you are a good man and we should treat you to a proper meal," declared Tariq during one of several deliveries of ration packs which I had liberated from the QM. "Not here though. My house is small and unworthy of such a visitor. We shall dine at my sister's house, in Rumaylah." I nearly choked on my tea. After a week spent largely soaking up the sun by the waterside I had almost forgotten about the malevolent little town on our doorstep, and it had never occurred to me that these people might be related to the occupants.

"I have not seen her in several months," he continued, grinning at me like an ape. "But I shall send word and we shall journey there tomorrow night." The "journey" was all of five miles, but I didn't point this out to him.

Like all the local fishermen the village headman had no vehicle, so the following evening I pinched a Recce Troop Land Rover and drove to the bridge to pick him up. He was already there, waiting for me, all a-jitter. I began to feel distinctly uneasy about the whole escapade and fervently wished I had adhered to the rules and brought someone else with me (single person journeys were strictly forbidden). But it was too late for such thoughts, so I focused instead on engaging him in conversation as we drove through the twilight. It was easier than I anticipated, since he clearly had a lot on his mind that he wanted to talk about.

"My sister, I sent her a message last night to say we were coming today," he chattered. His sister, it transpired, was a childless widow whose husband had died of TB a decade earlier. "Normally she would be overjoyed to see me because, praise Allah, she and I have always been very close, though I don't see her as often as I should." I nodded sagely and bade him continue. "But this morning I get back a message saying something is wrong and we should not come. Pah! Of course I must go. If something is wrong, I must find out and put it right, yes?" I continued to nod, feeling that all-too-familiar sensation of imminent danger approaching. But there was nothing to be done but keep driving, and before I knew it we were entering Rumaylah.

Tariq's sister lived in a fairly substantial house near the end of the high street – not far, in fact, from where I had been when the Recce Troop patrol came under fire almost two weeks earlier. No-one answered the door when we knocked, so Tariq rapped his knuckles against an adjacent windowpane. Still nothing. I could tell immediately that he was uneasy and felt a sudden rush of fear grip me. I quietly undid the press-stud that held my pistol in its holster, while Tariq hammered on the door once more. Finally I heard the bolt being drawn back, and the door opened a few inches.

"In the name of Allah, what kept you, woman?!" he exclaimed.

"Tariq, please, it is not good, you must leave at once!" she answered in a forced whisper.

"Don't be ridiculous, I haven't seen you in months," he replied forcefully, shoving the door open with the flat of his hand. She tried in vain to push it closed but he barged his way inside, cursing as he went. "Come, Harry," he commanded, waving me in behind him. I hesitated for a second but despite my feeling of unease I could hardly refuse to go inside, so I dutifully followed, stooping under the low doorway.

Inside, a commotion broke out. Tariq found himself confronted by two men, strangers who immediately told him he should leave before he caused trouble. Not one to be ordered around, he refused and just before the situation turned ugly, yours truly burst through the door. My arrival took everyone by surprise. Tariq's sister – who was much younger than I had imagined and not bad looking with it – shrieked and covered her mouth, while her two guests looked startled and froze, evidently not sure what to do. A more menacing pair you would be hard pressed to find this side of Hereford, both dressed from head to foot in black, one sporting a full beard, the other a couple of days' stubble and an eye patch. A Mexican stand-off ensued for a few seconds while everyone considered the situation, until the stalemate was broken by the bearded devil producing a Kalashnikov rifle from under his robes. I practically shat myself as he swung the barrel in my direction, and wasted no time hurling myself in his direction – there was nowhere else to run and in my panic-fuelled frenzy my only thought was to prevent him pointing the rifle at me. I crossed the room like an Olympic sprinter and caught the fellow, rifle and all, at full tilt while he was still wrestling with the safety catch. The two of us hit the floor like a sack of potatoes and I wasted no time stuffing my fist into his face. I was bigger than my adversary and with a strength born of fear I'm pretty certain I would have got the better of him, but his one-eyed colleague had other ideas and started laying into the back of my head with his fists. I yelped and rolled over, witnessing Tariq and his sister staring open-mouthed at the melee unfolding in front of them. Before I could shout for help the gunman crawled away from me and jumped to his feet. Flat on my back, I found myself staring up at my two assailants, one of whom was delivering well-aimed kicks at my nether regions while the other was about to administer the coup de grace with his AK47. In the nick of time I remembered the pistol on my hip, which thankfully had remained in its holster throughout the ruckus despite its unclipped cover. I grabbed it, whipped it out, pointed it squarely at the chest of the gunman, fired, and missed. It's easily done, I assure you, especially if you're distracted by some maniac attempting to kick seven bells out of your wedding tackle. Nevertheless, the effect was immediate: my two assailants turned tail and ran, barging past Tariq and his sister in their haste to be through the door. I fired at them again as they exited the house, but succeeded only in destroying a vase and knocking a slab of plaster from the kitchen wall. Silence descended and for a second I lay staring up at the ceiling, wondering what on earth I had gotten involved with. My contemplations were short lived though, as Tariq's sister threw herself on top of me, howling with delight and proclaiming me the hero of the hour. It wasn't an unpleasant experience (she seemed not to notice that my legs were still shaking with fright) and I might have chanced my luck with a quick fumble if her brother hadn't been stood watching and applauding. As it was I came over all British stiff-upper-lipped and shrugged it off as if these things happen every day.

Given the experience I had just been through, I was in no mood for hanging around – I wanted to be back safely inside the Headquarters as quickly as possible and almost said as much to Tariq. But he seemed in no mood for listening, his sister was already rustling up dinner for the three of us, and she was most insistent that we stay so that she could tell us the whole story. I calmed my nerves by gulping down half the contents of my hip flask before offering it to Tariq, who glanced guiltily at his sister before swallowing the remainder.

A short time later dinner was produced (and a remarkably good spread it was too, all things considered). As she served the food I got the chance to have a better look at Tariq's sister, whose name was Pasha. She was a pretty, lissom thing who moved in a rather graceful manner, taking immense care over everything she did. She kept glancing at me through large hazel eyes, then looking away, embarrassed, when she saw I was taking an interest. She could have been no older than thirty five, which would have made her very young indeed when she was widowed – I was frankly amazed that no-one had swept her up after her old man passed away. Under different circumstances I would have gone out of my way to spend more time with her, but in the meantime I was simply curious to know the background to the earlier dramatic events.

"I sometimes take in lodgers for a little extra money," Pasha told us, hesitatingly. "Two weeks ago, these two men appeared, visitors to the town, and asked if they could stay. Of course I said yes – there is nowhere else for them to stay and anyway I need the income." Tariq and I nodded and he gestured at her to continue. "As soon as they move in, I know there is something wrong. They tell me I must stay indoors and not interfere with them. Of course I refused, then they show me the guns and insist I do as they say. So I have been a prisoner in my own home for two weeks now." I half expected tears, but none came. She's made of stern stuff, this girl, I thought to myself. "These men, it turns out they are from Iran. They come to start an insurgency with the local men, who we know are hotheads and stupid enough to believe anything they are told." She sneered as she spoke about them and I began to get a sense of why she was still single – in her opinion no-one in the town measured up. "They tell these men that if they get rid of the British they will own all the oil, and that this place can become a powerful Muslim state." The penny was beginning to drop. She looked at me as she explained: "So that is why you have had such a hostile reception in our town. Most of the young men want to get rid of the British, and the rest of the town is too afraid of these men to be seen to welcome you. It's all so silly." And with that she let out a deep sigh and began topping up the teacups, as if the entire episode was already forgotten. Unexpectedly it was Tariq who became animated, leaping up and down and declaring "We must hunt down these dogs and kill them!" I could think of no worse idea and I was prepared to tell him, too, but fortunately Pasha was able to calm him down before he got completely out of control. She continued to apologise profusely for the hostile reception the Brits had received, and insisted I stay for the entire evening. I would have refused but she began producing all manner of deserts – sugary little things, similar to the stuff you get in North Africa, which I adore – so I stayed and stuffed my face until I felt physically sick.

It was past midnight when Tariq and I eventually said our farewells. Pasha hugged us both and loudly declared me her "liberator", much to the amusement of her brother. "Come visit me again," she demanded, and I swear she winked at me as she said it. I dropped Tariq back at the canal bridge and caned the Land Rover mercilessly along the desert highway that led back to the GOSP, eager to be back behind the wire and in the safety of a camp guarded by dozens of Marines. No-one remarked on my solitary arrival so I quietly dumped the Land Rover alongside the other Recce Troop vehicles and stole silently through the compound, clambered back onto my rooftop, and collapsed exhausted into my sleeping bag. Perhaps it was the excitement from earlier in the evening, but I was as restless as a stag in rutting season, and it took me hours to drop off. I remember fantasising about tupping Pasha before eventually falling into a troubled sleep, during which I suffered nightmares about being executed by a firing squad made up of mad Iranians, my old headmaster, and the Brigade Commander.

When the bright sunshine of the next morning eventually woke me I felt as if I had barely slept at all.

My solo escapade was strictly against the rules so I was unable to tell the Headquarters staff anything about the previous evening's happenings. But I did make a point of loudly telling the morning briefing that I had solved the riddle of Rumaylah's hostile reception, and that since I knew the Iranians had scarpered we could expect somewhat warmer greetings from now on. The news was well received, and my deduction proved correct: within a few days the entire Assault Engineer troop was employed renovating the schoolhouse, while the rest of the Commando reverted to its usual modus operandi of low-level patrols and dishing out biscuits and sweets to the kids.[3]

42 Commando spent a further 10 days stuck out in the desert, much of which I spent sunbathing and reading countless books and magazines that Roddy and the boys sent from home. The Marines spent their time running endless laps of the camp and lifting weights, while I watched idly from my rooftop. The only visitors to the camp were Americans, soldiers and civilians working for Halliburton, who came to survey the oil infrastructure. They may say that oil wasn't the primary motive for war but Dick Cheney's boys were on-site less than a fortnight after the bullets stopped flying. Frankly, I didn't much care what the motive for the campaign was. With no armoured warfare to worry about and Rumaylah quiet once more there was virtually nothing for me to do – which is exactly how I like it.

The Marines weren't the only people getting bored. A squadron of the RAF Regiment was stationed nearby, and they were evidently in a more self-destructive frame of mind. A couple of their number blew themselves up by driving a Land Rover into a minefield, apparently because they wanted to take a look at a burned-out Iraqi vehicle, whereupon the Engineers were scrambled to extricate them – a dangerous task which I wouldn't do for all the tea in China. The extraction was successful, or at least it would have been if one of our Air Force comrades hadn't ignored the white tape which marked the safe lane the Engineers had cleared through the minefield. Instead, despite the warning shouts from hi colleagues, he stepped over the tape, trod on a mine, and blew his foot off. Since the damned fool had driven into the minefield in the first place this would have been poetic justice but for the fact that the explosion injured one of the Engineers. The whole foolhardy episode was difficult enough to believe but was equalled the next day by the news that one of his colleagues had deliberately injected himself in the leg with atropine, a highly toxic chemical which is used to negate the effects of nerve gas. Compared with this idiocy, running hundreds of miles round and round the GOSP was an entirely harmless activity – but all this madness was a clear sign that we needed either a meaningful tasking, or to be sent home. I need barely tell you how delighted I was when we eventually received the news that it was the latter. The rumour-mill had been rife for weeks and now that our return home had been confirmed, morale shot up.

Of course, like every military journey, the return took inordinately long to facilitate. 42 Commando was moved en masse to the port of Az Zubayr, where we were housed in enormous corrugated steel warehouses for over a week. The waiting was interminable, but eventually a convoy of ancient buses arrived, I found a vacant seat, and we were whisked over the border to Ali Al Saleem airbase in Kuwait and thence flown back to the UK. Of course, a direct flight would have been far too sensible, so instead the RAF made us waste a day in Cyprus. The aircraft finally landed at Brize Norton at 1 a.m. on a chilly night in mid-May, and I was delighted to find that my return had not gone unnoticed by my regiment, since a driver was waiting dutifully for me – a huge relief, since I had no desire to spend days in Plymouth with the Royal Marines when I could take centre stage in a cavalry unit where I would be the sole returnee from the Gulf.

The goodbyes took only a few minutes – the quicker the better as far as I was concerned, for I was eager to put some distance between me and the Marines without further delay. Perhaps it was just good manners on their behalf, but they seemed genuinely sorry to see me go.

"Well done, Harry," said the CO, gripping me by the hand. "You've had a better campaign than the rest of the staff combined," he added, grinning. "Now bugger off and get some rest – you've earned it." On this last point I wholeheartedly agreed with him, so I wasted no more time and jumped into the waiting car. The last I saw of 42 Commando was a queue of men waiting patiently to board a line of coaches. For a moment I felt a pang of sorrow as we departed – although in retrospect it might have been wind, brought on by the awful RAF food. Good luck to you all, you bloody madmen, I thought to myself as my driver accelerated into the night.

NOTES

1. The wetlands which were home to the Marsh Arabs were drained by the construction of upstream dams by the Ba'ath regime. There were many motives for this but the primary one was probably ethnic hatred: the Marsh Arabs were largely Shia Muslims and mistrusted by Saddam's Sunni henchmen. Their lifestyle, now a thing of the past, is vividly depicted in Gavin Maxwell's *A Reed Shaken by the Wind*.
2. HumInt: Human Intelligence.
3. Iranian (and other) agitators were reported throughout southern Iraq in the immediate aftermath of the war, though none were ever brought to book.

11

My welcome home was every bit as triumphant as I had hoped, and didn't I just love it. I slept for most of the first day, but the evening was another matter – the boys in the mess gave me a hero's welcome, breaking open the champagne and demanding to know every last detail of the deployment. They got what they wanted – I gave them chapter and verse, and of course the battles got larger and the gallant deeds got more outlandish with every bottle of booze. After a largely liquid dinner the CO joined the fray, probably in an attempt to prove he could still hold his drink. He got royally pissed and kept slapping me on the back, shouting "Good show, Harry, bloody good show!" I had fully intended to hit the town but after months in the wilderness the comfort of the mess seemed plenty sufficient for my first night back, so I propped up the bar and plied myself with bubbly until well past three. All in all it was quite a night.

The following morning I gave Roddy the slip and ducked out of camp to meet Charlotte. She looked an absolute picture – although given a four month period of abstinence (well, almost) I dare say I would have found a female sumo wrestler attractive. In any event she wasted no time in taking me home, practically tore the clothes off me, cooed over the scar on my leg, then pinned me to the sheets and pleasured herself atop me for a good hour or more.

"Oh Harry, darling, I've missed this," she muttered, nibbling my ear as she ground away down below. "Really, it's been too long."

I didn't believe that for one moment – the randy little tart had probably been through half the mess in my absence. But then she had written to me several times a week, and sent endless text messages whenever possible, so maybe there was some truth to it. In any event I didn't much mind – she was a talented lover and I spent a thoroughly enjoyable day getting shot of several months of pent up tension.

My rehabilitation into the QRH took very little time, whereupon I took my post-operational tour leave, which amounted to just over three weeks. I spent most of it swanning around the countryside visiting old pals, playing polo, gate-crashing the occasional wedding, and sponging tickets to Henley and Wimbledon from the Pagets (the better-bred side of my family has always been well connected when it comes to the Season). A thoroughly enjoyable three weeks it was too, being feted as a returning hero everywhere I went. But before I knew it the holiday was over, I was back at the regimental depot, Iraq was a fading memory, and I was pushing a pen for a living once more. Summer gave way to autumn and the interminable exercises on Salisbury Plain that are the blight of any cavalryman's life, and the only thing of note which changed is that Charlotte and I became an item. It seemed only fair to make it public after almost six months of seeing her on the sly, and anyway her sexual prowess was, if anything, growing – she certainly became a lot more adventurous (I won't go into the details here, you'll have to use your imagination. She certainly did).

Christmas arrived and was the usual tawdry family affair, followed by a spectacularly drunken New Year's Eve, in which I disgraced myself by staggering out of a fancy dress party and vomiting onto the leather seats of Charlie Valdez-Welch's open-top MG. (Serves him right too – I ask you, what kind of buffoon drives around with the roof down in January?) I finished the night back at Charlotte's place – she wasn't best pleased by my bedraggled appearance and refused to go near me, so I spent what little was left of the night sprawled on her sofa. My drunken slumber was interrupted by her screams of excitement at about ten o'clock – an ungodly hour when one has only been asleep since five. I fervently hoped that whatever caused the squealing didn't involve me, but of course it did.

"Haaaarrrrryyyyy!" shouted the little minx as she scooted into the lounge, dressed only in a long t-shirt. She jumped on top of me, pounding me excitedly with her fists. I could still taste the bile in the back of my throat and was on the verge of gagging, but the news she announced washed the hangover clean out of my mind. "Guess what?!" hollered Charlotte. "I just got a text message from Roddy and . . ." she paused, grinning, while I rubbed my eyes. "You're in the New Year's Honours list. You've been awarded the Queen's Gallantry Medal!"

I could barely believe it myself but it was true nonetheless, printed in black and white in the morning newspapers. Numerous names from 3 Commando Brigade and 42 Commando were also listed – the CO got an OBE,[1] while the CO of 40 Commando received a DSO.[2] But there were plenty of medals awarded for bravery too, including at least one Military Cross, several MiDs[3] and a fistful of Queen's Commendations for Valuable Service. The Navy and Air Force received a fair number, as did 16 Air Assault Brigade, and the boys in 1 Div – although God alone knows what they did to deserve them. Lastly, it was heart-warming to see a few old chums in 7 Armoured Brigade receive recognition for their part in the proceedings. But each time I scanned the list, one name stood out above all others: Captain Harry Flashman QRH, awarded the Queen's Gallantry Medal.

The reception at the Palace took place a few weeks later, and a fine affair it was too. I, of course, was in uniform while Charlotte rushed out and bought herself a new frock from Harvey Nichols (she looked quite a picture in it too). So many medals were being dished out from the Iraq campaign that the reception was somewhat overwhelmed by the military, but there was no shortage of celebrities too. Palace officials and minions rushed around, clucking advice as they vainly attempted to herd us into the right place at the right time.

Charlotte spent the day by my side giggling and gushing. "It's just like being in Hello magazine, Harry!" she hissed in my ear as she busily pointed out one TV star after another, most of whom I wouldn't have known from Adam. For my part, I spent a thoroughly enjoyable few hours toadying with luminaries from the armed forces – one never knows when such groundwork will be rewarded.

I had met the Queen before of course, but I still found myself surprised by how much smaller she was in the flesh than she appeared on TV. She had evidently been well briefed and seemed quiet knowledgeable about the campaign, chattering away pleasantly as she pinned the gong on my left tit.

"They tell me you were involved in several actions," she commented discreetly. "You must be delighted to have got home safely."

"Ma'am, you have no idea what a relief it was," I replied, with devastating honesty.

"Well done, Captain Flashman. Very well done indeed." She smiled at me for a moment, then plodded on down the line to the next deserving soul to be decorated. If only you knew, I thought to myself.

A couple of days later I found myself back at the QRH Regimental Headquarters where I spent the day strutting around, terribly pleased with myself, knowing I was the object of a great deal of professional envy. The CO bumped into me in the mess during lunchtime and asked me to visit his office during the afternoon.

"I have a little something to discuss with you," he remarked over the salad counter, and winked conspiratorially. "Drop in at three o'clock and I'll fill in the details."

For a moment I was all a quiver – I wondered if I was being sent away again. I consoled myself with the thought that it was still too soon after Iraq, and anyway the British forces weren't planning any new deployments, or at least none that I knew of. It was probably some mundane task, designed to take the shine off my new gong.

I knocked on his door at the allotted hour and was summoned inside, where he waved me into one of his voluminous leather armchairs.

"Harry, first let me offer my heartfelt congrats on your recent decoration," he started. "It really is an honour to have you serving in the Regiment right now. I'm delighted for you."

I stammered some thanks and wondered where the conversation was leading.

"I have been chatting with the appointing people recently," he continued. "I think you have proven your mettle often enough, young Flashman, and it's high time we recognised the full extent of your abilities."

So far so very good, I thought to myself. Now for the punch line.

"I'm delighted to tell you that you've been picked up for promotion." With that, he reached across his desk and thrust out his hand. "Well done, Major Flashman. Or perhaps I should say, Major Flashman QCG!"

So the Iraq war had at least one happy ending: mine. Decorated, promoted, and most important of all, unharmed. I'm not saying for a moment that I deserved any of the accolades that came my way that spring. But I know better than to look a gift horse in the mouth. And, should UK Plc decide to go to war again, I take heart from the fact that my newly elevated rank should keep me safely behind a desk and out of trouble...

NOTES

1 OBE: Order of the British Empire.
2 DSO: Distinguished Service Order.
3 MiD: Mention in Dispatches.

Epilogue

I am not normally a spiteful woman, as those of you who know me will testify (I hope). But when I stumbled across Harry's wartime diaries recently I couldn't resist taking a peek. His writing is, I think, much better than his often boorish spoken manner – and he is remarkably open and honest in the written word, unusually so for someone who usually holds back so much in the vernacular.

I read much of Harry's commentary with shock and surprise. No longer will I look upon him as the dashing hero or fearless warrior. He is obviously nothing more than a coward and a liar, a fake Fendi in a world of designer handbags, a cheap crystal in a princess's tiara, and I despise him for it. But even this I could have forgiven, were it not for his confession that, whilst on *active service* in Umm Qasr, he was deliberately and consciously *unfaithful* to me with some enlisted hussy from Australia. Most men, it seems, were happy enough to serve their country, endure the hardships and privations of war, and return home as heroes to loved ones and families. Only one man (at least to my knowledge) found time and energy to go seeking carnal knowledge of other coalition troops – and then had the sheer affront to accept a medal for valour *from the Queen* in the certain knowledge that he has not a courageous bone in his body.

Therefore, dear reader, I have taken the decision to publish his diaries, albeit in an edited format which I trust makes the whole sordid tale a little easier for you to digest. Harry uses rather a lot of military acronyms in his journal, most of which I have attempted to explain in the footnotes, with a little help from my brother – I hope you found them helpful.

I trust that in doing so I have exposed Harry Flashman as the coward he really is, not to mention a cad and an unfaithful fiancée to boot. I need hardly add that the engagement is OFF – I hope never to clap eyes on the filthy animal ever again.

Yours etc.
Charlotte Woodstock